Summer had wanted a three-week escape from her chaotic life. Now she was well and truly stuck. Or maybe she could still get out of this rodeo.

She inhaled a deep breath. "I'm sorry. I think we're suffering from a major communication breakdown. The bottom line is that I cannot be separated from my horse. This is unacceptable. I was led to believe there would be adequate accommodations for us here."

"Well," Levi returned in a flat tone. "There will be in about two weeks when you're due to arrive."

Before she could open her mouth to let him know they'd be leaving but would not be returning in two weeks, her trainer Theo interjected, "I'm sure we can figure something out." He asked Levi, "Can you recommend somewhere we could stay until you've sorted out your renovations? There must be a ranch nearby with an empty stall and room for a motor home, right?"

Levi scrubbed a hand over his jaw. "Let me think."

"Ours does," Levi's ten-year-old daughter chimed in. "We have room. You could stay at our place. We've got empty stalls and a full hookup for an RV."

Levi barely squelched a groan.

Then his kind, precocious and unfortunately solicitous daughter reached out a hand and made everything even worse. "Welcome to Wyoming, Ms. Davies. My name is Isla Blackwell. It's an honor to meet you."

Now Levi knew for certain that he was in trouble.

Dear Reader,

Problems. Ugh. A not-so-fun part of life we all have in common. But I think how we choose to solve our problems is what sets us apart. And there are so many ways: Is it better to deal with a problem straightaway? Or set it aside, gain some perspective and settle it later? Then again, maybe just ignoring a problem altogether is the answer?

Professional equestrian Summer Davies is running from her problems while former rodeo star Levi Blackwell is tackling his head-on. Of course, bringing these two together doubles their troubles to a comical degree, while adding a romance then compounds them exponentially. Piling on the complications are a cheating almost fiancé, an embarrassing proposal video, a town on the verge of destruction, a legacy at risk, ex-wife trouble and plenty of typical Blackwell family chaos to keep things interesting.

And while I can't say *Wyoming Rodeo Rescue* ultimately answers the question of which problem-solving method is best, I think the story illustrates how much easier it is to face our trials with someone we love. Hope you enjoy Summer and Levi's engagingly problematic and fun-filled path to their happily-ever-after.

Thanks so much for reading!

Carol

HEARTWARMING

Wyoming Rodeo Rescue

———

Carol Ross

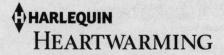

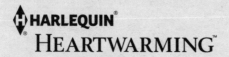

ISBN-13: 978-1-335-58466-3

Wyoming Rodeo Rescue

Copyright © 2022 by Carol Ross

Recycling programs for this product may not exist in your area.

Harlequin Enterprises ULC
22 Adelaide St. West, 41st Floor
Toronto, Ontario M5H 4E3, Canada
www.Harlequin.com

Printed in U.S.A.

Carol Ross lives in the Pacific Northwest with her husband and two dogs. She is a graduate of Washington State University. When not writing, or thinking about writing, she enjoys reading, running, hiking, skiing, traveling and making plans for the next adventure to subject her sometimes reluctant but always fun-loving family to. Carol can be contacted at carolrossauthor.com and via Facebook at Facebook.com/carolrossauthor.

Books by Carol Ross

Harlequin Heartwarming

Return of the Blackwell Brothers

The Rancher's Twins

Seasons of Alaska

Mountains Apart
A Case for Forgiveness
If Not for a Bee
A Family Like Hannah's
Bachelor Remedy
In the Doctor's Arms
Catching Mr. Right
The Secret Santa Project

Visit the Author Profile page
at Harlequin.com for more titles.

Amy, Anna, Cari, Mel & Kathryn

For this book, more than any other, your friendship, encouragement, support and especially the laughter carried me to the end.

Thank you.

CHAPTER ONE

"LYING SNAKE," Summer Davies whispered, the chill of betrayal spreading through her and turning her blood to ice. "This cannot be happening..." With her fingers numb and trembling, she tapped the play arrow on her phone's display as if watching the video again would somehow change the outcome.

Later, much later, after the shock had subsided, Summer would marvel at how the entire calamity that followed could have been avoided if only she'd received the video at a different time. Seriously, at any other point during the day, things would have gone exponentially better. That morning, for example, before riding practice, when her back wasn't screaming in pain, would have been ideal. But any time during would have been suitable because even though she wouldn't have checked her phone until afterward, she would have had time to process, calm down, think and then devise a plan before she saw Braden. With a clearer head and her feet encased in sensible shoes, she wouldn't have acted so rashly. Or, at least, not quite so…publicly.

Instead, she received the video via text message while standing in the foyer of Chauncey's, one of Louisville's chicest restaurants, waiting for the hostess to show her to the table where Braden was already seated. She'd been contemplating setting off to find him on her own, but part of Chauncey's charm was the historic venue, a grand mansion chock-full of nooks and crannies and halls and stairs and balconies. He could be anywhere, and she was in no condition for a hike. Then again, she wasn't thrilled about an evening out at all.

What she really wanted was to get off her feet, kick back with her tiny, perfectly imperfect terrier turned rescue dog, Nugget, and stream a few episodes of *Baking Bad*, her new favorite cooking show. But because Braden was already prickly about her bailing on their last two dates, she'd forged ahead. She'd only worn the three-inch heels because Braden had requested she show up tonight "to the nines," his not-so-subtle way of reminding Summer to swap her riding gear for a dress. Since the shoes had been a gift he'd brought her from a recent trip to Milan—that she'd yet to wear— she knew the gesture would make him happy.

She was sincerely regretting the impulsive attempt at relationship compromise.

It was slightly annoying how Braden felt the need to make such a wardrobe request at all. Sure, she might frequent the occasional social outing straight from practice. Mostly gatherings with fellow equestrians, though, and rarely anything important where she'd be "seen." Braden, on the other hand, would never take the chance of being caught anywhere looking anything less than perfect. Then again, Braden liked being seen. Made a point of it, which, she had to admit, was a bonus when it came to landing—and keeping—the big-dollar sponsors.

That, along with his model-worthy looks, dashing charm and edge-of-reckless riding style, made him one of the most popular personalities in the world of professional equestrian sports. Everyone loved Braden Keene.

Summer, on the other hand, not so much. As her coach and friend Theo kindly put it, she didn't have the patience for publicity or a natural flair for networking. She was embarrassingly unphotogenic; her focus, nerves and intensity translated through the lens as grumpy, snobby—or worse. Fortunately, her innate talent, hard work and devotion to her horse, Sacha, resulted in a consistently high ranking. She had to work at the rest. Thankfully, her biggest sponsors like Juniper Saddle & Leather, Bundy Jump Co. and Matilda Specialty Motorcoach were all very specific to her sport, where her performance mattered more than her persona.

This was why she and Braden were so good together. Being seen with Braden boosted Summer's social cachet. While for Braden, being paired with Summer elevated the professional regard he received. They were a match made in Louisville, as her father, Roland Davies, liked to say. A concept that advertisers had noticed, too, and one that would secure her a comfortable existence for the next year while they publicly played out their engagement and subsequent wedding plans. A massive ad campaign was being designed around it. Just the notion of living so blatantly in the spotlight caused her chest to constrict to a lung-crushing degree, although Braden, Roland and her agent, Ingrid, kept reassuring her it would all be fine.

They weren't even engaged yet, and speculation was already raging about their relationship. When was the wedding? Where would it be held? How big was the ring? What will the merging of two such powerful equine families do to the sport? Can you imagine what their stables are going to look like? Won't their kids be cute?

Summer didn't want to think about any of that right now, or for the next several weeks, for that matter. They'd agreed to put all wedding talk on hold until after the Meadows Cup next month. That's when they were scheduled to "officially" announce their engagement and begin the photo shoots, appearances and filming. Even now, *not* thinking about it had her thinking, which sent her head spinning—a perfect example of why she needed to stay focused. This would be the most important competition of her life to date.

As teammates, Braden Keene and Summer Davies were predicted to place high. But Summer's secret hope lay with the individual eventing title. A championship at Meadows would cement her standing in the international circuit. More prize money coupled with higher-dollar endorsements *of her own* were the key to her financial independence, something she absolutely needed to achieve. Not only for her sake, but for her father's, too. *That's* what she was thinking about when her phone chimed.

Expecting a text from an impatient Braden, she was surprised to see a number she didn't recognize. The message read:

You deserve to know the truth. He's not who you think he is.

Tension shot through her, her mind going straight to her father, to the issues he'd been having—another massive source of stress that had lately been taking a toll. Squinting at the blurry, frozen image of a man and woman on the screen, Summer quickly realized the man's hair wasn't nearly dark enough to be her dad's. His was darker blond, thick and wavy, too. Like Braden's.

Wait, was it Braden? One thing she was certain of: the woman was not her.

Curious now, she stepped outside to a discreet smoking patio shared by the lounge. No one was there, so she leaned against the wall and hit the play button.

Now she realized the man was indeed Braden. Shirtless and in the arms of a strange woman. No, that wasn't accurate. He was the aggressor, for lack of a better term. The woman was in *his* arms. Not that she wasn't amenable because her hands were all over him, too, threading through his hair, gripping his neck and finally settling around his shoulders until… They were equally in each other's arms. Both…*armed*? She nearly chuckled, but the feeling passed quickly because soon they were both shirtless, too, which wasn't at all funny. And then they were kissing and…

More. So much more. More than enough to get the idea of where things were headed. Finally, the video ended with a merciful, albeit predictable, cliff-hanger.

A knifelike spasm clenched her lower back, stealing her breath with its depth and intensity. Bending at the waist, she placed her hands on her knees and inhaled deeply until the worst of it passed. She straightened, steadying herself with one hand by gripping a concrete ashtray-planter-thing. And then, inexplicably, she watched the video again.

This time, she examined the footage more carefully, watching for signs that it was fake or that the man wasn't truly Braden. The brief flash of his tattooed shoulder confirmed the worst as he'd gotten the tattoo shortly after they'd started dating. When it ended, she continued to stare numbly at the screen, struggling to land on an emotion—humiliation, disappointment, anger, despair…

Seconds passed until another text from the same number appeared:

I'm sorry. But I thought you should know before.

Summer glanced around, suddenly feeling vulnerable and exposed. Was she being watched? What did the *before* refer to? Before what? This evening's date? The Meadows Cup? Just the thought of receiving this video on the eve of a competition vaulted anger straight to the top of her tumbling heap of emotions.

A text from Braden followed a few seconds later:

Hey, beautiful. Where are you? I thought you'd already arrived. Are you OK? I miss you. I ordered that cheesy crab appetizer you like. But you have to promise not to eat it all because I want you looking extra hot for next weekend's party. ;)

"Ha, ha, ha," she cackled. "He *misses* me? Somehow, I do not believe that is true." Not that it was at all funny. Nope, and the near-evil edge in her tone probably should have served as a warning that she needed to take some time to process what she'd seen. But it didn't. Not even a little bit.

Stepping back inside the foyer, she was immediately accosted by the hostess.

"Oh, Ms. Davies, there you are! Thank goodness! Mr. Keene was getting concerned, and that had me worried. My name is Gwen. I'll show you to your table. Right this way." Without waiting for a response, the woman took off at a hurried clip.

Easy for her to do in her practical, comfortable ballet flats, Summer acknowledged as she followed, her own condition requiring a more measured pace and a dedicated effort not to limp.

"New shoes," Summer explained when she caught up to Galloping Gwen, who'd stopped to wait for her at the first intersection.

"I understand! Isn't that the worst?" she gushed, her face a mask of sympathy as she eyed the sparkly heels. "They are gorgeous, though."

Gwen slowed her pace but kept tossing worried glances over her shoulder. Glances, Summer knew, that had everything to do with not disappointing Braden Keene and very little to do with Summer's well-being. They trekked through the large dining area, down a long hall, up a set of stairs and onto a landing where they hung a left into the Emory Ballroom.

Summer couldn't help but pause because the space was magnificent. Most of the entire wall opened on to a vast expanse of balcony with small tables skillfully arranged to provide privacy. Twinkle lights and the glow from tabletop candles evoked romance, as did the subtle strains of orchestral music emanating from well-placed speakers. Summer knew these were the best tables in the house, reserved weeks in advance.

Gwen herded her to the far corner on the balcony's edge, which delivered a stunning view of the lake below. And yet, even with all of these clues, Summer still did not anticipate what was coming, distracted as she was by the cheating video looping through her brain.

Then suddenly, there he was, the star of the show. Braden. Picture-perfect in a black suit with an ice-blue tie that complemented the shade of his eyes. His dark blond hair was stylishly gel-ruffled, and when he caught sight of Summer, his face lit with an electric smile.

That smile. An alluring mix of sincerity, mischief and mystery, it consistently earned him admirers of every variety. The money-maker, his agent dubbed it because it not only landed him sponsorships but also lucrative ads and magazine covers. Summer preferred the term *rakish*, often teasing him about both its appeal and its dark power.

Always courteous, the consummate gentleman, he stood as she approached the table.

"Summer." Her name whooshed out with an eager, relieved breath. "There you are." Glancing at the hostess, he cooed, "Thanks so much, Gwen. You're an angel." She departed with a blush and a brilliant smile.

"You look spectacular," he said to Summer, dipping his head to brush a kiss to her cheek. Drawing back an inch, he added a whispered, "Thank you for dressing up for me. You won't regret it. And the shoes, too. I'm… Wow."

"Yeah," Summer replied flatly and took a step back. "Huge mistake all the way around."

"What?" A furrow appeared between his eyebrows but was quickly squelched when he grinned. "I know you don't like heels, but trust me, your legs look fabulous. You can thank me later."

"Doubtful. Can I please sit now? We need to talk."

"Yes, we do need to talk," he responded eagerly. "But, um… Hold on one more second, okay? Stay there." He glanced over her shoulder, and if the circumstances hadn't been what they were, she would have seen that for the signal that it was, too. So many missed hints and overlooked clues.

"Braden, I—"

"Summer," he interrupted softly, the magic of his smile now aimed at her. "I love you. I think you're the most incredible, talented, dedicated woman I've ever known…"

He went on, but Summer quit listening. It was too late. She'd missed her chance at avoiding an altercation because as he stood before her, expression radiating affection and tenderness, he *looked* so perfect. He looked like a man in love. When she *knew* it was all a lie. He was a lie.

A lying snake. Why did he think she needed to hear his lies, too? The video said it all.

It was all too much. Really, it would be too much for anyone to take, right? Okay, maybe not *anyone*, but Summer had certainly reached her breaking point.

"Braden—"

He dropped to one knee. "Summer Francesca Davies."

Oh. No. He. Is. Not.

One arm swept forward, hand cradling a small blue velvet box.

But he was. And *that's* when things went more than a little sideways.

"MOLLY!" LEVI BLACKWELL SHOUTED into the empty space of his office. "This cannot be happening," he then muttered, rereading the email as if that would help. As if the words would somehow rearrange themselves and not spell disaster.

He tried again, "Molly? Are you still here?" As if she could help even if she was.

"Where else would I be?" Molly answered, gliding through the doorway of what she'd dubbed the "command center" of the Eagle Springs rodeo grounds. For a woman of seventy-four years, she could flat out move. And toss hay bales like a man half her age. Standing before him, she heaved a sigh that could rival his ten-year-old daughter Isla's on the woe-is-me scale. "When you have me working overtime every single day."

Usually, Levi found Molly's antics entertaining, but he was currently too keyed up to remind her that her work was voluntary. And not only was she a volunteer, but she'd also invented her own job title and position as executive assistant and publicity supervisor. Not that he wasn't grateful for her help every single day in the last couple of months since he'd taken on the project of rebooting the town's iconic rodeo. Truthfully, he didn't know how he'd have made it this far without her. And the notion that after all their hard work, it was now crashing down around them was unbearable.

Molly was one of his gran's best friends, which was why she'd initially insinuated herself into this project. Years ago, his grandmother, Delaney Blackwell, or Denny as she was more commonly known, had been instrumental in establishing the rodeo. The annual event had helped earn Eagle Springs, Wyoming, its very own dot on the map. For decades, it had been a vital part of the town's identity—one that had grown into a crucial slice of its economy.

All that was before a respiratory ailment had devastated the local equine population, contributing to the rodeo's closure and ravaging Denny's ranch, the Flying Spur, too. When this calamity of circumstances had left Gran short of cash, a loan against the property had proven the solution. Until she'd gotten sick.

As kidney disease wreaked havoc with her body, medical bills piled up fast, infection struck her livestock, and just when things seemed like they couldn't get worse, the bank decided to call in the loan. Aggravating the situation, as well as Gran's nerves, was the ambitious developer Xavier Howard, a man with deep pockets and pie-in-the-sky plans waiting on the sidelines to gobble up the ranch.

Levi felt that now-familiar rush of distress at the thought of anything happening to his gran, or the Flying Spur, his childhood home, while she could still walk its fields. His four siblings felt the same, and three of them, Corliss, Nash and Wyatt, currently called the ranch home. He and his sister Adele both had homes in Eagle Springs, but the Flying Spur would always own their hearts.

This was why the siblings had agreed to come to Gran's aid and divide the debt into five pieces—a task that sounded much simpler than it was, especially when none of them was exactly flush with cash.

Levi was arguably the worst off of them all. The rapid decline of his financial position was a similar, albeit less life-threatening, complement of his grandmother's—new home, divorce, accident, unemployment—in that exact and unfortunately quick order. Resurrecting the rodeo had seemed like the perfect solution to all his financial problems.

The profits from the rodeo would go toward his share of the Flying Spur debt. At the same time, a successful outcome would segue into his new business of expanding the property into a multiuse event venue. After settling on terms with the property owner, Curtis Holloway, he'd then poured a good chunk of his remaining savings and energy into the endeavor. With only two months to plan the event, he'd had no choice if he wanted to put on the best rodeo the town had ever seen.

Now this wrecking ball had landed in his inbox, smashing his plans to smithereens.

"Have you seen this email from Trace Baylor's assistant?"

"Well," Molly replied wryly, "you're going to have to be a little more specific. We've received approximately three thousand emails from Trace Baylor's people. Quite frankly, I think his assistant has a crush on me."

"He's canceling." Levi glanced up at her and then back down at the screen. "Correction—he canceled." Then he read, "'Dear Mr. Blackwell, It is with sincere regret that I write to inform you that Trace has suffered an accident and the injuries he's incurred will prevent him from hosting and performing at the Eagle Springs Rodeo.'" He paused. "It goes on, but that's the important bit."

"Oh dear," Molly said, finally absorbing the seriousness of the situation. Shifting her reading glasses into place, she moved around the table where she could view his laptop screen. "Let me take a peek."

Levi was pretty sure Molly read it twice, too. Or possibly three times, before she responded with a flatly toned, "Huh."

"Huh?" Levi repeated. "That's all you've got?" Molly was never short on commentary or opinions.

"What do you suppose that man was doing riding a dang bull?" The email also briefly explained how the injury had occurred.

"He was a bull rider."

She rolled her eyes. "Thanks for that breaking news bulletin, Scoop. *Was* being the operative word. I mean, I thought he was retired."

"So did I."

It was a good point. As far as Levi knew, Baylor hadn't competed for several years and now enjoyed a successful career as a stand-up comedian with a Western flair. He'd found his niche performing at rodeos, fairs and other similar events. Getting him to agree to a gig in Eagle Springs had been a major coup. More than that, Levi had staked the event's success on Trace's performance. Tension crept upward from the base of his skull, tendrils branching rapidly, threatening a headache. This was a nightmare.

Apparently, Molly needed more time to register the extent of the catastrophe they were facing because she was still stuck on the how. "What was he thinking? A good rodeo rider knows when to quit, and wiser words have never been spoken."

"Oh, yeah? Who said them?"

"I did. Didn't you hear me? *You* quit, didn't you?"

Levi tried to smile but couldn't quite pull it off. "I appreciate that, Molly, but let's try and focus here. This is an unmitigated disaster. It is the absolute worst thing that could have happened right now. I don't—"

"Whoa there, Shakespeare," Molly interrupted, clapping him on the shoulder. "That's a respectable amount of drama, but I'm not sure words like *unmitigated* and *absolute* apply here."

Levi noted Molly's casual demeanor. Was she purposely underreacting to counter his reaction? Trying to keep him calm? The notion was endearing—or would be if he wasn't already freaking out.

"I know what you're doing, Molly, and I appreciate it. I do the same thing to Isla, but it won't work. This is the end. We're done. We've sold tickets based solely on Trace's appearance. His stand-up show is sold out, too.

We will have to issue a statement, offer refunds and appease angry fans.

"There's no way we can find someone willing to host the event, knowing that people were expecting to be entertained by Trace. Not to mention the damage to my credibility, to my future business of event hosting. It's not like we can just pull the next name from our vast waiting list of interested celebrities who are dying to come to Eagle Springs, Wyoming, with only three weeks' notice."

CHAPTER TWO

"WILL YOU MARRY ME?"

Summer was stunned. She couldn't even speak. The entire spectacle was shocking and so, so…ill-timed that she was having a difficult time even believing it was happening. Braden, on bended knee, in the middle of Chauncey's, asking her to marry him less than five minutes after catching him with another woman. Granted, she'd "caught" him via video, but still, it was just…ludicrous.

Not to mention appalling and, and, and *brazenly* disrespectful.

Misreading her silence, Braden reached out, took hold of her hand and slipped the ring on her finger. The move was deliberate and smooth to the point where she knew he must have practiced—a notion she might have found endearing prevideo.

With her fingertips tucked firmly in his grasp, Summer looked down at the dazzling display now perched upon her finger, an enormous diamond surrounded by glistening blue sapphires and an array of smaller stones. Braden gently lifted their joined hands and the jewels electrified as they caught the light.

"It fits perfectly," he said in a low, satisfied tone. She could feel his intensity as he awaited her response. Every inch of his body radiated confidence in the affirmation he knew he was about to receive. When she finally shifted her eyes to meet his, they seemed to sparkle as brightly as the gems.

Pouring it on even thicker, he continued, "This ring isn't anywhere near as dazzling as you, my beautiful Summer, but I hope it will suffice." He flashed the smile before sobering again. "Summer, you are my love, my heart and my best friend. It feels like I've waited forever for this day. There's no one else who—"

"Stop," she interrupted, head shaking in disbelief. "Just…stop." No one else? How dare he? Anger flared hot and fierce inside her, a force of nature that she couldn't control. The ring felt like a white-hot brand on her skin. Off, she needed it off! Twisting her hand from his grip, she then yanked it from her finger.

She went to give it back to him, to simply get the *thing* away and out of her life. But when she raised her hand, the gems caught her eye again, and another thought occurred to her. Braden didn't know her at all. Cheating aside, everything about this ostentatious display proved it.

They'd discussed their impending nuptials. With the ad campaign on the horizon, they'd needed to prepare. They'd touched on all the key elements like proposal locations, length of engagement, ceremony dates—rings! Even certain specific wedding details like cakes, flowers and colors had been narrowed to a significant degree. Aside from the surprise timing, nothing about this proposal landed anywhere close to her preferences.

"No," she whispered. "We are not doing this right now."

Braden's lips twitched, but his grin held. "I know we agreed to wait, but I couldn't. And I know how much you like surprises." He winked.

"*You* couldn't? What about me?"

"Summer, you are killing me here. Now is not the time to be joking around."

"Joking around?" she repeated, her fingers tightening into a fist. The stones felt sharp and biting against her skin and, she noted, surprisingly heavy. Too heavy. Like a… A weight. A burden. One she could not bear for another second longer. She didn't plan her next move. She wasn't even thinking beyond making the unpleasant sensation stop, and like some sort of involuntary muscle movement, it just…happened.

"This is definitely a joke, all right," she muttered. And then, angling her body so that she faced the lake, she drew her arm back and launched the ring with a nice arcing throw.

"Summer!" Braden's tone was shrill now with a mix of surprise and horror. He popped to his feet.

Kerplunk.

She actually heard the thing hit the water. Ripples fanned out from the spot. People seated on the first-floor patio below looked out and then up toward the balcony, wondering what could have caused the commotion. A pair of swans paddled closer, hoping perhaps, that treats were falling from the sky.

"Looks like someone else didn't like their appetizer," a voice quipped. Muted laughter ensued.

Summer chortled nervously and gave the audience a breezy wave. An older gentleman returned the gesture.

"What in the world is the matter with you?" Braden hissed softly through a significantly less dazzling smile. "That is a flawless three-carat diamond with heirloom sapphires in a platinum setting. If you didn't like it, all you had to do was say so. How am I going to—"

"Well, that explains the splash, doesn't it?" Summer interrupted. "That rock certainly had some heft to it. Glad I didn't hit one of those swans—probably would have knocked it cold." Another bubble of laughter burst forth, and she squelched it with one hand across her mouth.

"Summer, honey, are you having some sort of breakdown? I know the pressure has been getting to you even more than usual lately. I haven't seen you like this since Springdale."

"Ha!" she barked. "Of course you'd automatically assume this was my fault. No, Braden, I'm not having a *breakdown*. I am, however, having a *breakthrough*."

"What is that supposed to mean?"

"Seriously?" Summer studied him carefully. "You can't think of a single reason why I might react this way?"

For the first time all evening, his poise wavered, the grin wobbling ever so slightly, a glint of not-quite-confidence flickering in the endless blue depth of his eyes. But he didn't answer the question. Or confess or beg for forgiveness.

Well, neither would she. Explain, that was. A few silent seconds followed while she waited for him to figure it out. Her focus shifted to her feet, probably because they were now quite literally throbbing with pain.

"These stupid shoes," she muttered. "You know what?" She bent one leg up behind her at the knee, ungracefully slipping off the heel and then repeating the motion on the other side. "I am never going to wear *these* again, either."

She made a show of holding the shoes aloft for a few seconds before tossing them over the balcony, too, with an added, "Buh-bye."

This time, the crowd below reacted even more strongly. Summer heard murmuring, a few gasps, a honk of surprise from one of the swans, followed by a chorus of snickering and what sounded like muffled applause.

And that act, she decided triumphantly, did not require an encore. Without another word, she turned and headed for the door. She'd only managed several victorious steps before noticing an unfortunately familiar face gaping at her from a table near the door. Off to the other side, Braden's best friend, Cort, and Cort's girlfriend, Nicole, were standing against the wall, looking baffled and concerned. That's when an already horrific situation officially turned into the worst night of her life.

"WHAT AM I going to do?" Summer lamented to her coach, Theo. Upon fleeing the restaurant, she'd gone home, packed an overnight bag, loaded her dog, Nugget, into her car and hightailed it straight to Theo's house, where she'd relayed the details of the evening's events.

"Carla Tillman was there. And I think Cort and Nicole saw the whole thing. Braden must have invited them to celebrate with us. Now that I think about it, there were four champagne glasses on the table. Ugh."

It was convenient when your coach was also your friend and closest confidant. Remaining at her place was out of the question; it was the first spot Braden would look. Since she lived in the "guest quarters," a detached one-bedroom cottage on her father's estate, his house was out of the question, too. Not that she'd seek solace there anyway. Her dad and Braden were tight. Too tight.

Braden's father, Gregory, and Summer's dad, Roland, were best friends. Gregory Keene and Roland Davies's bond stretched all the way back to their college days and contributed to the larger problem: Summer and Braden had grown up together. They knew the same people, hung with the same crowd, frequented the same places.

There was precisely one door where Braden would hesitate before knocking, and that was Theo's. Her coach seemed to be the only person who'd never fallen under Braden's spell.

At thirty-eight, Theo was a decade older than Summer, but he'd been her coach for ten years and felt like family. At least, their relationship was how she imagined it would be if she had a brother—a shared sense of humor, plenty of bickering and unwavering support delivered with brutal honesty. As an only child, Summer had no clue how a sibling connection would truly feel.

Theo had no family, save for an aunt he adored who lived out West. Years ago, after the end of a brief marriage, he'd declared himself a bachelor for life. Not that the single women of Louisville, and everywhere else he traveled, didn't continually try to change his mind.

Handsome features set to curious, Theo asked, "Do you know the woman?"

"Of course! So do you. I told you it was Carla Tillman." The biggest gossip she knew, possibly the biggest gossip in all of Louisville, had witnessed Summer's meltdown. Part of it, at least. How much she had observed was the big question. Had she seen Summer throw the ring? The shoes? How much had she heard? Their voices hadn't been loud. Music was playing in the background, and it was not like they'd had a huge fight.

Cort and Nicole had undoubtedly seen enough. Cort could be trusted. Probably. But Nicole couldn't keep a secret to save her life. Cort would do his best to convince her for Braden's sake, but...

But once word leaked out, and some version was bound to, there was no way to spin things where Summer wouldn't look like an insensitive lowlife. She could already imagine the chatter. *Poor Braden. Summer didn't like the ring, so she threw it in the lake! Such a spoiled brat. He's always been too good for her. What does he see in her anyway?*

How long before it was all over social media? How long before her father found out? When would her agent, Ingrid, call and say her sponsors were bailing? Another flush of anxiety washed over her as the myriad possibilities and likely repercussions pelted her from every direction.

The biggest one slammed into her like a loaded freight train. If there was no wedding, there would be no ad campaign. Summer was counting on that money to get her through the next year until she and Sacha could rack up some big wins and secure enough sponsorships to stand on their own two feet and four hooves.

Theo steered her back on point. "Not *that* woman. I'm referring to the woman in the video with Braden. Who is the cheat-ee?"

"Oh. Um, no. All I could see was her back side—long silky blond hair and tiny-bikini tan lines."

"Hmm."

"I don't even care about that." Well, she *did* care. Of course she did. Undoubtedly, the heart breaking-aching part would sink in soon. It was just that she had so many more pressing problems to contend with first.

"How big was the ring?" he asked.

"I don't know…" She shrugged a helpless shoulder. "Big. He said it was a three-carat diamond and platinum something-or-other with sapphires and a bunch of smaller diamonds, too. It was impractical and flashy and just way, way over the top. Like something Elizabeth Taylor would have worn. I can't believe he thought I'd want something like that! I'd need some sort of cart to push my own hand around. And how could I wear it when I ride? I'd probably get it tangled in the reins and strangle myself. If I didn't lose it first."

"True." Theo snuffled out a laugh before reminding her, "You do realize that you chucked *thousands* of not-hard-earned Keene dollars into that pond?"

"Theo." Summer flattened one palm to her forehead. "You are not helping."

Her stomach ached, especially when it occurred to her that she could probably support herself and Sacha for an entire year with what that ring cost. Braden had an entirely different concept of money. He'd never comprehended, or respected, the disparity in their financial situations. Riding was more like a hobby for him. For Summer, it was her life.

Getting to this competitive level was expensive, and she'd only managed with her dad's help. Help she could no longer in good conscience accept. If she didn't figure out a way to start earning more than the cost, she would have to give it up. And if she couldn't ride, what would she do?

Theo waved her off. "Don't worry—he'll recover the jewels. It won't be cheap, but he'll dredge the pond or hire divers or whatever." He belted out another laugh. "The damage to his ego might not be so easily remedied, however, and that's the part I am really and truly enjoying. I wish I could have seen his face…" Laughing, he looked skyward as if imagining the scene again.

"Theo," she groaned. "This isn't funny."

"I know," he agreed in a somber tone while his grin underscored the lie. "Okay, but Summer, it is a *little* funny. Surely, you can see that, and following it up with the shoes was…" He looked down at her now comfortably sneakered feet. "Epic. I am so proud of you. Not to mention, there's a couple grand he *cannot* recoup."

Summer felt a smile slip into place. "That part I don't regret. I can't believe I even wore those stupid things for him. What was I thinking?"

"I don't know," Theo replied softly, catching her gaze and holding it tight. Summer knew he was intimating way more than the ring or the wearing of the shoes. He'd never understood what she saw in Braden in the first place. "He deserves way, way worse."

"That's probably true," she conceded.

"No, Summer, it *is* true. I hope you see that now. And on that note, let's talk about you posting the video. Maybe leak it to the press. Trish at *Iron Horse and Trail Magazine* would love to have the scoop on this, and she'd be fair. She likes you."

Theo didn't have to add that she was one of the few remaining reporters who did. Summer didn't enjoy the spotlight the way Braden did and especially disliked being interviewed after a ride. She had a reputation for being standoffish and uptight when the truth was that she was riddled with anxiety. At the Springdale show a few months ago, she'd pulled her microphone off midinterview and walked away—straight into her motorcoach, where she'd had a full-blown panic attack. Something she hadn't experienced for years, not since she was a teenager.

Theo went on, "Or put the video out there yourself before the rumors start flying. You control this narrative. Out Braden as the lazy, entitled, lying cheater that he is, and for once in his life, let him get exactly what he deserves."

"You know I can't do that."

Theo eyed her carefully before asking, "You're not going to marry him now, are you?"

"Of course not!" she cried. "But the last thing I need now is a scandal. I'm on thin ice as it is after Springdale. And you know very well that I've already spent most of my advance, which I will have to pay back if there is no wedding."

A few months ago, after securing the ad campaign with Braden and carefully calculating her finances, she'd quit her part-time job to train full-time and focus all of her energy on competing. "Now I have to figure out a different way to…" Pay for her life, she finished silently.

Now Summer wished she hadn't even seen the video, at least not until next month. She voiced that thought and then added, "You and I both know Braden was right about one point—things have been extra difficult lately. The stress has been getting to me between my finances, Dad's issues, my back problems and this upcoming wedding stuff. I'll admit that."

Theo didn't argue. He knew it as well as she did. He'd been trying all sorts of strategies to help her manage the anxiety—diet, yoga, deep breathing exercises. Last week, he'd downloaded a meditation app on her phone.

"And now this…" she trailed off helplessly. "I would do anything if I could put all of this on hold until after the Meadows Cup."

"Anything?" Theo asked, tilting his head thoughtfully. "Do you mean that?"

"Absolutely," she confirmed. *"Anything."*

"Do not mess with me, Dad," Isla Blackwell implored. "Please. Not about something this important." She paired the request with a beseeching, almost challenging expression. Her eyes narrowed into a piercing hazel stare while her mouth formed a straight flat line, underlining her resolve.

Spunky, Gran liked to call her great-granddaughter, always coloring her quiet determination into a positive quality, undoubtedly because she could see how Isla had inherited the trait from her.

"Not messing with you," Levi reiterated. "Summer Davies is going to host and perform at our rodeo."

When Molly had suggested the professional equestrian as a replacement for Trace Baylor, he'd had his doubts. Prepared for his uncertainty, Molly made some good arguments, pointing out the rising popularity of show jumping and how plenty of riding clubs, like Isla's, were teaching the skill. Sure, Summer Davies might not attract the same raucous, boot-stomping crowd as Trace Baylor, but any horse aficionado was sure to be impressed. And wasn't this high-society, English-riding, fancy-pants equestrian world a potentially lucrative avenue he could pursue with his future business venture? Imagine the connections he could make! The swanky horse shows he could host!

That last one tipped him over the edge. Besides, it wasn't as if he had a multitude of options here. And he wasn't going to lie;

making his daughter happy was proving to be an added bonus.

"Yes! I cannot wait to tell Nell that Summer Davies is coming here." Isla flopped back dramatically onto her neatly made bed. Bed making was a chore she'd dutifully executed every day since Aunt Adele had gifted her the expensive horse-covered duvet and sheet set for her tenth birthday. He often marveled at his sister's creative problem-solving skills when it came to kids. Like a jack-in-the-box, Isla popped back up and threw her arms around him. "You are the best dad ever!"

Levi's heart squeezed tightly inside his chest, releasing a burst of love so intense he could barely breathe. If only that was true. If only he could give his little girl a dose of joy like this every day.

The divorce had been hard on her. Kylie had moved to a neighboring town. And while that was fine with Levi, it meant huge changes for Isla, adjusting to a custody schedule and bouncing between two homes.

The worst part was that Isla didn't like Kylie's fiancé, Brett. Levi couldn't blame her; he didn't care for the guy either. It infuriated Levi how often they left Isla with a sitter so they could go out dancing or over to a friend's house for game night. Despite Levi offering to be that babysitter, Kylie always refused, insisting that it was still "her time."

Levi accepted plenty of blame for the long-blooming problems that ended their marriage. Although ironically, when they'd met, Kylie had been enamored with all things rodeo. She'd been head over heels for Levi, her "real cowboy," and ambitious on his behalf. But like many things in life, the reality hadn't matched the fantasy, and ultimately, the life-style hadn't suited her.

She didn't enjoy being on the road and increasingly chose to remain behind. Meanwhile, Levi poured every penny of his earnings into his property and custom-built barn home, which Kylie grew to resent, accusing him of caring more about his "pets"— the animals—than he did her.

Convinced a baby would make her happy, they'd conceived Isla, but motherhood had only made matters worse. She'd complained endlessly about being lonely and how she didn't want to be a single mom and hadn't signed up to be a "zookeeper."

At least Kylie had been the one to leave, allowing Levi to keep the house. Isla loved being here in their untraditional home, where she still had her horse-themed bedroom and the bulk of her belongings. Thankfully, like

Levi, she adored their little farm, consisting of a small misfit herd of cows, goats, llamas, sheep, chickens, donkeys and of course—the horses.

Riding had always been a way for father and daughter to bond. Since the divorce, it had been Isla's escape and one that seemed healthy and therapeutic. Levi bent over backward to make sure she never missed her riding club meetings, lessons and events.

"Wait…" Isla said, her expression morphing into doubt and making her look her age again. "Will I be able to meet her?"

"Absolutely!" Levi assured her. "She's staying here in Eagle Springs."

"Where? Please tell me you're not putting her at the Barn Door Inn?"

"Of course not," he managed to say with a straight face. "She's here for the rodeo, so Molly has her all set up at Finley's Boarding House." Finley's was basically a hostel for traveling cowboys needing temporary digs and the rodeo crowd looking for a cheap place to bunk.

"Da-Da-*Daad*!" Isla sputtered, wide-eyed and clutching Dixie, her favorite plush horse. "No! Finley's is for cowboys."

"But she's *like* a cowboy, though. I mean,

she rides horses. Pretty sure she'll want to hang out with the other cowboys."

"No. Summer Davies is *nothing* like a cowboy."

"Sure, she is. Finley's is perfect. They have free coffee in the lobby, donuts on the weekends and *two* vending machines." He held up two wiggling fingers for emphasis. "Plus, they change the sheets on the beds every single Sunday." The twitch of his lips finally gave him away.

"You're joking." Isla punched him lightly and then exhaled a relieved breath. "That is so disgusting."

Levi busted out a laugh. "Listen, sweetie, Summer Davies is no different than you and me. Eats, sleeps, laughs, cries, puts her Wranglers on one leg at a time."

"Wranglers? Ugh! Summer doesn't ride in blue jeans. She wears these…" Isla stopped talking and gave her head a frustrated shake. "Never mind. You don't get it! She's a huge celebrity."

Huge seemed like a bit of an overstatement. Levi doubted the average person had even heard of Summer Davies. He hadn't until Molly told him. But his daughter had, and who was he to argue the point? He'd had posters of rodeo stars on his bedroom walls when he was Isla's age.

The skepticism must have shown on his face because Isla went on, "Dad, listen. People like Summer, they are used to five-star hotels with lobster and champagne and hot tubs and towels folded like swans, and, and, and all that fancy stuff. You need to find a *nice* place for her to stay. Nell said the Suttons are renting their house out on one of those travel sites for ritzy vacation homes. Maybe you could talk to Bill Sutton and—"

"Isla, relax." Chuckling, he reached over and patted her knee. "She's bringing her RV. When I said I didn't know where she was staying, I meant I wasn't sure where she was going to park it yet. Hopefully, we'll have the hookups ready at the rodeo grounds. And besides, anyone who travels in an RV can't be all that different from us regular folk, right?"

CHAPTER THREE

"I HOPE THEY HAVE decent sushi in Eagle Springs," Summer commented from the passenger seat of the custom-built class A Equine Motorcoach. She was trying to locate the town on the map of Wyoming she'd pulled up on her iPad so she could peruse the area's shops, restaurants and services. Nugget lay curled contentedly on her lap.

Amidst the chaos and the minutiae of packing herself, Nugget and Sacha for a last-minute three-week journey, she'd forgotten a few things. Her straightening iron, for one. And there'd been no time to purchase enough of Sacha's supplements or her face moisturizer, both of which she would run out of at some point. There wasn't room to pack enough feed and supplies, so they'd need both a feed store and a health food shop. A good massage therapist would be nice, too, because sitting in this vehicle for hours on end hadn't done her back any favors. Before leaving town, Theo had loaded them up with grocery staples, but he hadn't had time for a haircut.

At the moment, though, hunger was edging into her number-one concern. "I could eat an entire platter of spicy tuna rolls right now."

They'd been on the road since yesterday, each taking a shift behind the wheel before stopping outside Lincoln, Nebraska, at a horse trainer friend of Theo's. There, they'd been able to exercise Sacha and board him for the night. This morning, they'd taken off early again, with Summer driving the first leg. After a quick stop for lunch, Theo had reclaimed the driver's seat, where he'd remained for the last few hours.

He tossed her an amused glance. "Summer, you do know where Eagle Springs, Wyoming, is located, right? Do you really want to eat sushi this far from the ocean?"

"I do now!" she cried triumphantly. "Here it is! The dot is so tiny I couldn't find it at first. Oh. Hmm. I can see how that ocean situation is a valid point. I wonder what types of food Wyoming is famous for?"

"I don't know," Theo guessed, "steak?"

Curious, she typed a quick search.

"Ding, ding, ding! You get points for steak. Also, chili, and rack of lamb," she reported.

"Yum, on all counts. But I'm not gonna lie, I will miss my tuna rolls."

Theo grinned. "You're going to miss a good deal more than that, I'm afraid."

Summer kept reading, filing away the state bird, flower, motto. She skimmed a brief article about the region's history and came away impressed that it was the first state to give women the vote. A tourism site revealed the place was awash with geothermal activity and hot springs, Yellowstone National Park was popular, the population was... Wait. What? She paused and read that last statistic again.

"Theo, did you know the population of Louisville is larger than the population of the entire state of Wyoming?"

That didn't seem possible. She looked up and out the window—at the vast expanse of... rolling hills against a blazing blue sky. Pretty, yes, but... But. Awareness mixed with trepidation as it dawned on her that she'd barely given any thought to where they were headed until now. Or, at least, what the "where" was all about.

She trusted Theo, and when he said he'd found her an easy paying gig that would allow her an escape from Louisville for a few weeks, that was all she'd needed to hear.

There hadn't been time to think about much more between packing and devising a story to sell her dad.

She didn't like lying—correction: omitting pertinent details—to her dad, but what choice did she have? They'd settled on a partial truth; Theo was whisking Summer and Sacha away for some focused, intense training before the Meadows Cup. Roland had lately been concerned about Summer's stress level, too, and how it might affect her performance, so he'd accepted the explanation almost without question. They didn't say where they were going exactly, and he hadn't asked. A testament, she thought, to Roland's own troubles and the cause of another spear of guilt. It had to be this way, she reminded herself; her dad couldn't be trusted not to tell Braden.

Braden. Her conversation with him had been an entirely different experience. An ordeal more exhausting than a four-day event competition, he opened with denial. Once Summer mentioned the video, he quickly moved on to excuses, claiming the "incident" had happened before he and Summer started dating. When she pointed out that you could see his tattoo in the video, he'd morphed "incident" into "mistake," and on it went.

The apologies were way too long in materializing, although once he got there, his teary-eyed performance had impressed her with its authenticity. The drama culminated in Braden begging for another chance. Impatient to put an end to the grueling conversation, Summer had told him she needed time and was leaving town to think things through.

He'd protested, but so what? She held all the cards, and in the end, Braden was eager to keep the real reason behind her ring toss to himself. They agreed that if any gossip hit the news, they'd laugh it off and call it a misunderstanding. It was also deemed practical to let everyone go on believing they'd be getting engaged soon. Summer was in no hurry for their sponsors to learn of their breakup. Not until she landed firmly on a Plan B.

"I did not know that," Theo answered. "But it certainly confirms my belief that there are entirely too many people populating Louisville these days."

"Or maybe not enough in Wyoming?" Summer pondered, feeling a twinge of concern. "Why *doesn't* anyone live here? Is there something wrong with this place?"

Like a scene from a horror movie, the vehicle slowed, Theo belted out a few bars of spooky music and said, "You're about to find out."

Summer looked up just in time to see a large painted answer to her question: Welcome to Eagle Springs! Home of the Eagle Springs Rodeo.

"DAD!" ISLA RUSHED into his office with her best friend, Nell McFee, hot on her heels. The girls loved exploring the rodeo grounds, chatting with the workers and reporting on their progress. His sister-in-law Harper, a social media influencer who'd volunteered to help Levi with promotion, had charged the girls with taking photos so she could do a series of before and after posts. It was a brilliant way to both involve Isla in the rodeo's production and keep her busy at the same time. Harper was awesome. Not only was he happy his brother Wyatt had found happiness, Levi felt lucky to have her in the Blackwell clan.

Admittedly, Levi had been more than a little suspicious of his sister-in-law's motives at first. Who wouldn't be when she'd married his brother in Vegas without knowing him at all, only for him to discover she was Brock Bedford's stepdaughter? Brock Bedford, the bank manager who'd called in the loan on the Flying Spur, partner of developer Xavier

Howard, and who, only a couple of weeks prior, had had Gran and his sister Adele arrested! Despite their inauspicious beginning, Wyatt and Harper had proven to be the real deal.

The girls halted before him, both wide-eyed and on the edge of breathless. "Here you are! We've been looking everywhere."

"Yeah?" Levi teased. "Can't believe you thought to look *here* in my office, where you find me every single day."

"Daaad," Isla drawled with a dramatic eye roll. "Please, stop kidding around. This is important."

He was grateful for a distraction from the paperwork he'd been tackling. Surprising how much "desk riding" this endeavor entailed. Although the work itself wasn't as tedious as he'd anticipated, but it was time-consuming. The phone was the worst. By the end of every day, he was so tired of talking on the thing he fantasized about pitching it out the window.

He composed his features to solemn and lowered his voice to match, "Yes, we are still on for Tucker's after we finish up here." He'd promised the girls a trip to the ice cream shop after they left for the day.

"Way more important than that." Isla

waved him off, and the fact that she did so had him listening. "*They* are here."

"They?" Levi repeated patiently.

"Summer Davies."

"And her horse," Nell added. "At least, we're pretty sure her horse is in there. Did you know she rides a Trakehner? I can't wait to see it in real life."

"Very sure, Dad. Like *very*."

"Oh, *that* they," Levi said and then gave his head a shake. "Sorry, girls, but Summer Davies can't be here already. She won't be arriving for…" He glanced at the calendar on the wall above his desk where Isla had drawn a horse and then circled the date marking Summer's arrival. "Another two weeks."

Despite the reassurance he'd given Isla a few days ago, they—meaning the rodeo facilities—weren't ready for guests. The grounds had been closed for nearly three years now. When the property's owner, Curtis Holloway, had retired to Arizona, it sat vacant for a year before an event company had taken over. But when a highly contagious equine disease swept through the town, they'd abandoned the project. No one stepped up to take their place.

Curtis, after deciding to sell the property, began liquidating equipment and furnishings. No buyer was forthcoming, and with the facilities empty and unattended, weather, neglect and Mother Nature had taken their toll. Grass and brush were growing wild all over the place. Mice had invaded many of the buildings, birds were nesting in the arena's rafters and a windstorm had torn a chunk off the stable's roof.

The tight schedule would have him working right down to the wire. The rodeo was only a few weeks away, but the buildings were still being cleaned and repaired. The arena was almost complete, but the floor was awaiting a topcoat of special sand, and the bleachers were only two-thirds refinished. The roof had been repaired, but the stall doors were being rebuilt, and the structure was only partially painted. But the biggest issue was the leaking pipe that had the water shut off.

To save time, and since he was in the process of purchasing the rodeo grounds and expanding the venue, he'd gone ahead and used his own money to replace the line.

Levi was grateful that he'd taken his great-uncle Elias's advice and settled on a price and terms for the property. It was basically a matter of signing the paperwork at this point. His gran might not be thrilled that her brother Elias, or Big E as nearly everyone called him, was in town to "help" get her through these tough times, but Levi was beginning to believe he had good intentions. Uncle Elias had set his mind to discovering a means to thwart Xavier Howard's plans to acquire the Flying Spur—and uncover the details of exactly how the vulture developer intended to hijack the entire town.

"Levi!" Molly hustled into the room behind the girls, confirming their announcement. "Summer Davies is here. Did you know she was arriving early? Never mind," she added, discarding the notion with the flap of her hand. "Of course you didn't. Where is she going to park that RV? We don't have any place suitable for her horse. We don't even have water!"

"Are you sure it's her?" he asked, hoping they were all wrong. "Could it be Jim? He has an RV." The plumber, Jim Hudson, had promised to be here bright and early in the morning to start on the water line. It was common practice for Jim to bring his trailer to a jobsite, stay the night and get started early. He lived way out of town, and this was going to be at least a three-day job.

"Not unless Jim has recently become the richest plumber in the world," Molly said dryly, obliterating Levi's remaining smidgen of doubt. "That doesn't look like any RV I've ever seen."

JUST AS SUMMER had failed to research their destination, so she'd neglected to vet their host. Theo had quickly stepped forward and introduced himself, allowing her time to form an impression of her very first Wyomingite, which sounded like some sort of mineral but was what people who hailed from the least populated state in the union called themselves. At least she'd managed to pick up a few useful tidbits in her much too brief cram session.

As she observed Levi Blackwell chatting with Theo, she tried to analyze her surprising reaction to the man. Why had she expected someone much older and less good-looking and way more…welcoming?

She estimated him to be in his late twenties or early thirties. He was tall and lean, with shoulders carved from stone and a jawline to match. He seemed too young to be retired from the rodeo and too handsome to be so… What? It wasn't that he was unfriendly exactly. Unenthusiastic, maybe? She wasn't sure, but something felt off.

"…and this is Summer Davies."

"I'm sorry?" Summer said, startling a bit when she heard her name. Pasting on a smile, she realized both men had turned toward her.

"Nice to meet you, Ms. Davies," he said, stepping forward to shake her hand. "Levi Blackwell."

"Summer," she replied. "Please, call me Summer."

For a few seconds, they remained hand in hand while his arresting gaze locked on to hers. Much more than the interesting green-gray shade of his eyes or his austere expression was what she saw there, what she *felt*.

But what was she feeling exactly? Empathy, she decided as she took a moment to study him. Levi Blackwell looked a lot like she felt. Tired, anxious and maybe a little grumpy, but trying not to show it.

Releasing her hand, he stepped away, tucking both his hands into the back pockets of his worn blue jeans. Then he did this particular sort of slow fidget, shifting his weight from one foot to the other, which generated another theory. She'd bet her favorite Juniper saddle this guy was in pain, too.

He said, "You folks arrived a bit earlier than we expected."

Had they? Summer flashed a questioning glance at Theo, who delivered Levi an apologetic grin and answered, "We did. I have an aunt in Jackson, but Summer had never been to Wyoming, so we decided to make a vacation of it."

When Theo said they were loading up the motorcoach and getting out of Louisville, she hadn't questioned him. But now she wanted to laugh at the idea of a vacation in this place. The least populated state in the nation wasn't exactly on her travel bucket list. No sushi. No spa. No thanks.

"I see. Well, this is pretty country for sure." Glancing at Summer, he added, "You're in for a treat. But we've been undergoing some significant renovations getting ready for the rodeo, and unfortunately, our lodgings are not quite ready to accommodate guests yet."

"Oh, don't worry about us." Theo casually tossed a hitchhiker thumb over his shoulder. "This tin can on wheels has everything we need. If we can get Sacha set up, all we need is power and water, and we'll be good."

"Sacha?"

"My horse," Summer supplied.

"Uh-huh." Levi brushed a hand across his jaw and then brought it to rest on his hip. "Well, that's the thing. See, we've got the water shut off for a major repair. And the stable isn't ready, either, and won't be for at least a week. We could put your horse in one of the corrals—"

"Corral?" Summer interjected a little sharper than she intended. But was this guy for real? "Are you serious? My horse can't stay *outside* in a *corral*."

"Oh?" Blackwell's brow traveled upward before descending again into a thoughtful crease. "That's interesting. I don't think I've ever met an *inside* horse. How does that work? Is it like a house cat where you have a litter box? Or a city dog that you put in one of those crates?"

Summer felt her cheeks heat with embarrassment even though she knew he was joking. Sort of joking, she amended because she could tell he'd been annoyed by her interruption.

"No. I didn't mean that he's never outside—I meant he can't *sleep* outside."

"It's early fall, though. Temps are mild. It's not raining or snowing. Twenty below, sure, then I agree that a horse needs to be inside but for a—"

"It's not about that," she interrupted again, trying to temper her impatience. "I don't need a lesson about suitable weather conditions for my horse. The temperature doesn't matter so much as his…" Trying *too* hard, she realized, because her voice sounded condescending even to her own ears.

This was one of the many reasons she was so terrible at publicity. She could never seem to land on the correct tone or the proper expression. She'd stopped short of adding the word *security*. She knew this guy wouldn't get it even as she wanted to add, *Sacha is my life, my teammate and the horse of my heart. Not to mention an investment that cost as much as a modest-sized home.*

But this Blackwell guy wasn't going to understand any of that. He was a rodeo man. A dude. A cowboy. His relationship with horses was different than hers. These people viewed animals as livestock, tools to be utilized. Not that they didn't care for them, of course, but her world was different. She treated her horse like she would a family member, better probably than many people treated their families.

"So much as what?" Blackwell prompted. "Does he have a medical condition?"

"No, but he always sleeps in a stall. He wouldn't be comfortable staying outside all night."

Blackwell stared blankly, and Summer could tell he was struggling with how to respond and possibly what to think of her.

Finally, he went with, "He wouldn't be *comfortable*? What does his comfort entail?"

"Look," Summer said, shifting on her own now-fidgety feet. "Sacha is a very valuable horse. He requires a certain level of care. For example, we have an evening routine, a ritual."

"Like what?" he asked, mouth hinting at a smile. But not the kind of smile that suggested he was laughing *with* her. Nope, she already knew this was going to be a joke at her expense. "A hot toddy and a bedtime story?"

Theo let out a loud surprised guffaw.

Summer felt a flare of irritation because this wasn't funny. Not to her. Ignoring his sarcasm, she focused on the issue. "Is there anywhere in this town that has boarding facilities?"

He lifted one shoulder. "Sure," he said. "My grandmother's place, the Flying Spur for one, but that's a ways out of town." Then he rattled off some more names.

"Great. Do any of them have a place where we can also park the motorcoach?"

"The...?" Blackwell drew out question-style while his eyebrows took another trip skyward. He turned and gave the vehicle an assessing once-over. "There's an *RV park* not far outside of town near the Blue Mist Run River. It's a pretty spot. I'm certain they can accommodate your…" He paused, seemingly to search for a word, and finally finished with, "you."

"What types of facilities do they have?"

"Full hookups as far as I know. Does your, uh…what was it again?"

"Motorcoach," she supplied, her jaw now so tight with tension it ached.

"Yeah, that's it. Does your *motorcoach* require something special beyond that, too? Perhaps a sleep mask for the headlights and a radiator massage?"

Theo laughed again.

Blackwell smirked, making her 99 percent certain he'd misunderstood her on purpose. Only that remaining sliver of a chance enabled her to respond with a tight-lipped, "I'm referring to *equine* facilities where I can stay *with* my horse."

What she needed was to get away from this guy before she said something she'd regret. Because what she did not need was for this backwoods rodeo clown to needle her into losing her temper. Again. Too bad she didn't have another ring to toss, or even better, a horseshoe to chuck at him.

"No, there are no, uh, combination RV

equine *glamp*-grounds around here that I know of."

"Glamp-ground?" Summer repeated, surprised that he even knew the trendy term for an upscale campground. Which wasn't even what she was looking for! "Listen, you need to—"

Theo caught her eye and shook his head. *Breathe*, he mouthed.

He was right. It wasn't worth it. As Theo repeatedly reminded her, all she could control was her reaction to a stressful situation. She couldn't control the cause—or the irritating, annoying, sarcastic cowboy who seemed to be purposely goading her.

Summer nodded and inhaled deeply before continuing, "Okay," she said calmly, reasonably. "I think we're suffering from a communication breakdown here. The bottom line is that I can't be separated from my horse."

"You…?" He bit off another word like maybe he was trying to rein in his frustration, too. He sighed. "I don't know what to tell you. I am trying to give you options, but—"

"Unacceptable ones. How are you planning to host a rodeo without adequate accommodations?"

"Well," he returned in a flat tone. "The accommodations will be more than adequate in *two weeks* when you're actually due to arrive."

That's when Summer's predicament, the situation she'd impulsively signed on for, began to sink in. When Theo had read her the email from his aunt's friend, it had seemed like a gift from fate. A rodeo in Wyoming was looking for a host who could also perform at the event. Theo had been wanting to take a trip out here to visit his aunt and look for some horses to buy. The fee was surprisingly generous and, with the free accommodations, would more than pay for the trip.

In her mind, this had translated to the temporary escape she craved: three Braden-free, Dad-free, drama-free, stress-free weeks in a place where no one knew her. She'd imagined her and Sacha practicing and working out their precompetition jitters without any distractions. All she had to do was announce some names and perform a quick riding exhibition at their little rodeo. Easy-peasy.

Except, she hadn't thoroughly considered the logistics of it all. Couldn't have known that dealing with this Blackwell guy would be the opposite of stress-free. Her stomach began fizzing with a whole new source of anxiety as she realized she now had to follow through. Three weeks with this guy seemed like an eternity.

Or…not? It wasn't as if she'd signed a contract. Clearly, this wasn't the retreat she'd been seeking after all. Composing her features into a glare, she met Blackwell's challenging expression while she formed the words to tell him so.

CHAPTER FOUR

BEFORE SUMMER COULD open her mouth to politely inform Blackwell and his smirk that they'd be leaving but would *not* be returning in two weeks, Theo stepped forward. "Levi, I apologize for the mix-up. That's my fault. But I'm sure we can figure something out." Then he asked, "Can you think of somewhere we could stay until you've sorted your renovations? There must be some riding clubs around that host equestrian events? Closer to a city, maybe? We could even stay in Jackson if we need to."

Summer snorted out a laugh. "Yes, by all means, let's head to the *city* and talk to the other four people who live in this state."

Blackwell leveled her a narrow-eyed look of confusion. "You say that like it's a bad thing."

She shrugged a shoulder. "I don't know why anyone would want to live in a town without sushi or a spa."

"Sushi and a spa?" He repeated before inhaling a deep breath, holding it in his cheeks, and then exhaling with a long sigh. "Unbelievable," he muttered. Then, "Listen, Ms. Davies, as much as I appreciate that you traveled all this way, I don't think—"

"Fine," Summer interrupted. "We'll go and—"

"We appreciate this opportunity," Theo interjected. "Truly, we do. Levi, again, I'm sorry. This misunderstanding is all my fault. I'm the one who didn't ask the necessary questions and clarify our travel plans. But we want to work this out. We're excited to be here, to relax, and have a much-needed vacation." He made a show of looking around like an option might pop up out of the ground and present itself on a silver platter.

Good luck with that, Summer thought. At this point, she was convinced the only answer lay in climbing back inside the motorcoach and heading east, although the thought of confining Sacha any longer gave her pause.

Theo tried again. "As I was saying, do you know of anywhere we could find a ranch with an empty stall and room to park our vehicle? Even just for the night?"

"Ours does!" Isla cried. "We have a spot. You could stay at our place. We've got empty stalls and a full hookup for an RV. We even have our own arena. There are lots of places to ride."

Levi barely squelched a groan. He'd been so focused on Diva Davies here that he hadn't heard Isla, Nell and Molly approaching. He'd been about to suggest the Flying Spur, where they had boarding facilities and room for an RV but was considering the ramifications. His family had enough problems without foisting a difficult boarder on them, too. He could only imagine his sister Corliss's face when Summer asked her where the nearest spa was. It would be funny, except it wasn't.

He realized he'd been half hoping she'd climb into her motor-mansion and disappear. If he didn't need her so much, he'd have already suggested it.

"That's a super idea!" an unhelpful Molly gushed. "Isla, sweetie, you are a genius." Sweeping a hand toward Levi, she informed their guests, "This guy has got a luxury RV hideaway you would not believe. He designed and built it for his in-laws. And let me tell you, his place is something special, too."

Levi had installed the deluxe space for Pete and Gloria, his ex-wife's parents. They enjoyed traveling in their RV, and after Isla was born, they'd made the trip from Cheyenne a regular occurrence. With Nash's and Wyatt's help, he'd poured a concrete pad, constructed a covered area next to the house, run power and water to the spot, and even added a brick-lined fire pit. The whole setup could not be more perfect, and yet he feared that this woman staying anywhere near his property could only be a nightmare.

"Molly?" Theo asked, extending a hand. "I'm Theo Lundy."

"Well, Theo." Molly grinned, looked him over and then went in for a hug. "I'm so pleased to finally meet you. Your aunt Stella says nothing but the sweetest things about you."

Theo's aunt was a friend of Molly's, which was how Molly had hooked them up with Summer, a turn of events Levi was rapidly regretting.

Then his kind, precocious, polite and unfortunately solicitous daughter reached out a hand and made everything worse. "Welcome to Wyoming, Ms. Davies. My name is Isla Blackwell. This is my friend Nell. We love horses, too. We've been counting down the days until you got here, and it's an honor to meet you."

"WE ARE *NOT* STAYING," Summer vowed in an angry whisper voice, which ended up sounding more like a breathy shout. At least she'd managed to wait until they'd climbed back inside the motorcoach, where she planted herself in the passenger seat. She yanked on her seat belt, which held fast, a mocking reminder to slow down and get a grip.

"I know," Theo said, calmly sinking into the driver's seat. "No water. Can you imagine? We have enough in the tank for about one more day, but I'm not thrilled at the notion of hunting down a water source every few days."

She released the strap with exaggerated slow motion and then pulled it again, before snapping the buckle into place with a satisfying click.

"Listen to me, Theo, we need to get out of here now." Nugget leaped into place on her lap and let out an agreeable woof. "See? Nugget agrees."

"We are. Stop worrying. We'll get Sacha settled at Blackwell's place, and all will be well." Then he lowered his voice to match Summer's. "What's with the weird whisper voice?"

"Blackwell is a condescending jerk face," she said, only slightly louder this time.

"How so?"

She huffed. "Don't pretend like you didn't see us *not* hitting it off."

"That would have been difficult to miss." Chuckling, Theo started the engine. "That doesn't make him a *jerk face*, though, does it? Maybe you two aren't going to be BFFs, but nothing I witnessed gives me the impression that he's an all-around, overall bad person."

"Ha! Trust me, he's a jerk face, and I am always right about people."

"You?" Theo laughed hard as he steered the vehicle onto the two-lane road.

"Why is that funny?"

"Summer, you cannot be serious. You are rarely right about people. You have to know this about yourself. You constantly make snap judgments."

"I do not!"

"Wren Cooper, Arianna Gilbert, Jonah Maxwell."

"Why are you randomly spouting off names of my favorite show jumping rivals?"

"Because those are three examples right off the top of my head of three humans who you disliked upon first meeting but later decided were nice people. Wren is even your friend now."

"That's not fair, and you know it—Arianna had just lost that huge competition when we met, and Jonah's dad had just died. And Wren is super shy until you get to know her, which takes a long, *long* time."

"Umm…" Theo drawled while slowly shaking his head. "You can see how you are making my point here? A snap judgment is one you make without all the facts."

Hmm. Well, those examples were not… untrue. Okay, so they were true-*ish*. "Fine," she conceded. "Possibly, at times, in the past, I have formed opinions a tad too quickly."

"Do I even need to mention Braden? You *knew* him forever, and you were still wrong."

Summer winced. "Ouch," she said because hearing this truth voiced aloud caused a fresh dose of painful humiliation.

"I'm sorry," Theo said. "That was going too far."

"It's okay," she answered softly. "You were spot-on about Braden. You warned me, and I…"

"I wanted to be wrong."

"I *wanted* you to be wrong."

How could she have been so off the mark about Braden? Sure, she knew they were different. He was the charismatic socialite to her happy homebody. He goofed off. She worked hard. And yes, he could be self-centered. But she was hyperfocused on Sacha, riding and her goals to the point where it was a relief that he gave her so much space. Most of the time. Although now she couldn't help but wonder what he'd been doing with all that "space."

Cue video reel, accompanied by a familiar current of humiliation.

Summer was grateful when Theo swung the conversation back to the present and more urgent matter at hand. "He has a cute kid—polite, smart, curious. That has to count for something, don't you think?"

She couldn't argue with that observation. Isla Blackwell was unequivocally adorable, as was her friend Nell. After politely introducing themselves, the girls had bombarded Summer with horse questions and engaging, intelligent conversation. That was, until the fun police, a.k.a. Levi Blackwell, had steered the girls back toward the office and told them to gather their things.

Then he'd pulled a tiny spiral-bound notebook and a pen from his shirt pocket and jotted down the address and directions to his place. Why couldn't he just text the address like a normal person?

Then he informed them that he had business to finish up, but they could "head out," and he'd follow in an hour or so to show them around. In the meantime, they could turn Sacha out into the empty pasture on the east side of the small barn. At least he'd had the decency to think about the fact that her horse had been on the road for two days and needed to stretch his legs.

"What do you think his wife is like?" Summer asked and then went on before Theo could answer, "Besides being a saint, obviously. But beyond that, don't you find it strange that he didn't call and ask her if she was okay with us staying there? I'd be so irritated if my husband did that."

"That's the way country people are, Summer. They're generous and polite and make people feel welcome."

She rolled her eyes and added a dubious snort. "So, by that logic, we could deduce that Blackwell originally hails from the big city?"

"He's letting us stay with him, though," Theo countered. "I can't think of anything more selfless and generous than opening your home to total strangers."

"We're not staying. You heard that part, right? Tomorrow, we are out of here."

"LEVI, THEY ARE total strangers!" Levi's sister Adele admonished after he'd filled her in on the circumstances. He'd dropped Nell off and then swung by her house in town to drop off the sleeping bag he'd borrowed for Isla's sleepover.

Close in age, Adele and Levi had grown up doing everything together, with younger brother Wyatt as their sidekick. They remained tight. A bond that had only strengthened when, after years of marriage, they'd found themselves single again at the same time. Levi's divorce seemed like a breeze compared to the death of Adele's husband. She'd been newly pregnant with the twins when he'd died. Having had plenty of baby practice with Isla, he'd given Adele all the support and babysitting his life could spare.

When Levi turned down Adele's offer of sticking around for pie, he'd had to explain about his guests because typically, nothing short of a gastrointestinal virus would prevent him from staying for pie. And Isla adored her two-year-old twin cousins, Ivy and Quinn, and was always happy to keep them entertained.

Adele glanced into the toy-cluttered living room, where Isla and the girls were stacking giant foam blocks on top of the ottoman. Lowering her voice to a whisper, she asked, "What were you thinking inviting them to stay at your place? They could murder you in your sleep."

"In Eagle Springs, Wyoming? Besides, did you not hear the part about them having an RV? An extremely large and fancy one that I can't wait for Big E to see."

Ivy toddled toward him, then stopped, chubby arms stretched high in the universal baby sign for "you can pick me up now." Levi gladly acquiesced, scooping her up and then planting a loud kiss on the top of her head. That earned him an adorable baby belly laugh. She patted his cheek, and Levi felt his heart melt. He missed this phase where there wasn't much you could do wrong in your baby's eyes.

Adele's entire demeanor lightened as she watched the interplay. "It's super cute how much she adores you." But she wasn't finished with her lecture. Expression back to determined, she frowned at him. "Haven't you ever read *In Cold Blood*? It happened in the middle of Nowhere, Kansas."

"No, Adele, I haven't. And please don't tell me about it. You need to stop listening to those true-crime podcasts. Although, with your track record lately, I'm wondering if your goal is to star in one." He'd lost count of how many times his sister had been arrested in the preceding weeks. Minor infractions all, but he was starting to wonder if Sheriff McMillan had it in for his sister.

"Funny," Adele returned flatly and then muttered something unflattering about said sheriff under her breath.

"What I was thinking was how I need a star attraction for the rodeo. Any attraction will do at this point. I don't exactly have a lot of options here—unless you're volunteering to juggle like you did when you won the talent show back in middle school?"

Adele grinned. "You couldn't afford me."

"Probably not, which means I'm stuck with Summer Davies. I don't like the woman, that's true, but I can't see her as a murderer."

That explanation was only partially true, Levi silently acknowledged. After thinking things through, he'd decided that his place was indeed the best option. There were several reasons for this. Location being the main one. The woman was clearly high maintenance with a superior attitude that would not play well with the more down-to-earth populace of Eagle Springs. Out at his place, she'd be farther from the goings-on in town and less likely to mix with people—people he needed for her not to annoy so they'd show up at the rodeo. Although once she saw his living arrangements, there was a danger she'd take off and be gone for good anyway.

His ex, Kylie, hadn't been shy about letting him know how off-putting his home was. "No woman would ever want to live like this," she'd informed Levi repeatedly. Levi told himself he didn't care. Like he'd told Adele, it wasn't as if Summer Davies was going to be living *with him* anyway. She had her swanky motor-palace, and she could use the barn, arena and corrals. That was it, no reason for her to even see the living quarters. They didn't need to mingle.

Except, Isla. How would he explain any of this to his daughter? She was so proud of their farm.

Okay, so it wasn't a perfect plan. If Summer did opt to stay, her proximity to Isla could potentially become a problem. Sure, she'd been nice upon first meeting the girls, but that was probably the ingrained politeness from her upbringing. How long would that last? How patient would she be with Isla following her around and asking millions of questions? Isla clearly had Summer Davies on a tall, tall pedestal, and even the idea of the woman brushing his daughter off caused a flicker of anger to ignite inside him.

Not to mention that he didn't want any of

that spoiled, entitled attitude to rub off on her. Levi would just have to make sure Isla wasn't allowed to spend too much time with her. Which, now that he thought about it, should be simple enough. Isla would be at her mother's for a week starting tomorrow. After they got home, Summer would be busy getting settled and coddling her precious horse. He could keep Isla distracted and out of the barn for an evening. That only left the morning.

In a fortuitous happenstance, he'd promised Isla an early trail ride, and he highly doubted Summer would be getting out of bed at the crack of dawn to clean her horse's stall. He was pretty sure that was Theo's role. They'd get an early start and make it an extra-long ride before they had to leave for town to meet her mother at noon. Next weekend, he'd make a new plan—if their guest was still around.

Then it dawned on him that tomorrow would mark the first time he'd ever been glad to see his daughter go, a thought that promptly earned Davies the Diva yet another black mark.

"Hmm. Where's she from? What do you know about her?"

"Kentucky," he answered. "And I didn't ask about her criminal history if that's what you're getting at, but you could ask the sheriff to run a background check for me the next time you're in jail."

"Enough already," she said and then rolled her eyes. "That gag has run its course. The rodeo isn't for another three weeks, right?"

"Yeah."

"Why did they show up so early?"

Levi felt a rush of irritation at this reminder. Because how much arrogance did it take to drive all this way and just assume the red carpet would be rolled out when you arrived?

He shrugged a helpless shoulder. "They're on vacation, I guess." He lowered a now-fidgeting Ivy, who ran squealing into the living room to tackle her cousin and sister. The three of them collapsed into a giggling heap.

Curiosity dancing across her face, Adele handed over a to-go container of pie and asked, "What kind of person takes their horse on vacation?"

"WHERE'S THE HOUSE?" a perplexed Summer asked, raising a flattened hand to shield her eyes from the rays of the late afternoon sun.

There were several structures, including an easily identifiable riding arena. She counted two barns, one significantly larger than the other, making it clear which was the small barn Blackwell had referenced. There were three other outbuildings, one of which appeared to be a chicken coop. A bright green tractor was parked near the smaller barn along with a faded, dusty ATV and an old flatbed truck. There were no other vehicles in sight.

An assortment of colorful cows of multiple breeds and horses grazed in a distant field. A closer enclosure held a smaller herd of goats, while another contained a smattering of sheep and a pair of llamas. For some reason, this variety came as something of a surprise. Several of the critters had moved to the fence line and were watching them curiously. The goats bleated loud friendly-sounding greetings, which made her smile even in her agitated state.

"I guess we should keep driving?" Theo pondered.

Summer puffed an impatient sigh. "See? Blackwell could have at least mentioned that we needed to drop Sacha off and then keep going. You can't even see the house from here! Ugh. I'll probably have to walk a mile to check on my horse. You know how inconvenient that is? No wonder he was so hesitant to let us stay. Maybe we can park here near the barn instead. It'll only be one night, and we—"

"Wait a minute…" Theo said, squinting off into the distance.

Summer looked around again, prepping herself for how miserable this was going to be. She wouldn't be able to sleep not knowing if Sacha was secure, which meant at least one trip in the middle of the night and another first thing in the morning. Blackwell's weather comment came to mind. A check of the forecast had revealed that it was already freezing here at night. She might have to purchase a warmer coat.

She didn't even want to think about how awful the trek would be in the middle of winter when it was blowing snow. Thanks to her self-imposed Wyoming crash course, she'd also learned the state was teeming with wolves, coyotes, bears and cougars, and it wasn't unheard of for livestock to be harassed—or worse. They could be hanging around outside where they'd pounce on an opportunity to harass her, too. Tomorrow could not come soon enough.

"I think they live in the big barn," Theo finally stated, pointing at the largest, gray-painted structure.

"What?" Summer repeated, the concept not registering. "No!"

"Yep. See how there are shades up there on

the second-story windows? And those colorful things hanging down sure look like flowers to me—pretty sure that's a deck on the upper story. I think Blackwell lives in a *barndominium*."

For a long moment, Summer couldn't process what she'd heard. But as she studied the evidence, her pulse kicked up its pace. "Blackwell lives in a *barndo*?" No. Couldn't be. No way was the guy they met cool enough to have a barn home.

It was Summer's secret dream to live in a barn home, or *barndominium* or *barndo* as they were often called, with her horses. Well, she would live *above* them on the second story, and it wasn't a total secret because Theo knew about it.

He was the only one who knew, including how she went so far as to collect barn home plans. Not that she would ever build one. Even if she could afford it, her dad would be mortified. Braden would never agree to live in such close proximity to any horse. He rode, yes, but he didn't tend to his horses. He had a stable full of staff for that.

But dreams were dreams, right? You couldn't really expect them to come true. If childhood had taught her anything, it was that, but fantasies were fun and had sustained her through those tough times.

Theo's grin was all cat and canary as if he couldn't be more pleased about these circumstances. "This must elevate Blackwell's standing somewhat, huh?"

"Hardly," Summer scoffed. "Where someone lives has absolutely no bearing whatsoever on who they are as a person." But even as she uttered the words, she knew she didn't entirely believe them. Because there was a small piece of her, an itty-bitty slice, and one she did not like at all, that was placated. At least, for now. Not that she was going to admit it.

"Do you still want to leave tomorrow?"

"Probably not," she answered primly. "We'll stay a day or two, see how things go. Call it a research trip."

Theo grinned. He knew she was lying, and she knew he knew she was lying. And they both knew it would take a lot more than Levi Blackwell's surly attitude to get her out of here now.

CHAPTER FIVE

"As you can see, each stall has a run attached. Food dispenser, auto water, heat and exhaust system…" Levi managed to relay all of this information matter-of-factly as if he hadn't poured nearly every penny of his rodeo earnings into building the place. Like he hadn't meticulously researched every single aspect of its design and then sweated and cried and shed blood over the construction.

After continuing down the aisle where stalls lined each side, he stopped at the end. A long hallway branched off from both sides, and he turned right. "Supplies are in this area." He pointed. "We keep the feed in there. Tack room is on the left." Hard to miss as the door was labeled with one of the cool rustic signs his sister Corliss had special ordered and gifted him. "Pretty much anything you could need is in there. Go ahead and help yourself. Ask if you can't find something—we probably have it. Behind that door at the end, you'll find bedding material—we use pine shavings, but the feed store in town carries chips and pellets if you prefer. Blue wheelbarrows for shavings, black for manure. Down there, out that door is the manure pile."

Summer's head seemed to be on a swivel, glancing here and there like she'd never seen anything like it. Then again, considering the world she lived in, she probably hadn't. He wondered if she'd ever mucked a stall. He imagined grooms and stable people, or whatever she called the hired help, doing all the heavy lifting.

"Where's Theo?" he asked because he assumed that was who would be doing her dirty work. He didn't want to have to repeat himself.

"Uh, I don't know." She glanced around absently as if only just realizing he wasn't around. "On the phone, I think. Do you mind if I...?" she asked, one thumb hitched while she sidestepped toward the tack room.

"Be my guest." Might not have the expensive supplies she was used to, but everything was neatly organized and meticulously tended. "Feel free to commandeer a spot for your tack," he offered politely. "Should be plenty of room on the far end." He kept a couple of spaces clear for guests who came over to use his arena or take a trail ride on the vast expanse of forest service land that bordered his property.

She disappeared inside. Levi waited, disliking the part of him that felt anxious about being judged. Maybe she'd find this all unsuitable and go stay somewhere else. But he didn't want that either, he reminded himself. He needed her. The rodeo needed her.

Several minutes passed before she re-emerged. Closing the door behind her with a soft click, she then stood facing him with her back against the door. Head bowed, she stared at the ground while seconds ticked by, and Levi tried not to fidget. She swung her gaze up to meet his, catching him off guard; there was a softness there he hadn't seen before, a sweetness.

As if she'd opened a door, he noticed more things, too, like the shifting deep blue shade of her eyes, more gray than blue, he noted, the color calling to mind a rolling bank of storm clouds over the foothills.

Her expression, however, was a mystery. She didn't look displeased exactly, but it was hard to tell what she was thinking. When she wasn't scowling, it was impossible not to admire other nice things about her, too.

Slowly, she patted the tack room door behind her with the flat of one palm and informed him, "There is a bed in here, a people bed."

"Yes, I know." Technically, it was a set of bunks, and there was also a recliner, television and kitchenette, but he was pretty sure she'd seen all of that, too.

Forehead crinkling, she dipped her head back down with a disbelieving shake. "I can't even..." she uttered so softly he wondered if she was aware she'd spoken aloud. No, he decided when the rest of her thought trailed off into silence.

Disappointment settled into him, along with a hint of embarrassment, more than he expected and way more than was comfortable. He refused to acknowledge the comment, to explain or justify his lifestyle, his desire to—

"Where will Sacha be staying? Will he be inside here with your horses and other...animals? There's a lot of them. But I noticed you have another barn, too."

"Yes," he answered tightly. "Not all of them sleep inside, though. And the goats bunk together in this double stall, and the other barn is used for storage."

"I see." She looked to where he pointed. "This is quite the, um, menagerie you've got here, huh?"

He chose to ignore the question because it was more of an observation, wasn't it? *Menagerie* was only a slightly more polite way to call his place a zoo. He didn't owe her an explanation about why he did what he did. It was none of her business.

"We'll put your horse down on the far end for now, away from our lot. Give him a few days to settle in and let everyone get used to the new-guy smell before we introduce him." On this point, Levi would not negotiate.

"Mmm-hmm," she answered with a series of head bobs while nibbling on her bottom lip. "That's good. I brought paperwork from his vet showing that he's up to date on everything."

He nodded even though he'd already made this assumption. That was common practice in the world of equine sports. "During the daytime, you can use the same field you did today. In a few days, we'll put Sacha in the adjacent corral and see how it goes, and then we'll decide from there."

The furrow in her brow suggested uncertainty.

"I can promise you he'll be safe. I'm right upstairs."

"Yes, of course he will." She added a tentative half smile before lifting a hand and pointing one finger straight up at the ceiling. "So, you, uh, you live up there, huh?"

Here we go, Levi thought, and said, "We do."

"What's that like?"

"Convenient," he answered simply, which was the understatement of the century.

Luxurious would be a better word, he decided. Wyoming weather was extreme, to say the least. After a lifetime of layering on whatever necessary gear parka, long underwear, stocking cap, insulated coveralls, rain jacket, wool socks, boots—to feed or check on an animal, and then peeling it all off again, multiple times a day, what else could he call it? Now when he opened the door at the end of the hallway and walked down those stairs that led directly into the stables wearing nothing more than jeans and shirtsleeves, he felt like a king. This barn was his castle. He might not have the big family he'd always envisioned, but he and Isla had each other and their fur-covered crew.

"Well," she said with a sigh. "This is…"

Levi waited, tense and unsettled, preparing for whatever condescending comment she might throw his way. Formulating a series of snappy comebacks so he could—

"I am very grateful and relieved," she

stated firmly. "From the bottom of my heart, thank you."

He stared at her, and he knew he was staring, but the declaration caught him off guard, as did the sincerity in her tone. Abandoning his collection of sarcastic replies, he went with an imaginative, "I'm glad. And you're welcome."

She exhaled loudly, a breathy sound of relief and satisfaction that left him feeling relieved, too, despite his earlier vow. Then she hit him with another punch: a smile, a real one, the kind where you can see the light and the joy shining out from the inside. That's when he realized Summer Davies was more than pretty. Quite a bit more.

Something shook loose inside him, something dark and bitter that had been holding tight ever since things went south with Kylie. It broke, scattered and then a new sensation formed and settled in the center of his chest. What was happening here?

Summer said, "Sacha is generally great with other horses. But he's still fairly young, and he's a stallion, so there's always an element of unpredictability. When he's, uh, constantly looking to make a love connection." Was she blushing? "Well, you know…" She flapped a hand. "Makes him silly."

Yes! Levi wanted to shout. *Attraction!* That's what this was about. It makes men silly, too. It was making him a little silly. Because that's all this was, this new *feeling* he had for her. So, she was beautiful, so what? It was more the shock of finding her attractive than anything. He hadn't been able to see it before because she wasn't a pleasant person, and this new realization had caught him off guard. But just because she was pretty and liked horses and approved of his boarding facilities didn't mean anything more than that.

Instead, he nodded. "I am familiar with those tendencies."

"Of course you are. You've probably seen all kinds of horse hijinks and shenanigans in your life as a rodeo star."

"Sure. But I wasn't—"

"Yep, he was a star," Isla confirmed, joining them. *Wow.* Levi hadn't even heard her coming down the stairs, probably because he'd been too busy gawking at Summer and rationalizing this new…revelation. Heat crept up his cheeks at the idea that his daughter may have noticed.

"Hello, Isla!" Summer greeted her with warmth and enthusiasm. "I was hoping to see you again."

"Hi, Summer. We'll probably be seeing a lot of each other for a while, huh?"

"I sure hope so."

Not if I can help it, Levi thought, reminded now of his mission.

Nugget let out an eager bark, jogged toward Isla, sat and then looked up expectantly. She laughed and scooped him up, and he licked her cheek. She giggled and complimented him, "You're so cute!"

Summer laughed. "He likes you, and he doesn't normally take to strangers so quickly."

They began chatting, and Levi heard Isla mention her horse Cricket, and Summer asked a question, but he quickly lost track of the conversation because again, he was distracted by her luminous smile and happy eyes. What had happened to elicit this dramatic change in her? Didn't matter, he told himself. This time he was prepared because he was way too old and experienced to get silly over a woman.

Isla was talking about her riding club, so he stole a glance at Summer, who appeared eager, interested. Tipping her head back, she laughed, and dimples flashed in her cheeks. Huh. He hadn't noticed that before. Cute. Was it his imagination, or did people with dimples look happier when they smiled?

"Right, Dad?" Isla asked.

"Mmm? Right," he answered without knowing the question because he figured he had a better than fifty-fifty shot at that being the appropriate response.

"Dad never brags. He says once you start bragging, that's when you get bucked off. But his record speaks for itself, don't you think?"

"Yes, I do," Summer agreed, shooting him a quick, approving glance. "You must be so proud of him."

Apparently, Isla had rattled off some of his achievements. Levi doubted Summer had a clue what any of those rodeo titles meant. Probably, she was bored to tears. It was time to wrap up this little chat.

"Super proud. My dad is awesome. So is our house. He designed it. Do you want to come upstairs and see my room? You will love it. It's all horses. Even the sheets on my bed." Bouncing on her toes, she couldn't keep the excitement at bay.

"Isla, no," Levi answered a little too quickly. He could kick himself for not stepping in sooner; things were already getting too familiar.

He felt two sets of female eyes land on him—one shooting daggers of disappointment and the other flickering with... What was that? Once again, he couldn't tell what Summer was thinking, but it so closely mirrored his daughter's expression that it left him disconcerted. And confused.

Since the daggers were all he cared about, he addressed Isla, "It's getting late, kiddo. We need to head upstairs and get ready for bed."

"It's not a school night," she countered logically.

"True, but you need to…" What did she need to do besides what she usually did, which was hang out with him here in the barn? "Uh, get your room picked up before bedtime."

"But I already—"

It dawned on him then that she'd probably been upstairs doing that since she'd invited Summer to see it. Prompting him to rush out another excuse, "We need to get to bed early so we can make it up to Hatchet Ridge tomorrow." The reminder of the trail ride he'd promised should help his cause.

Brow furrowing, she countered, "But it won't take long, and my room is clean."

"It will take longer than you think," Levi said, irrationally wishing his daughter would quit being so logical. "We still need to eat dinner and feed…" Everyone was fed! "The cats."

"The cats?" she repeated, clearly perplexed. And why wouldn't she be? The cats came and went as they pleased through their very own cat door and ate whenever they wanted. "But—"

"Yep, forgot this morning. I bet they're starving!" That sounded so goofy. He was a terrible liar. "And your mother will not be pleased if she picks you up tomorrow and you're all worn out for her birthday party." That much was true, at least. Kylie was militant about the parenting agreement, even though her time with Isla seemed to be as much about Levi's time without her.

This birthday party was a perfect example. They shared custody and agreed that Isla would be allowed to visit on their respective birthdays regardless of what the calendar decreed. That was why she had to go home a day early, which would be fine, except Levi knew Kylie and Brett were planning a huge party, one with catered food, a band and an open bar. Not the kind of party a ten-year-old would enjoy and where she'd ultimately spend the bulk of the evening with a babysitter.

Isla's face crumpled with confusion as she looked up at him, and Levi could see her struggling to make sense of his disjointed excuses. She wanted to argue; he could see that, too. Guilt pooled inside him as he willed his child into compliance. Or maybe it was his stern expression. Either way, it worked.

Nodding somberly, she said, "Okay, well, maybe some other time then. Good night, Summer." Face a perfect picture of brave dejection, she turned, slumped her shoulders and shambled toward the door. The only thing missing was an accompaniment of sad violin music.

"Good night, Isla," Summer called after her. "Don't worry! Like you mentioned—I'll be around for a few weeks. I'd love to see your room whenever we can work it out."

Guilt flooded through him, and he vowed to make tomorrow's ride an extra-long one to make up for his daughter's disappointment. Disappointment, he assured himself, that would be unimportant in the grand scheme of life. Parenting was hard. Everyone said so. Doing the right thing for your kid wasn't always easy, but it paid off in the long run. People said that, too, although the underlying, unanswerable question was one he often pondered: Just how long was this "run," and would he be too exhausted by the end of it to appreciate this promised outcome?

To Summer, he said, "Good night, Miss

Davies. If you guys have any questions or need anything—you've got my number."

SUMMER WATCHED LEVI hustle away while several important observations coalesced in her mind. One, he did not want her to go upstairs and see Isla's room. Two, thanks to Isla's disclosure about him designing this place, now she absolutely *had to* get up there, and the sooner, the better.

Three, circumstances seemed to indicate he was divorced. When combined with one and two, this led to a myriad of questions. The first of which was why wouldn't he want her to see his house?

Was he hiding something? Maybe he was some sort of criminal, and the barn was an elaborate cover... *Rein in your imagination, Summer.* Blackwell might be arrogant and uptight, but he wasn't the type for nefarious deeds. The guy was a bachelor with a young daughter, and she and Theo had shown up unexpectedly. A simple explanation was more likely.

Perhaps the place was a mess? Maybe he wanted time to get things tidied up. That made sense. Probably, he'd invite her up once he'd had a chance to break out the feather duster and the vacuum.

That roused the next set of questions: How long had he been divorced? Who in their right mind would divorce and leave this property behind? Were he and his ex good at being divorced? Meaning, did they put Isla first?

As a child of a bitter divorce, that last musing landed hard on her heart. Memories of her own traumatic experience bombarded her. For the billionth time, she reminded herself that her dad might not be perfect, but he loved her. It took her many years and much therapy to accept that her narcissist mom loved her, too; she just loved herself more.

The simple fact that Levi spent time with Isla suggested positive things about their father-daughter relationship. For Isla's sake, she hoped Levi's ex-wife was nothing like her own mother.

An entirely unrelated question occurred to her. When exactly had she started thinking of him as Levi instead of Blackwell? What did that mean? He didn't appear to be quite as bad as she'd initially believed, leading her to wonder if Theo could possibly be correct about that snap judgment thing? And my goodness, he was easy on the eyes, too.

Plus, he smelled good. She was a sucker for a nice-smelling man. Not that she was *interested*, per se, so much as she found him more interesting than she'd initially assumed. Possibly she needed to settle things with Braden before she even thought about another man, which she most certainly was not doing.

"Hey." A voice sounded close to her ear while a hand landed on her shoulder.

With a jump and a gasp, she turned to find Theo standing behind her.

"You okay?" he asked. "You were a million miles away."

"Yeah, fine. You startled me, and I was, um, thinking."

"About what?" he quipped. "Moving in?"

Summer couldn't help but chuckle. "Can you believe this place? How can my luck go from rock-bottom to *this*…" Letting the word hang there, she lifted her hands and did a twirl. "Look at this place! I feel like I've won a lottery or something."

"Sure," Theo agreed, clearly amused. "A very specialized lottery, but I'm extremely pleased to hear you say this because I found a car, a pickup, which is even better. I'll bike into town tomorrow and get it." They often rented a vehicle when traveling in the motorcoach, especially if they planned to stay in one location for more than a night or two. "Then we can go shopping and get settled in before I head to Jackson."

Summer gave him a playful glare. "You weren't even planning on getting me out of here, were you?"

"No." Theo shrugged a shoulder. "But we can still go if you want to."

"You know very well I don't—you just want to hear me say it."

"What I want to hear you say is that you were hasty in judg—"

One hand came up to chop off the end of his sentence. "Nope. Not going to happen. I admit nothing. The only thing I like about Levi Blackwell is his *barndo*."

And his daughter, she added silently, because who wouldn't adore that sweet girl? Talking to her made Summer happy, the horse obsession reminding her so much of her own at that age. Okay, and every age since. But that was it.

Wait. Also, his eyes. They were such an intriguing color, the way they kept changing from green to gray to blue and hinting at more depth of emotion and intelligence and mystery than she would have guessed.

Which reminded her of all these animals because what was the deal with this *variety* of critters anyway? She would never have pegged him for a goats and llamas kind of guy. How did he make money with this sort of ragtag ranch? Wool? Milk? Maybe he was a knitter, or perhaps he was making goat cheese: chunky knits and organic cheese, both very trendy at the moment. Unlikely, as there weren't enough of any one species to be profitable, although the image of Levi processing animal fiber and cheese…mongering, or whatever you called cheese making, made her smile.

But she also knew very well how much a house like this must have cost to build. He couldn't have earned this much money on the rodeo circuit, could he? She added all of these to her growing list of questions.

That was *all* she liked about him though— his house, his daughter, the animals and his eyes.

CHAPTER SIX

LEVI CHERISHED HIS MORNINGS. Especially in the fall when the sun began to rise and the blazing, constantly changing colors glowed like fire across the frosty, glittering landscape. Around midmorning, the cold would melt away, leaving the earthy scents of hay, pine needles and compost that mixed with the pleasing aroma of pumpkins still ripening in his garden. Today promised warm sunshine in a Wyoming-blue sky, and the forecast called for a light breeze, perfect conditions for a morning ride.

Descending the stairs, he could hear the animals already stirring in their stalls, ready to greet him. Nothing better to kick-start the day than barn chores. Mornings with his critters were his therapy. Lately, between worrying about Gran's health, the fate of the Flying Spur, his financial future and all the accompanying rodeo stress, he needed these peaceful moments more than ever.

Ordinarily, when Isla was here, she helped

with all animal-related chores. Not only was it a fun way to spend time together, but it was also a chance to teach her, instill responsibility and reinforce her love for horses. But not today when speed was the top priority.

Like him, Isla hit the ground running in the mornings. If he completed the chores before she awoke, they could eat breakfast, saddle the horses and take off, lessening the chances of any further Isla and Summer interaction.

Last night had been tough. Isla had headed straight down the hall to shower and get ready for bed. When he'd gone to her room to say good-night, he'd avoided her questions by explaining how Summer wasn't their guest in the typical sense of the word.

"She's more like a…" He searched for a suitable descriptor and landed on "A business associate."

"You think I'm going to pester her, don't you?" his perceptive child had asked, leveling him with her narrow-eyed truth-detecting glare.

"No, of course not," he'd lied. "I just want you to be aware that Summer isn't like a family member or friend that we invited to stay with us. She's here for the rodeo. Does that make sense?"

"I guess. But…"

"But what, sweetie? It's okay—you can ask me anything."

"But she could become our friend. That's how you make friends, by spending time together, right?"

How was he supposed to answer that? He hadn't known last night, and he still didn't know.

In order to avoid any misunderstandings, he'd been firm. "Summer isn't here to make friends, so let's not put her on the spot by inviting her to go places with us or asking her into our home."

The deflated look on her face had tugged his heartstrings so hard they'd nearly snapped. She'd cleverly countered, "What if *she* invites *me* to do something?"

"Sure," he'd answered because, at that point, he couldn't bear causing her more disappointment. "That would be fine. If it's something you want to do." Also, the answer felt safe because he was positive that would not happen, especially if he stuck to his plan. "Remember, she is extremely busy, so that probably won't happen."

"Yeah, probably won't," she'd responded sadly, another ice pick jab to his heart.

Why had he ever agreed to let this woman stay here? Levi had then gone on to break two of his own parenting rules. First, by allowing Isla to stay up past her bedtime to watch a Halloween cartoon. And second, by giving her something out of guilt. Both infractions that he irrationally blamed on Summer Davies.

How did he explain to his ten-year-old daughter that bad influences came in all kinds of packages? Even ones who were prettily wrapped and loved horses as much you did.

The moment he stepped through the door into the barn, Bosco let out an enthusiastic bleat. Luna greeted him with a loud whinny. A hodgepodge of other calls chimed in, easing his guilt and nourishing his soul. He headed straight for the large stall, opened the door and stepped inside.

"Good morning, goats!"

After a round of pats and praise, he pressed a button, opening the exterior door that accessed their barnyard playground. They all hustled outside, except for Bosco, who waited patiently for Levi to open the interior door. Together, they went inside the barn for their morning rounds. Bosco knew the routine and enjoyed his status as barn mascot. Who needed a dog when they had a goat? It was still painful for Levi to think about what the poor guy had gone through before he'd joined their troupe.

"Hey, pretty lady," he said, stopping next at Luna's stall. "You got your beauty sleep, didn't you?"

"Good morning," a voice chirped from behind him. "Thank you! Yes, I sure did. Slept like a rock. It is so *quiet* here, isn't it? I wasn't expecting that."

Levi spun around to find a grinning Summer standing behind an empty wheelbarrow.

"Oh, um, yeah, no..." Flipping a thumb toward Luna, he continued mumbling like a flustered teenager. "I didn't mean..." But only, he told himself, because he'd been caught talking to his horse and because he was surprised to see Summer this early. It had nothing to do with the fact that she did indeed look like she'd gotten plenty of rest. The kind that made her skin glow and her storm-cloud eyes shine. Her dark brown-red hair was in a ponytail that she'd pulled through the back of a baseball cap.

"What?" she asked, calling him out on his perusal. She glanced down at herself, brushing some wood shavings from her barn jacket, which he noted had a rip in one sleeve. "I know I'm a mess, but..." Beneath that, he could see a faded blue thermal top. With a guileless expression, she looked at him. "You do think I'm pretty, right?"

He didn't answer. Because… So many because-es. The most obvious of which was a resounding yes. But also, because she was joking with him like they were *friends*, precisely what he'd told Isla they were not and would never be. And then because, even in barn clothes dusted with wood chips, she wasn't anything close to looking like a mess. But he certainly wasn't going to tell her that either, was he?

"I'm joking!" she added when he didn't reply, her tone now thick with laughter. "I'm sorry—it's probably too soon to be messing with you like that. I knew you weren't talking to me." She gestured at Luna. "Who could compete with that gorgeous *grulla* anyway? American quarter horse?"

He tried to cover his awkward lack of response with a chuckle. *Grulla* was the term for the mare's unusual shade of gray. Similar, he suddenly realized, to Summer's eyes. "What I meant was that I'm usually alone down here."

As if objecting to Levi's pronouncement, Bosco sounded a loud maaah and ambled toward Summer.

Grinning, she stepped to the side of

the wheelbarrow to greet him with open arms. Behind her, Levi could now see into Sacha's stall, where fresh wood shavings lined the floor. He also couldn't help noticing how Summer's legs were encased in a pair of snug riding pants tucked into sensible barn boots—worn ones. No Theo in sight. Pretty much all the evidence he needed to deduce that she was no stranger to these chores after all. Huh.

"Looks like someone takes issue at not being recognized for his highly important role as barn helper," she joked before gesturing around. "Besides, you are hardly alone down here."

The goat wasn't shy and didn't stop until he'd cozied up to her side. Summer seemed unfazed. Reaching out a hand, she scratched his neck, which prompted Bosco to move even closer, burying his head in her armpit. She laughed, and the sound held such genuine delight that Levi felt himself grinning. Okay. Possibly, maybe, he'd misjudged her. Slightly.

"Good gracious, you are handsome!"

"Thank you," he quipped, with absolutely no thought or regard to his own rule of not engaging.

"Good one," she said with an approving grin. "I set myself up for that."

"Sorry about his manners. He's looking for a treat, and I just realized I forgot them upstairs."

"Oh." Her eyes darted to the doorway. "Do you want me to run up and get them for you?"

What? The question snapped him out of his momentary enchantment and propelled his stomach into a nervous churn. "No! I mean, of course not." He waved a casual hand, hoping to temper his overly enthusiastic rebuff. "I'm in a bit of a rush."

"In that case, are you extra sure? I'm all finished, and I could pop up there and grab them while you get to work."

"I'm positive. I'll make it up to him later."

"Well, can he have one of Sacha's treats?" she asked, patting her pocket. "Carrots?"

"Sure," Levi said. "But I'm warning you—he will not forget where it came from. Wicked smart, goats are—especially this one, and when you're not looking, he *will* eat your pocket."

She chuckled. "Thanks for the heads-up. I'll be sure to keep it well-stocked." Reaching into her pocket, she retrieved a carrot stick, which she offered to an enthusiastic Bosco. "Thanks again for letting me use your arena. I checked it out last night, and it's fantastic. I've got an important horse show coming up next month, and I'm incredibly grateful to have such a nice place to practice."

"No problem," he said. "That's what it's for."

Summer's gaze latched on to his, and Levi felt that same pleasant sort of tightness squeezing his chest. A few silent seconds stretched between them, and he knew he should get going.

Before he could manage to form the words, the door opened, and Isla rushed inside the barn. "Dad! Why are you doing chores without me? Why didn't you wake me?" Noticing Summer, she skidded to a halt. "Oh. Summer, hi! Good morning."

"Good morning to you, Isla. How are you? I had a quick chat with Cricket this morning. I can tell he's smart, and he is every bit as handsome as you claimed. Can't wait to see you ride."

Isla beamed.

No doubt, this was the conversation he'd spaced out on the evening before. The Arabian gelding was a fine horse. Two years ago, Levi had taken a chance on the five-year-old bay. He'd been lame with a bad case of white line, which was why Levi had been able to purchase him so cheap. Between the magic touch of his farrier, who happened to be his ex-sister-in-law Helen, the vet, and plenty of TLC, they'd cleared it up.

Then his brother Nash, Helen's ex-husband, had generously helped rehabilitate and train him with Isla, teaching her in the process. Cricket had wound up healthier, confident and more bonded to Isla than Levi could have ever dreamed. When it came to horses, his brother had the best instincts he'd ever seen. Not as much when it came to his relationships, but who was Levi to judge? At least Helen was a good person and an excellent mother. Their five-year-old son, Luke, who'd inherited both the Blackwell love for horses and his dad's equine sense, was one of Levi's favorite tiny humans.

"What are you up to this morning?"

"We're going on a trail ride today," Isla answered. "We get to ride on miles and miles of forest service land that borders our property. That's why Dad bought this place. It's every bit as pretty as Yellowstone park, but hardly anybody rides there. There are waterfalls and hot springs and so many wild animals. Last month, Dad and I and Nell saw a bear. It was across the valley and eating berries, so we weren't scared."

"Oh my goodness, that all sounds incredible! I would love to see a bear. We don't have any of that stuff in Louisville. Well, Kentucky might have *some* of that stuff, but not as much, and I certainly never get to see any of it where I ride, that's for sure."

Isla slid a look at Levi, and he could see her struggling once again to *not* invite Summer along. How could he have ever anticipated that raising a polite child would prove so inconvenient? He saw so much of his sister Adele in Isla, and usually, this kindness and sweet nature made him proud.

Hoping to ease her angst, he explained, "Summer is going to be riding today, too, kiddo. She's practicing in the arena. She's got a big horse show coming up."

"I know," Isla said. "The Meadows Cup. Summer is going to be the *eventing* champion."

Summer chuckled. "Well, I hope that prediction comes true."

Eventing? Levi had no idea how Isla knew all of this, but that was enough conversing about it. "Well, Isla, let's get our crew fed so we can get out there. It won't be morning for nearly long enough."

"That's so true!" Summer agreed, moving around behind the wheelbarrow. "This is the best time of the whole day. I should get going, too. First practice in our new digs, and then

Theo and I have some shopping to do." Her voice was cheerful, but when her gaze flickered over to Levi, her smile looked forced, and her expression hinted at the same confusion and disappointment he'd seen the day before.

Now he felt like a double jerk. What he didn't know was why. And even more concerning was why did he care?

Braden: Summer, where are you? Everyone wanted to know why you weren't at Kelly and Roarke's party last night. Tell me where you are, and I'll be there in a heartbeat. Please let me make this up to you. I love you. Call me.

Summer swiped at the screen to make the text go away. Too bad it wasn't that easy to make all her problems go away.

A niggle of guilt coalesced inside her as she realized she'd forgotten to call Kelly and tell her she couldn't make it to their engagement party. Kelly and Roarke were mutual friends of Summer and Braden's.

"How's it going?" Theo called out, approaching the arena where she and Sacha had just finished an easy ride through their paces.

"Hey," she said and urged Sacha toward the fence, where they halted.

Reaching through the slats, Theo stroked Sacha's muzzle. The horse snuffled with pleasure and nudged his hand for more.

"He did so great this morning." She was pleased with how well Sacha was settling in. Levi's cushy accommodations and professional setup made it easy. "He seems relaxed and focused." And so had she been before Braden's interruption. "We did the best half pass and—" Her phone buzzed with a call. The word *Dad* popped on to the display above his grinning face. She winced.

Ignoring the call, she set it to silent. "Now that you're back, I'm turning this off."

"Braden, I presume?"

"A text from Braden and then a call from Dad, back-to-back. I'll call Dad later. Braden is trying to guilt me into telling him where I am by pointing out how I missed Kelly and Roarke's party. But the good news is he wants to make it up to me. Isn't that nice?" She rolled her eyes. "Can you make up for cheating? How would you even do that?"

"Only you can answer that," Theo said in a wry tone that effectively conveyed his own opinion on the matter. "But knowing Braden, he's going to try."

"Which is why I don't want to tell him

where we are. I don't even want to think about this yet." Summer dismounted.

Theo opened the gate so she could lead Sacha through. They walked toward the field to turn him out. "You don't have to—that's why we're here. If he loves you like he claims, he'll wait. He'll give you the space you're asking for. It's only a few weeks."

Summer nodded. She wanted that to be true.

"Have you heard from Ingrid?"

"Yep." She'd talked to her agent this morning. "So far, I'm in the clear as far as gossip goes. She didn't mention anything about Braden or Chauncey's or videos or rings." Summer had made a point of instituting regular checks on social media herself in case word leaked out. "So, I stuck to our story— we left town for some privacy and intense training."

"I like how true that's already turning out to be. What did she say about that?"

"She sounded thrilled. Didn't even ask where we were. Said she's working on new endorsements, but for the short term, she's clearing my schedule to allow me to focus. As long as we're back before the cup, we're good."

"That's perfect." Theo opened the door to the barn, and they all headed inside.

"How was your morning?" Summer asked him as he loosened the girth on the saddle.

"Good. I strolled around Eagle Springs, scoped things out. You know that dot you found on the map?"

"Yeah?"

"Well, it's to scale."

Summer busted out laughing. "Oh boy."

"No problem finding feed for Sacha and Nugget's dog food. But this afternoon, I'm going to head to the nearest outpost where they have more people-things to buy and get the rest of the stuff we need."

Summer grimaced. "How far?"

"I called Levi for advice, and it depends on which direction I go, but regardless, it's a drive." She made a face, and he said, "You don't have to come with me. Give me your list and keep your phone on."

She beamed. "Thank you, Theo."

"I mentioned to Levi that we needed fresh produce, and he said we could help ourselves to his garden, so maybe check that out while I'm gone and text whatever else you need."

"That's nice of him," Summer commented, ignoring how the mention of his name made her stomach feel fluttery.

All morning, she'd kept replaying their encounter in the barn. Things had gone so well; she'd turned on the charm, he'd lightened up, they'd joked around and she was confident they'd turned a corner. It was nice. Thing was, she needed to *stop* thinking about it in this way that made her stomach flutter.

But, ugh, the way he'd sweet-talked his horse before he knew she was there, and he had a goat for a pet—one that followed him around like a puppy. Then he'd *looked* at her, and she'd looked right back, and the air had gone all crackly. At least, her air had. She had no idea what he was feeling or thinking because then Isla had appeared, and he'd made a point of not inviting her on their trail ride. Again.

Why was she still thinking about this? She didn't know anything about him.

"He's a good guy," Theo declared confidently.

Summer slid him a look. Did he suspect something?

"This rodeo is a big event, much bigger than I realized, and Levi Blackwell is kind of a rock star in this town."

"What do you mean?"

"While I was in town, I stopped by this restaurant called the Cranky Crow for breakfast and to get a feel for the place. Find out the best spot to buy feed and supplies and your straightening iron.

"I kid you not, rodeo was the topic of conversation at the table next to me. Apparently, Eagle Springs's rodeo has been shut down for a few years now. The owner of the diner is a woman named Harriet, and she stopped by my table, ostensibly to see how my food was, but in reality to find out *who* I was. We chatted, she asked me a few questions, I asked her a few.

"She told me Levi's grandmother Denny Blackwell started the first rodeo in this town. Over the years, it grew to be a huge deal—economically and for the town's collective pride. And now Levi, Denny's grandson, former rodeo star and hero of Eagle Springs, is attempting to restore it to its former glory. People love him for it, and they love their rodeo around here."

"Wow." Summer recalled reading how rodeo was the state sport of Wyoming. "Yikes. No pressure," she joked.

"And get this, the profits from the rodeo are going toward helping his grandmother."

"What?"

"Yeah, she's been sick and has all these medical bills and a big loan payment due on her ranch. Levi and his brothers and sisters are helping her pay it off."

And now she knew some things about him, didn't she? Nice things. Things that were doing nothing to calm those flutters. "This woman told you all of this?"

Theo grinned. "I may have heard that last bit from Lilah."

"Who?"

"The waitress who also agreed to go out with me."

Summer rolled her eyes. "Of course she did."

"Apparently, a lot of people are quietly calling it Denny's Last Rodeo. She's very beloved in this town."

"Oh my gosh, that's so sad." No wonder Levi seemed so tense when they'd met. The man had far more important problems than caring about where Summer could park her RV, and yet he'd opened his home, or the bottom floor anyway, for them. She needed to find a way to make this up to him or apologize at the very least.

"It's even worse than that. He had to issue refunds to a bunch of ticketholders who were coming to see Trace Baylor, who you are replacing."

"Wait a minute." A surge of nervous adrenaline flooded her bloodstream, raising her voice a few octaves. "He went from Trace Baylor, the comedian, to me?"

He grinned. "Yep."

No wonder the paycheck was so generous. Why hadn't it occurred to her to ask this question? Same reason she hadn't asked any other questions before she'd hopped in the motorcoach and fled West.

"Why would he do that? Theo, what have I signed up for? I can't sell those tickets. I can't sell any tickets, and especially not *rodeo* tickets."

"Calm down," Theo said with a grin. "He knows that, and you don't need to. That's not your job. Ultimately, people are coming for the rodeo. And for Denny Blackwell."

She groaned. "That might be even worse. How will these people take to a show jumper performing at their precious rodeo? Are they going to throw rotten food at me when I don't rope something or get bucked off my horse?"

Theo laughed. "Would you stop? They're going to love you and Sacha. The equestrian world might be diverse, but it's in agreement about the most important thing, and that's horses. Horses don't care what type of saddle you strap on their backs, and neither do people who truly appreciate talent and skill.

Western, English, bucking, roping, jumping—
doesn't matter. They want to see an impressive ride. They want to be wowed. You can do
that. You might not be known in their world,
but you've got plenty of fame in ours.

"Once word gets out around town that a
professional show jumper is performing at
their rodeo, folks will be curious. Trust me—
worlds will collide."

CHAPTER SEVEN

LEVI WAS RIDING HIGH on his successful morning maneuverings: amicable run-in with Summer, smooth distancing between Summer and Isla, fun ride with Isla, minimal conflict in his handoff of Isla to Kylie, followed by two hours of uninterrupted work at the rodeo office.

He was looking forward to a visit from Gran and Big E, who were stopping by to check on rodeo progress and offer last-minute advice. A construction crew was hard at work on the stables, Jim was on schedule with the water line fix. The restrooms still needed tile, and the painters hadn't shown up, but there was still time. It was shaping up to be a good day. So good, in fact, that it didn't even occur to him to be annoyed when his phone rang.

He answered. Curtis Holloway, the current property owner, greeted Levi warmly, inquired after the health of his family, chatted about the weather and then proceeded to ruin not only his day but likely his life as well.

"I'm sure you understand, Levi," Curtis explained after informing Levi of the reason for his call. "This offer is substantially more than yours. Fifty thousand dollars is a lot of money for Monica and me." His tone somehow managed to both demand and plead for understanding. "You know, with Monica's mom living with us now, we could sure use that extra cash to add on another bathroom. And with Monica having to drive her to the medical clinic in Phoenix every week, our gas bill has doubled. In fact, all our bills have increased in ways we didn't budget for."

Levi bit down hard on his bottom lip. It was all he could do not to rail at Curtis, shame him and remind him they had a deal. And they *did* have a deal, didn't they?

"I didn't realize you had it on the market," Levi somehow managed to reply.

"I don't. This guy called out of the blue."

A vibration indicated Levi had another call coming in. A quick glance at the screen showed it was Kylie. He didn't have time to listen to any of her usual complaints, like about Isla's coat smelling like horse, how her jeans were stained from playing outside or that the birthday gift he'd helped her choose wasn't quite right. He tapped Ignore and prepared to ask Curtis how it sat with him breaking their agreement.

Curtis beat him to the punch, "My attorney said it was a good thing we haven't signed any papers yet so we could bring this negotiation back to the table. And our Realtor Gary assured me this offer was in the ballpark, what with the real estate market going crazy like it has been lately. You know, if that new town gets built like people are saying, it might not even be enough."

"I see." Two words. That was all he could manage. It was almost funny how he'd believed that Trace canceling was the worst thing that could happen. Not even close.

The arrival of a text from Kylie was like an exclamation point:

Call me. Please, Levi. I need to talk to you. I have the best news ever! Super important—do not delay!

Yeah, if she was hoping all the *I*'s and *me*'s would prompt him to return the call quicker, she was sorely mistaken. The last thing he wanted was to hear her best news ever when he was receiving his worst.

"But don't worry," Curtis went on. "Gary said— You know Gary Smith?" He did, but

Curtis continued with his nervous rambling before Levi could confirm. "'Course you do. Well, he's our Realtor, and he said you still have an opportunity to beat Howard's offer. I told him that, too—that I had to let you take a crack at it."

Howard could only be Xavier Howard. Hearing that name aloud descended Levi's nightmare into new depths. Howard was behind this. Levi should have seen it coming. Well, he had. Sort of. He hadn't believed it *would* happen. Or even that it *could*.

Thanks to Wyatt and Harper, they now knew that Xavier Howard and his "investors" wanted to buy up all the land in Eagle Springs so they could bury it under a lake and build a "new and better town" farther up the mountainside. Even with all the information they'd uncovered, though, Levi had been dubious.

The whole plan seemed outlandish to him, like the scheme of a delusional con man or the plot from an over-the-top television drama. Even the proposed town's name, Mountain Ridge, sounded contrived. And realistically, it wasn't possible to buy up *all* the land in an entire town, was it? No, because there'd always be people in this town who wouldn't want to sell.

People like the Blackwells.

Levi had been smug in his belief that just like his gran, he would hold out, too. In this small but vital way, he would help thwart Howard's plans. Technically, Curtis was correct; they hadn't signed the paperwork. But they had made a deal, and this was still Wyoming where your word and a handshake meant something. No, not something— everything. Had times really changed so much?

Another incoming call from Kylie. *Ignore.* A text followed, which he didn't open.

Fifty grand over the price they'd settled on made his musing a stupid one. Levi couldn't beat that offer. He'd already overextended himself on the original agreement. But he'd been okay with that; it had seemed fair. Back then, even *Gary* had thought so. Confident about their agreement and determined to make the rodeo a success, Levi had spent money on the improvements.

Somehow, he managed to get through the rest of the conversation without unleashing his anger on Curtis because the stark truth of it was that he wasn't *legally* bound, not in the big-city sense. Not in the *Mountain Ridge* way. How depressing. Levi was struck with the sense that the world was passing him by. It wasn't the first time he'd felt as if he was holding on to principles others had left behind.

His spirits sank at the idea of Eagle Springs going the way of Aspen, Breckenridge or even Bozeman, where property values skyrocketed, and the locals were soon priced out of their homes. Their small-town way of life would be commandeered and made over into a caricature of what some city folks thought it should be.

"If you're trying to crush that phone, son, you'd have better luck with a hammer."

Levi looked up at the broad man filling the door frame. His great-uncle Elias, also known as Big E, was looking pointedly at Levi's hand, still gripping the offending bearer of bad news.

"Xavier Howard," Levi managed in a strangled tone. He lowered the phone to his desk and gave it a disgusted toss.

"I'd like to crush *him* with a hammer," Gran said, stepping into the room to stand beside her brother.

Big E huffed a laugh. "I'd be happy to help with that, Delaney."

"Pfft," she snorted. "Don't need your help with that either."

Levi mustered a semblance of a smile. Despite Big E's efforts, Gran still wasn't quite ready to concede that his help was proving useful—or that his presence was growing on her.

When Levi didn't expound, Gran said, "Levi? That look on your face has me concerned. What did that wretched man do now?"

His inclination was to evade. Gran had been through so much with all of the ranch problems, and now kidney disease was kicking her while she was down. He couldn't stand the idea of upsetting her further. But he also knew there was no point in keeping this from her. Molly and Harriet were her best friends. With Molly working for him and Harriet owning the Cranky Crow, combined with a lifetime of doing business and establishing connections here, the woman had her very own spy network.

Levi sighed. "Howard made Curtis an offer on this property. Way above the price we'd agreed on, and now Curtis is waffling."

Fire flared in Big E's blue eyes before they deliberately narrowed. Mouth forming an angry, determined line, he slowly shook his head.

"He can't do that!" Gran's expression turned

fierce. Fists clenched, jaw tight, her entire body emanated anger. "You had an agreement! Curtis Holloway knows better. Born and raised here, he was in the same class as your father."

"I thought we did, too."

"Last I checked, this was still Wyoming. The Eagle Springs type, too, not some would-be mockery of a town called Mountain Ridge where money matters more than community or family or ranching."

Levi did smile now at the way her thoughts echoed his. Moments like this, he didn't have to wonder where he and his siblings had inherited their integrity, sense of honor and love for this small town.

"How much more?" Big E asked.

This was the part where Levi could hem-and-haw and say he wasn't sure exactly to keep her from worrying as much. But again, there was no point.

"Fifty thousand."

Gran went pale. Now she looked like Levi felt, and he hated that he'd inadvertently caused it.

"Why so much?" Big E wondered.

"What do you mean?" Levi asked.

"Well, fifty grand seems excessive, doesn't

it? Like he's making a statement. Like he's making things personal."

Big E had expressed this opinion already, that Xavier Howard seemed almost reckless in his quest to "buy" the town. Levi hadn't given much thought to the why because he'd been too busy feeling comforted that he could help stave off the how. But suddenly, now that he was a victim, the theory made a lot of sense. Why fifty grand when ten or twenty would suffice?

"I don't know, Uncle Elias… Maybe you're onto something with that theory. There does seem to be an awful lot of money flying around where he's concerned."

A light rapping sounded on the door frame, and an uncharacteristically somber Molly newly returned from a late lunch at the Cranky Crow stepped inside.

"Sorry to interrupt," she said, "but I've got news. Denny, I hate to tell you this, but Harriet just told me she has confirmation that Jacob Kelter has gone to the dark side."

Gran erupted with an angry visceral sound like an outraged growl. "That jackal!"

Levi felt his already sinking spirits plummet.

"Who's the dark jackal?" Big E asked.

Molly explained, "Jacob Kelter owns the

old granary building, and he's decided to sell to Xavier Howard. He'd agreed to wait while Denny, Harriet and I tried to find a buyer for the place. Someone who'd be willing to take over and reopen the business or even repurpose it into a new business. It's a beautiful building filled with cool old treasures."

Levi couldn't help but wonder if Adele knew about this. He said to Big E, "Gran and Jacob's dad, Elijah, go way back. She helped Elijah get the business going, and I don't think any other structure is quite as iconic to Eagle Springs."

"That seals it," Big E stated confidently. "Not that I needed further confirmation. Someone is targeting you, Delaney."

"But why?" Gran interjected.

"That's what I intend to find out." Big E scratched his chin, thinking it over.

"I don't understand why we need a whole new town," Levi said.

"You don't," Big E said shrewdly. "I'm starting to wonder if the point is more in the demolishing of the old town than the building of the new one."

"Regardless," Denny stated in a firm tone. "Enough is enough." She looked at her brother. "Elias, as much as it pains me to admit it and confounds me to believe this is happening, you need to get on the road to Colorado."

Big E had already been planning the trip to Xavier Howard's stomping grounds to do some amateur investigating into the man and his company.

"How long will you be gone?" Levi asked. Because, despite what Gran maintained, Levi could see a difference in her now that Big E was around. There was a spark in her eye and a bounce in her step, and he didn't care whether it was anger or irritation or resentment that was the cause. She wouldn't be feeling any of those things if she didn't care.

"As long as it takes," Big E said and headed for the door.

"WHO ARE YOU?" a voice demanded from behind Summer, where she was kneeling on the ground in Levi's garden inspecting pumpkins. "And what do you think you're doing?"

Summer had been here awhile, pleased to find so much still growing in October—potatoes, kale, squash, broccoli. And pumpkins! So many glorious pumpkins, she couldn't decide which one to pick or what to make first.

Turning to face the source, Summer sat back on her heels and looked up, assessing the situation and trying to process the confrontational tone. With one hand, she shielded her eyes from the sun. A beautiful blonde woman stood before her—hands on hips, head tilted, eyebrows dipped into a scowl. Short but curvy, she wore tight blue jeans tucked into a pair of gorgeous knee-high leather boots that she'd paired with a form-hugging, chunky knitted tunic. Her makeup was heavy but impeccably applied. Long loose white-blond curls hung past her shoulders. Somehow, the whole package made her look country chic and yet out of place at the same time. Like one of those ads where the model is standing in a muddy barnyard wearing expensive but very clean boots.

"I'm sorry?" Summer said. "Is there a problem?"

"There certainly is if you don't have permission to be on this property or to pick those pumpkins."

"What? You think I'm..." She struggled to articulate the thought because it was so absurd. "Why would I drive out into the middle of nowhere to steal produce?"

"Is that what you're doing? Do I need to call the police?"

"The police?" Summer repeated.

"Mom!" Isla said, rushing up to them,

backpack slung over one shoulder and a bulging duffel bag in hand. "Calm down! She has permission. This is Summer Davies."

"Who?" she snapped, her face contorted with confusion.

"Remember that video I showed you of the woman in the show jumping competition? This is her. This is Summer Davies, professional equestrian. Show jumper, eventer and soon-to-be Meadows Cup champion."

"Yes, of course, I remember. I just didn't expect to see her *here* on our... On your daddy's place. Picking *your* pumpkins."

So, this was Levi's ex. A knot of tension formed in Summer's chest, and she recognized the uncomfortable mix of jealousy and nerves for what it was. Why she felt that way, she would have to analyze later. Because mostly, she was confused that Levi hadn't mentioned his ex would be stopping by. She distinctly remembered him saying that he and Isla were meeting her in town today after their ride.

Summer stood. Even though she was still wearing dirty barn clothes and a baseball cap, it seemed like a good idea to meet this woman on a more level playing field. Her gaze traveled over Summer with an assessing, blatant look of curiosity that bordered on hostile. Hmm. Was she jealous, too? Summer couldn't help but wonder what had gone wrong in the marriage.

The woman's attention lingered on Summer's dirt-smudged hands. Bristling under the scrutiny, sarcastic retort dancing on her tongue, she stayed silent, pondering Theo's assertion about her rush to judgment. As if prompted, the Braden video flickered through her mind. What if Levi had broken his wife's heart? Then again, what if she'd broken Levi's?

Summer had no idea what kind of relationship they had, but it didn't matter. This woman was Isla's mother, and Summer wouldn't do anything to upset this sweet, innocent kid or jeopardize their blossoming friendship.

Instead, she set her expression on respectful and dialed her tone to polite. "Yep, I'm Summer. Nice to meet you. You must be Isla's mom. I'd shake your hand, *but*…" She emphasized the word and held up her hands as evidence. "You do not want these filthy paws anywhere near that gorgeous manicure." Leaning forward, squinting, she pointed at the other woman's nails. "Look at those beauties! Are those tiny palm trees?"

Summer almost laughed as the woman's

contentious scowl was shattered by her own smile. "Thank you!" Giggling, she lifted her hands for inspection. *Gotcha*, Summer thought.

"And, yes, they sure are palm trees. It's my birthday today, and my fiancé, Brett, surprised me with a manicure."

"How sweet! Happy birthday!" Summer gushed. "Sounds like you've got yourself a good one. Better hang on to him."

"Oh, I plan to," she said, the snip now officially snipped from her tone. "You don't know the half of it. The manicure was only part of the surprise." Then, as if remembering both her purpose and previous irritation, she let out a huff. "That's actually why I'm here. I'm trying to track down Levi. I've been calling and texting, but he won't answer. I assumed he was out riding or, or…*saving* something." Rolling her eyes, she gestured toward the distant foothills. "The cell service is terrible out there, but half the time, he uses it as an excuse not to answer his dang phone."

"Oh," Summer replied. "Well, as far as I know, he was going to the rodeo grounds today. Haven't talked to him since this morning when he and Isla went riding."

Kylie had the same miffed look of confusion again, and Summer realized she was probably speculating about why Summer had been here at the crack of dawn. How to explain?

"Mom," Isla jumped in to save her, "Summer is Dad's, um, business associate. She's here for the rodeo. She and her friend Theo came early, but the water isn't ready, so Dad is letting her park her motor home in Grandpa and Grandma's spot. She brought her horse, and she's using our arena to practice."

"Oh! Well, how nice." She nudged Isla with her elbow and added, "Maybe she can give you some tips on that English-style riding you like."

"Mom!" Isla said, wide-eyed with horror by her mother's suggestion. "Summer is training for an important competition, and she doesn't have time for stuff like that."

"I always have time to talk about riding." Summer grinned at her. "Isla, are you interested in learning how to jump?"

"She sure is," Kylie said. "Talks about it *all* the time."

Summer looked at a pink-cheeked Isla who confirmed, "Yes, but Dad said—" Frowning, she bit off the end of that sentence and started over. "I mean, I know you're super busy, and I would never ask you to help me."

"Why not?" What had her dad said?

"Um…" Her gaze slid toward the ground before she answered, "Because it wouldn't be polite."

What was going on here? Summer wanted to quiz her further, but something told her to wait until her mom wasn't around. "That is very thoughtful of you, but discussing horses is perfectly polite where I'm concerned." Summer added an encouraging wink.

Isla bobbed her head but looked far from convinced. On the contrary, she looked miserable. Poor kid. Summer didn't know if it was due to Kylie's pushy suggestion or if Levi had cautioned her against asking for help? Or both.

Summer felt compelled to add, "I'm glad your mom mentioned it." Even though the real question was, why hadn't her father? "We will certainly be discussing it later."

Kylie beamed. "See, sweetie? If there's one thing that I learned being married to your daddy, it's that horse people *love* talking horses. They can horse-talk till the cows come home." She laughed hard at her joke. Summer didn't see how it was quite that funny, but she faked a chuckle, determined to keep things amicable.

"Anyway, I am thrilled to meet you, Summer. Sorry about the misunderstanding. We can be touchy about trespassing around here. I'm Kylie Carlisle. Used to be Blackwell, Levi's ex-wife. I took my maiden name back after the divorce."

"I understand," Summer said with an agreeable nod. "I can assure you that I am not a pumpkin thief. Levi said we could help ourselves to the garden."

"I'm sure he did," Kylie responded wryly. "Generosity is my ex-husband's middle name. Normally, he'd have more of this harvested by now, but Denny's rodeo is consuming him these days."

Turning to Isla, she said, "Pumpkins are something else you and Summer here have in common. Isn't that fun? I like pumpkin spice lattes." The phone in her hand chimed with a text. "Maybe that's finally your father..." She tapped on the screen and then sighed. "Nope. I take that back—unreliable is Levi Blackwell's middle name."

With another pained expression, Isla looked down again, nudging the dirt with the toe of her boot. Summer could see she was struggling with whether to defend her dad. She was definitely at the age where statements like that, that once flew right over her head, were now landing with full force. Summer recognized it because she knew the feeling very well, that sudden realization that people—parents in particular—and situations like divorce and custody arrangements weren't quite the way they seemed. She'd been around the same age as Isla when her parents had divorced.

Back then, these types of backhanded compliments and sarcastic gibes had been her mom, Bethany's, favorite form of passive-aggressive warfare. Instead of turning Summer against Roland, though, it had made her wary of Bethany. In retrospect, she could see how it had resulted in Summer's massive loss of respect for and distrust of her mother. The outcome had been inevitable; only one parent could ever have won the war. But Summer had been the casualty. She so badly wanted to caution Kylie but knew it wasn't her place.

Instead, she steered the conversation back toward the point. "Well, is there something I can help you with, Kylie?"

Kylie opened her mouth, closed it and then, keeping her lips pursed, quickly checked her phone. Thinking. She tapped out a quick text before tucking the phone into her back pocket. Lifting her hands, she brought them palm to palm, interlocked her fingers and squeezed them together like a prayer.

With a nervous smile, she met Summer's gaze, inhaled and then whooshed out a breath. "As a matter of fact, there might be."

CHAPTER EIGHT

BOTTOM LINE: LEVI FORGOT.

Sure, there were times when he purposely delayed returning his ex-wife's calls or texts. But that was because he didn't want to hear her complaints or field her demands. Or listen to her chatter about Brett and their lavish lifestyle. Unless they were talking about Isla, he'd rather not speak to her at all. That was not the case here.

Today was a perfect storm for not remembering. First, it legitimately slipped his mind because of Curtis's phone call. Then he left his phone in the office when he went outside with Gran and Uncle Elias, so he didn't see the string of texts that followed Kylie's first message, which would have reminded him. And finally, when he'd realized he'd forgotten his phone, he was spending time with his gran and couldn't think of anything less worthy of his uninterrupted attention.

But, of course, it had to be the one time it was important *to him*. Because that's what bad days were like, right? Just when you thought things couldn't get worse, a new catastrophe set you straight.

After assuring Big E that he'd drive Denny back home to the Flying Spur when they'd finished their visit, they all walked outside, said their goodbyes and waved as he drove away in his motor home.

Then Levi forced himself to set his panic and anger aside and focus on his gran and the reason she was here—rodeo business. Regardless of who Curtis sold the property to, or what Xavier Howard had planned, this show still had to go on, so to speak. Years ago, Denny Blackwell had started the rodeo in Eagle Springs, and Levi did not want to let her down.

Leaving him no doubt they were on the same page, she turned to him and said, "Let's see what you've done with this place."

Conscious of her medical condition, Levi allowed her to set the pace, and by the time they'd finished the tour, he could see fatigue setting in. To be fair, he was getting tired, too, because she insisted on inspecting nearly every inch of the place—barns, stables, arena, concessions—even the parking lot and the refurbished restrooms. They ended in the arena, where she scaled a few flights of the newly renovated grandstands and took a seat. In typical Denny Blackwell fashion, she'd opted to save all relevant commentary for the end.

Levi joined her.

Leaning back, she let out a loud sigh. A moment of silence stretched between them while she looked around, taking it all in and gathering her thoughts.

"Well," she finally said. "Times have certainly changed."

Uh-oh, Levi thought, his stomach churning nervously. Seeing the updates and alterations through her eyes, he wondered if he'd changed too much, gone too far. His bank account certainly thought so. Once more, he tried to put his personal finances and the current dilemma with Curtis out of his mind.

Denny said, "First rodeo I ever organized, we had one corral. Lined up a bunch of flatbed trucks and hay bales for the spectators who didn't want to stand around the fence. Course, most of the spectators were also participants. We had this bull get loose, and he chased Junior Buckley clear across the hayfield that used to border this south side." Chuckling softly, she shook her head at the memory.

Smiling, he said, "I've done a few that weren't much more than that."

"Yes, you certainly have. First time I ever saw you rope in a competition was right here. I think you were, what—about ten years old?"

"Yes, ma'am. Junior rodeo. I won this fancy blue satin ribbon. Prettiest thing I'd ever seen." Grinning, Levi formed his hands into a dinner-plate-sized circle. "I was hooked."

Inspired and with dreams of future ribbons, he never went anywhere without a rope on his belt. From that day on, he spent every spare minute lassoing everything from furniture and sawhorses to his siblings, much to their irritation—with the exception of Wyatt, who was a good sport as a calf stand-in. The Flying Spur had had cattle back then, too, so he'd gotten plenty of hands-on experience. Roping had remained his best event and the one that had secured him every cowboy championship he'd won.

"Angus said you had the fastest hands he'd ever seen, and I knew right then we were going to lose you to the circuit." Angus Ferndale was Eagle Springs' winningest rodeo champion, Levi's lifelong idol and a friend of both his and Gran's. Years of wrangling and rodeo meant he now used a wheelchair. One of Levi's goals was to make the facilities not only accessible but welcoming for Angus and anyone with a disability.

"You didn't lose me, Gran."

"I know it." She nodded. "And I am just so…relieved."

Surprise jolted through him. His grandmother had never expressed anything but pride in his chosen profession—that and encouragement.

Then she turned to face him, and Levi could feel her truth-detecting glare narrowing in as she asked, "You really done?"

"I am."

"Good. I hope you mean it."

"I do."

"You know how many cowboys I've seen busted to pieces who've said the same thing? But once they heal up, those shiny buckles start hypnotizing their brains again, and it's like they forget all about the pain and suffering."

"I've seen plenty of that, too. But that's not me. I don't need to get back up on a horse and prove something to myself. It was my decision to stop. Sure, the accident and the timing helped me along. But it was the best thing for me, and the best thing for Isla."

Retiring from the rodeo had been the right move; he only wished he'd had a more solid backup plan in place. And now the one he'd finally settled on was slipping from his grasp, and possibly the entire town, too.

"You're a good dad, Levi. Your dad and uncle grew up without a father, and I was always afraid that would come back to haunt me in my grandchildren. So far, thank my lucky stars, that has not been the case."

"Dad always said you were enough of a parent that he never missed having a father."

Levi knew his grandmother had hoped that one of her sons, Hudson or Barlow, would choose to stick around and run the ranch when she was gone. The sad truth was that neither of them had a true passion for ranching. Levi's parents, Hudson and Elizabeth, had taken their share of the Flying Spur in cash and retired to Arizona. Uncle Barlow had never been around much, busy as he was with his oil business.

Thankfully, the trait had only skipped one generation. His own sister Corliss had never wavered in her desire to live at and run the Flying Spur. All four of his siblings had a love for the lifestyle and felt invested in ensuring its recovery. Wyatt, a cowboy for hire, was back home and doing his part by working on the ranch. Corliss and Nash had joined together to purchase, train and sell a quartet of cutting horses. And Adele was working over-time buying and selling antiques with plans to revive the livestock auction.

Gran's mouth curved with a small smile as she waved a breezy hand. "I know that's not true, but I love your father for saying so. Sometimes I wonder..." Head shaking, she looked off into the distance, her expression turning somber. "If I'd only..."

Levi felt a catch in his chest as he waited, hoping she'd finish that statement because he could see something pressing on her mind. It wasn't like his gran to have regrets. Or, at least, he'd never heard them. Delaney Black-well was a decision-maker, a doer, a tackler-of-life. But then again, she'd never faced a life-threatening illness. He imagined that would prompt a fair amount of looking back and a few what-if's.

Gently, he urged, "If you'd only what, Gran?"

Inhaling a deep breath, she then exhaled sharply and said, "I wonder how different my life would have been if only I'd chosen the man who was good for me instead of the one who I loved—and thought I could change."

Gran didn't talk about her past much, but Levi knew that once upon a time, there were two Wesson brothers in her life. When she was only nineteen, she'd essentially been engaged to one of them when she'd decided to run away with the other. The decision had cost her dearly. Like Gran and Big E, the Wesson brothers were children of a wealthy Montana ranching family. Her marriage to the oldest brother, Frank, heir to the Wesson empire, would have joined two very powerful families. Instead, her elopement with younger brother Cal had caused scandal and family strife.

By all accounts, their grandfather Cal Wesson had been a good-looking, sweet-talking charmer with a troubled soul. An expert wrangler and gifted horse trainer, he was also a gambler who spent more money than he earned. Newly married and heavily in debt, Cal made plans to capture, train and sell some wild horses to get them on solid financial ground. Instead, he'd been killed, leaving Gran pregnant with twins, destitute and estranged from her family, her beloved older brother Elias included.

It would be evident to anyone who knew her and this story how that long-ago abandonment had shaped her. A lesser person might have given up. But not Delaney Blackwell. She'd not only persevered; she'd thrived. Mixing equal parts grit, determination and stubbornness with an incomparable work ethic, she'd gone on to build the Flying Spur from nothing. By her own admission, it had been a long, hard, uphill road.

In the process, she'd poured her talents, time, money and energy into this town, too, including the rodeo, a crowning achievement. People adored her for it and respected her accomplishments. It was devastating to see her forced to fight for them both all over again, especially when she wasn't healthy enough to bring her A game.

That's why Levi couldn't give up; he refused to accept this town could so easily fall. Curtis was giving him a chance. Maybe if he made enough money from the rodeo, he could strike a new deal. Or maybe Big E would find a solution in Colorado that could help them thwart the development. A lot of maybes, too many to ease his mind much, but enough to press on. At this point, he had no choice.

"You can't change people, Levi. And if they won't change for love, they won't ever change."

He nodded his agreement.

"When you first meet someone, especially when you fall in love, they're at their very best. They naturally put their surest foot forward. Nothing wrong with that. We all do it.

But what complicates everything is the love glasses."

"Love glasses?" he repeated, even though he could see where this was headed.

"Yes, and they are a mighty powerful prescription indeed. All the feelings and hopes and dreams make it impossible to see clearly. But next time you find love, Levi, you need to force yourself to take those glasses off, and then you need to look hard. If the woman isn't who you want her to be in that moment, she isn't ever going to be."

Truer words had never been spoken, as Molly might say. Why hadn't his gran given him this talk before he'd married Kylie?

With her typical grandmother-style telepathy, she explained, "I knew Kylie wasn't right for you. But I also knew, from my own experience, that there wasn't anything I could have said to change your mind. You kids were young, and I feared that telling you would only cause heartache for us both. After what happened to me, I would never do anything to drive you kids away. So, I opened my heart to Kylie and hoped for the best."

"I'm so sorry about what happened between you and Uncle Elias, Gran. I can't imagine one of my siblings turning their back on me."

It was difficult to imagine Big E doing that to his sister, either, but Levi knew very well that the passage of time had a way of changing perspectives and priorities. Still, Big E was a brave man coming here to face his sister, and Levi admired him for sticking around when she'd told him more than once to get lost. His uncle was clearly determined to, if not right the wrong he'd done, then help with the problems she was facing now.

"Me, too, kiddo. I wouldn't want that for you either. It was rough. And not only that, I hurt a good man in the process. I lost two friends, including Elias."

"You're talking about Grandpa Cal's brother, right? Frank Wesson."

"Yes. If he'd only…" She stopped. "Never mind. That's enough *if only's* for one day. The most important thing is that I got your dad and your uncle out of the ordeal—and you grandkids are the real prize."

Levi grinned because he knew that Gran helping raise himself and his brothers and sisters hadn't been easy, either. With his brazen resentment of authority, a knack for finding mischief and risky career choice, he knew he'd been the cause of more than one sleepless night. But they'd each been challenging in their way.

His oldest sister, Corliss, unfailingly loyal and mama-bear protective, was also frustratingly stubborn. Younger sister Adele's big heart and good intentions made her generous to a fault. Then there was the baby of the family, Wyatt, whose free spirit, devil-may-care manner and seemingly incurable wanderlust caused them all to worry endlessly. But on the trouble scale, none of them could compete with firstborn Nash, whose uncanny similarities to their grandfather, good and bad, had probably given Gran half the gray hair on her head. Thankfully, they'd grown up and out of the worst of their faults. Mostly. At least, they were trying anyway.

"And now, you've got Isla. Raising kids by yourself is difficult, but sometimes I imagine how two people who don't see eye to eye trying to raise one would be even worse. I know Kylie doesn't make it easy on you."

"No, she does not." He still didn't understand the depth of Kylie's disappointment with him. She'd been the one to cheat and the one to leave. Setting that aside, his issue with her was that she didn't always put Isla first. Not that he expected her to do so *all* the time, but the way he saw it, their daughter played second fiddle to her mother's new relationship way too often. As much as he wanted to blame that on Brett, Kylie was the only one responsible for her behavior.

"Be the better person, Levi. Don't ever let your ire for Kylie distract you from Isla and what's best for her."

"I won't, Gran."

"Speaking of Kylie, Harriet told me she saw on Facebook how that boyfriend of hers bought her a trip to Mexico for her birthday."

Figures, Levi thought. Big Bucks Brett loved to buy her whatever she wanted.

"Harriet said they're leaving tonight. Who's watching Isla? I assumed since it wasn't you, it must be Kylie's parents, but I thought you told me they were going to Florida for the winter."

Only *then* did Levi remember that he hadn't yet returned Kylie's call.

"*RESCUE* GOATS?" SUMMER CAREFULLY repeated while she doled out another handful of pumpkin to the crowd of goats and sheep gathered around her and Isla. From the other side of the fence, a cow mooed loudly, asking for more. Inside their coop, the chickens clucked and chirped over the bits she and Isla already tossed inside. Nugget trotted around the periphery, stopping to sniff an occasional nose, seemingly pleased by the array of potential new friends.

"Yep," Isla said proudly. "Almost all of our animals are rescues. Not the chickens and most of the horses, but everything else—the bull, cows, mules, llamas and the goats. Even the cats. Dad saves all kinds of animals."

"Your dad rescues animals?" Kylie's earlier statement came back to her about Levi "saving something" now made sense.

"Uh-huh, rodeo rejects mostly. Dad prefers to call them retirees." She giggled. "You know, the animals that are done performing. Like they get old or hurt or just plumb worn out. Like cowboys. That's how it started anyway. He adopted this bronc no one else wanted—the brown sorrel with the white spots?" At Summer's nod, she went on, "That's him, that's Checkers. Only Daddy and Uncle Nash can ride him.

"Then came the goats. First was Homer." Isla patted the adorable guy. "Someone let him loose in the foothills for the wolves to eat because they didn't want him anymore. Dad heard about it, and he and Aunt Corliss went out and found him. He named him Homer because he figured he'd had lots of adventures out there in the woods. Julia came next—she got dropped off at the animal shelter, and Dad thought Homer could use a friend. They're besties now."

Bosco was next to her, and she placed a gentle hand on his neck. "A rodeo friend called Dad about this guy. He was so sick when he got here. We didn't think he'd make it. When the vet came out to look at him, she asked Dad if he was sure he wanted to try and make him well because it would take a whole lot. Dad said yes, and then we slept downstairs in the barn for days because Bosco was too weak to stand or eat or anything, and he had these bad sores from living in a tiny, dirty pen. Now he follows Dad everywhere." She motioned toward the two final goats. "Juniper and Cleo came as a pair."

"That's…um." Summer felt like a golf ball had lodged in her throat. As if he knew he was the topic of conversation, and as Levi had predicted, Bosco ambled close and sniffed Summer's pocket. She chuckled and offered him a piece of pumpkin. Satisfied, he then nudged her hand so she'd scratch his forehead. Tears prickled behind her eyes. She did her best to quash the emotion, but the image of Levi Blackwell, tough guy rodeo star, nursing the sweet, floppy-eared goat back to life was overwhelming. This guy was just so…

good. And nothing like she'd thought. *Darn you, Theo.*

Almost to herself, she muttered, "Do men like this truly exist?" Caught up in her existential pondering, she didn't catch Isla's disappointed expression.

"I know," she said sadly. "My mo…" She clipped off the short-sound vowel. Scrunching her face with frustration, she started again, "Lots of people think Dad is silly because it costs money to keep animals that aren't useful. But Dad doesn't care. He says how much more useful can an animal be if it brings you joy?"

Summer felt her heart clench painfully inside her chest because the word Isla had cut short was clearly *Mom.* She could only surmise that Kylie hadn't approved of Levi's unintentional and growing rescue sanctuary. And Isla's defense of her dad's choices heightened the sensation because it was apparent to Summer that she wanted to say these words to her mom, too.

"No!" Summer said quickly. "No, Isla, I wasn't going to say I think it's silly. I think it's amazing and wonderful, and your dad is amazing and wonderful for doing this."

"You do?"

"I do! Nugget is a rescue dog. He's small,

with short legs, and his color is off, so the breeder was going to…" She paused as she wondered if maybe this topic was too dark for a ten-year-old.

But Summer forgot she was talking to a ranch kid. "Put him down?" Isla finished for her. "Some breeders still do that if a dog doesn't match their standards or whatever. That makes me so mad."

"Me, too. That's what happened with Nugget."

"So, you rescued him?"

"I did." Summer grinned. "But if you ask him, he'd say he rescued me."

"That's funny." Isla's smile was as bright as the sun. "Dad says the same thing about Bosco."

CHAPTER NINE

LEVI WAS BESIDE HIMSELF by the time he'd driven all the way out to the Flying Spur to drop off Gran. He knew he'd hear about it later from Corliss when he didn't come inside to visit, but it was impossible to focus on anything other than Isla. If Kylie was on her way to Mexico, where was his daughter?

He could only assume that's why she'd called, to let him know where she was going and where she'd be leaving Isla. The rambling string of texts she'd sent revealed nothing. Levi couldn't think of a single person outside his family, Kylie's parents or her sister Lissa where he'd want Isla to stay for any length of time beyond one night. Lissa lived in Missoula, and a quick call revealed that she didn't know about the trip, and yes, their parents were in Florida for three months.

For somewhere around the millionth time, he wished he hadn't agreed to allow Kylie to retain the custodial parent role. Why hadn't he addressed this babysitting issue in the parenting agreement? The answer being, of course, because he'd assumed she'd be reasonable, and he'd believed she would put Isla's best interests ahead of her own.

Kylie wasn't answering her phone, and he alternated between worrying and wondering if this was payback. The rational part of him knew this was unlikely because he also knew his ex-wife. The simple, painful truth was that after she'd unloaded their daughter on whoever she'd talked into babysitting, her problem was solved. Kylie's thoughts and energy were now solely focused on Brett and their vacation. She had no reason not to answer; she was only being her typical self-centered self or was already on an airplane.

Levi called Marla, the babysitter Kylie regularly used when she and Brett went "out," which often lasted until the wee hours of the morning. Marla hadn't heard from her but suggested he try Kylie's best friend, Leanne. When she didn't answer, he left a message and hung up.

He was almost home when Kylie called.

"Kylie," Levi demanded, "Where is Isla?"

"Um, hello to you, too, Levi."

"Answer the question."

"Wow, grumpy much?"

"Kylie, I'm—"

"You're not home yet?"

"Home? No." This tendency of hers to dodge his questions with pointless ones of her own was maddening. "Where. Is. My. Daughter?"

"Chill, Levi! *Our* daughter is at home."

"Home, what home?"

"Her home, *your* home. I dropped her off hours ago. I thought you'd be there by now."

"Dropped her off?" A whole new type of fear coursed through him. "Where are you?"

He tried to stay calm. Isla was ten years old. Under normal circumstances, that was conceivably old enough to be left home alone for short periods of time. But these circumstances were anything but normal. Most people didn't live on a farm where heavy equipment and livestock were a part of life. Or on property that bordered forest service land teeming with bears, wolves, cougars and coyotes and where the nearest human neighbor was more than a mile away. Nor did she have a cell phone yet, one point where he and Kylie agreed.

"Oh!" she chirped and then giggled. "You are not going to believe this, but I am at the airport waiting for our flight to Puerto Vallarta!" She topped that off with an excited squeal. "You know how I've always wanted to go to Mexico?"

To Levi, the statement sounded more like an accusation than a question because he did know. When they were married, she'd told him approximately eight million times. He'd promised to take her "someday" after he'd finished the house and their finances were on firmer ground.

"Yes," he answered tightly.

"Brett surprised me with a trip for my birthday. Can you believe it? He's been planning it for weeks. But, you know, he's not used to being a stepdad yet, so he didn't make any arrangements for Isla, and I had to do something."

"You had to do something?" he repeated flatly.

"Well, yeah. Our plane leaves in like an hour. Anyway, we'll be gone for two weeks, and you've always said how I should come to you first if I need a sitter. So that's what I did. I thought you'd be happy."

Levi didn't point out that she'd only finally taken him up on this offer when she'd been desperate. "We'll adjust the parenting plan when I get back. From Mexico! I don't have anything to wear! But Brett said to put my flip-flops and my bikini in my bag, and I can

buy whatever else I need when we get there."
Another squeal.

Levi lost track of her words while she
droned on. He could not believe his ears. He
was stupefied. Who was this woman, this me-
monster who couldn't stop talking about herself and what she wanted? Not to mention
that his grandmother had found out about her
vacation plans via social media long before
he had.

Brett. The man should have called Levi and
given him a heads-up. This guy was going to
be Isla's stepdad, and that's what a good step-
parent would have done.

Anger rushed in, hot and fast, like a forest fire.

He tuned in to hear her say, "Our hotel is
beachfront, and I—"

"Kylie," he cut her off, "I appreciate your
coming to me first to babysit. I honestly do.
But what were you thinking of, dropping her
off all alone? I don't know why you thought
I'd be home by now, but she is not old enough
to be left on her own for this long."

"Levi! I didn't! Your friend Summer is
there."

"My... Summer?"

"Yes! She seems super cool, by the way."

A sort of giddy relief washed through him,

leaving him almost light-headed. Summer would take care of her; he knew that much. Irritation still remained because it didn't change what Kylie had done and the inconvenience she'd undoubtedly caused Summer. Somehow, he needed to make her see that.

"She is not my friend, Kylie. She's just parking her RV at my place. I barely know her."

A pause, and then, "Well, I think she's terrific. And Isla adores her, and she, um, offered to babysit."

"Isla is ten and a very sweet kid. She adores pretty much everyone who treats her kindly. You may as well have dropped her off at the Barn Door Inn and asked some random guest to babysit her."

Kylie scoffed. "You're talking like Summer is some sort of criminal or something."

"How do you know she's not?" he shot back. Adele would be so proud.

"Come on, Levi! You need to dial it back."

"No, Kylie, you need to grow up and start putting your daughter first."

She gasped. A rattling sounded, followed by some muffled chatter, and then, "Brett says to hang up. You can't talk to me like that."

"Brett says, huh?" He saw red. "I don't give a flying spur what Brett says. This is none of his business. And, Kylie, if you hang up on me, the next time we talk, it will be through my attorney."

"Oh, is that right, Mr. Cowboy Tough-Guy?" Brett's deep voice boomed through his pickup.

"This doesn't concern you, Brett."

"That's where you're wrong, *Le-vi.*" Levi had no clue why the man insisted on saying his name with that exaggerated and immature enunciation. "Kylie is my concern now, and you need to accept that. But you know what doesn't concern me?" He went on without waiting for a response, "Your threats of attorneys and such because you and I both know very well that when it comes to any legal action, I will bury you. I could buy and sell you a hundred times."

Levi hated how true this was. Brett had far more money than he did—a fact he enjoyed flaunting. Whether right or wrong in any case, Brett and Kylie could continue the court visits forever. "Brett, put Kylie back on."

"No can do. Time to board. Adios, muchacho."

ISLA OFFERED THE USE of her dad's kitchen for the pumpkin harvest. Summer was so overwhelmed with temptation that indecision froze her in her tracks. She could not have choreographed a more perfect means to get inside Levi's home. And with him gone, she could look around at her leisure, take photos, make notes…

In the end, she couldn't do it. Didn't feel right. There was a reason Levi didn't want her there, and she needed to respect that boundary. Especially since her respect and other confusing emotions for him had grown exponentially in light of recent revelations. So instead, she and Isla were working in the motorcoach's tiny kitchen.

Evidence of their efforts littered every surface, and the mouthwatering scents of cinnamon, nutmeg and cloves permeated the small space.

When a knock sounded on the door, Isla was settled at the table, working on her second muffin and a tall glass of milk.

"Come in!" Summer called from her spot in front of the stovetop, where she was stirring a batch of pumpkin soup.

The door opened, and a frowning Levi entered. With laser-like focus, his gaze zeroed in on a grinning Isla. Summer watched while the tension faded from his features, replaced by an affectionate smile for his daughter.

"Dad! Hi!" Isla called with a wave. "Guess what? Summer likes pumpkin as much as I do. Can you believe that? You want a muffin? They have cream cheese *inside* of them. They're *sooo* good. This is my second one. Not gonna lie, probably will spoil my dinner. But don't worry, I'm drinking milk, and I had an apple earlier."

Summer chuckled. It was so nice to see this kid relaxed and happy. When Kylie had first left, she'd seemed relieved but also rather tentative. That had faded pretty quickly, and now they were buddies for sure. Summer silently admitted that Theo was right about this, too—to have produced such a cool kid, the apple couldn't have fallen far from the Blackwell tree.

"Uh, hi," he said, walking over to the table and planting a kiss on the top of Isla's head. "Looks like you ladies have been busy."

"Super busy," she informed him. "We've had so much fun. We were going to go for a ride, but Summer wanted to talk to you about that first. So, we picked and cleaned and chopped and then cooked a whole bunch of pumpkins and then baked all of this stuff. Did you know nutmeg is a giant seed?"

"Nutmeg?"

"Yeah, we grated it fresh on this tiny grater

for the muffins. We took the pumpkin guts and scraps out to the goats, cows and chickens and then made extra muffins so we can put some in the freezer."

"Oh. That's…" His eyes swept the place, taking in the bowls of pumpkin, mounds of muffins, loaves of bread and cookie sheets scattered with salty seeds before landing on the steaming pot. "This is all… Wow."

"Try a bite," Isla said.

He did.

"What do you think?"

"Hmm," he said after chewing thoughtfully. "I'm going to need another bite to make sure…" He snatched the muffin from her plate.

"Dad!" Isla giggled as he finished it off.

"Delicious!" he finally declared and placed another on her plate.

So. Cute. Summer thought, and felt herself melt into the floor. And then, finally, he got around to looking at her. Their eyes met, and then held, and Summer *felt* the words before he ever spoke them aloud. "Thank you, Summer."

She wasn't quite sure what he was thanking her for exactly—the food or the babysitting. The latter seemed most likely, although it didn't matter. Or rather, she didn't care because other things were being conveyed, too. Sincerity, for one. A bit of surprise, for sure. And approval, maybe, or admiration? Whatever, all of it combined to make her feel all warm inside. *Appreciated*—that was the word she was looking for, and my goodness, it felt *nice*.

If Isla hadn't chimed in, Summer wasn't sure how long they would have remained in that eye lock.

"We picked out pumpkins for Halloween, too. It's going to be awesome, and Summer said she'd help me carve that haunted house. You know the picture I showed you?"

"That's very generous of her. Summer, are you sure?"

"Are you kidding me? I can't wait. Love to carve pumpkins."

Levi smiled. But then he sighed and slowly shook his head.

Isla's little face scrunched with concern as she watched him. "Dad, are you okay?"

"Yes, honey, I'm good now that I have eyes on you. Not very happy with your mother, but that doesn't have anything to do with you."

Isla looked back down at the table.

Like she'd been zapped, Summer's entire body tensed. Even her lungs went tight. *"No!"* she wanted to shout. *That statement has everything to do with Isla.* Kylie had done this, too. What was wrong with parents that they couldn't keep their comments about each other to themselves? Or, at least, out of the ears of their children.

Unclenching her teeth, she found a breath. *Not your business, Summer.* What she could do, however, was divert. She was a master at that.

Putting on a cheerful face, she went for a subject change. "Like Isla said, we've been having a blast. This is the best day I've had in forever. I need to thank you, too, Levi. When you said Theo and I could help ourselves to your garden, you failed to mention it was like a farmer's market, which happens to be one of my favorite places in the entire world."

"Is it?" he asked, his voice ringing with surprise. "That reminds me, Theo said you had plans to go shopping today. I'm sorry if—"

"Oh, *pfft.*" She waved a breezy hand. "I didn't go. He ended up going somewhere... far away, so I gave him my list. Theo's a good shopper, and I don't like shopping."

"You don't like to shop, but you like the farmer's market?"

"Well, sure. That's not typical shopping, though, is it? It's outside, and there's all this delicious fresh produce and baked goods. I appreciate all the work that goes into growing your food, too. It's so easy to lose sight of that these days, don't you think? Grocery stores are kind of weird when you think about it, everything all clean and shiny and bundled up and wrapped in plastic."

"I do," he stated and then chuckled. "I agree with all of that. So, you, uh, you cook this food you buy at the farmer's market?"

"Well, yeah," she said. "I wouldn't say I'm a *great* cook, but I try. I don't have a huge repertoire, but I make a few dishes pretty well. And I can steam vegetables like nobody's business. Anyway, when Isla and I were swapping pumpkin favorites, she mentioned she'd never had pumpkin soup. Which happens to be one of my specialties, so..." She flipped one hand over as if presenting the pot. "Soup. It's what's for dinner."

That made him grin, and Summer liked that, too. Making him smile as much as possible was a new goal.

"I've never had pumpkin soup, either."

"Lucky for you, too, then."

Eyes glittering, he teased, "But is it as good as sushi?"

"Better," she fired back and then laughed. He was funny! Calmly, she kept stirring the soup while something stirred inside her, too. She had no illusions that she'd won him over so easily. She recognized he was grateful for the help with Isla, but still, this thawing felt good. Not to mention, friendship would be the best way to earn an invitation upstairs.

Isla wiped her mouth with a napkin. "Dad, is it okay if I go see Cricket? I want to give him some pumpkin, too. I'm so excited that I get to spend two whole weeks here. I wish I could see Cricket every day all the time."

"Of course, honey. I wish that, too."

Since she and Isla had already discussed making this visit, she had a baggie filled with pumpkin. She handed it to Isla, who trooped outside.

Levi immediately filled the silence, taking a seat. "Summer, I can't thank you enough. I am incredibly grateful you were able, and willing, to spend the day with my daughter. I hope it wasn't too much of an inconvenience."

Summer turned off the stove and moved over to the table to take the spot kitty-corner to him. And then instantly regretted sitting so close. The table was small, and she could feel the heat coming off him.

The air seemed to buzz around them, bombarding her with all these *feels*. Blinking slowly, she tried not to meet his eyes because she feared he'd somehow see her thoughts—and the pulse now pounding in her neck. She attempted one of Theo's deep-calming breath techniques, which she quickly realized was another huge mistake. All she inhaled was Levi, and he smelled divine, like soap and sandalwood with hints of leather and horse. A fantasy seized her, one that had her snuggling close and burying her nose against his neck.

"Honestly," she tried to say, but her throat was so dry she had to stop and cough. Embarrassment warmed her cheeks. With a shaky hand, she reached for her water bottle, took a sip and tried again, "It was no big deal. I enjoyed it, and Isla is smart and funny and delightful."

"It is a very big deal to me." He raked a hand across his jaw and then focused intently on her. Summer couldn't *not* look at him now because his gaze was pulling at hers. Her eyes found his, and focused, and she knew he was feeling this force, too. This time warmth heated her from the inside out. "Summer, there is so much I want to say to you. I don't even know where to begin."

CHAPTER TEN

THAT WASN'T EXACTLY TRUE. Levi didn't want to talk at all. He wanted to kiss her, and the impulse was so strong all previous thoughts scattered. He liked her being this close where he could analyze and appreciate every feature: the perfect shape of her lips, the subtle glow of her sun-kissed skin, the scattering of freckles dotting her nose. His fingers itched to touch her cheek, to discover if it was as soft as he suspected.

She was so beautiful, and also, he realized, a bit of a mess. A very, *very* appealing mess, and how could he have ever thought she was high-maintenance?

Splatters of pumpkin decorated the front of the oversize faded blue sweatshirt she wore, and it looked like it was about one wash away from falling apart. Tendrils of unruly reddish-brown hair escaped her high, messy ponytail, and she had a smudge of flour on one cheek.

Blue-gray eyes melded to his as she answered with a gravelly whisper, "Okay."

"What?" he asked, his gaze dropping to her mouth.

"You wanted to tell me something?"

"Hmm?" He looked up, inhaled through his nose and then exhaled a sharp breath. "Yes, I do. I owe you an apology. When you first got here, I wasn't as nice to you as I should have been. I was sarcastic and rude and thinking only about my own problems."

"Levi, no, you don't need to apologize. I appreciate the sentiment, and sure, you were a bit...sarcastic. But I've been planning to apologize to you for the exact same thing. I didn't even stop to think about what you might have going on or how our early arrival might be inconveniencing you. I know I came across as difficult." Wrinkling her nose, she added a slight cringe, and it was about the cutest thing Levi had ever seen. "I *am* difficult where Sacha is concerned. My horse is my life and my livelihood."

"I get that. But there's more—I assumed things that clearly aren't true. I misjudged you, and I'm sorry. You are...a lot different than I thought you'd be. A whole lot."

Eyes sparkling and dimples wrestling with a smile, she said, "Yeah, you, too. According to Theo, being *judgy* is sort of my thing. And I thought you were a jerk face."

"Jerk face, huh?"

"I was absolutely convinced. When we left the rodeo grounds, I wanted Theo to keep driving. If it weren't for Sacha, I'd be somewhere, *anywhere*, else right now. I agreed to stay one night, and then we were going to leave the next day. So, as you can see, I owe you an apology, too."

"No, you don't. I *was* a jerk face. I didn't want Isla hanging around you. I was afraid you'd be a bad influence, and here you are entertaining her—gardening, baking, taking care of my animals."

"A bad influence," she repeated, eyebrows drawing together, lips compressing thoughtfully. "That explains a few things."

Levi grimaced, watching her face while the pieces snapped into place in her mind.

"Did you tell Isla not to talk to me about riding?"

"Not specifically, but I told her you might be too busy to spend time with her, not to ask too many questions and not to invite you to do things with us."

Her eyes flashed with gray-blue sparks. "Like, come upstairs and see her room?"

"Yes."

"Ouch. Was I *that* horrible that you wouldn't want me spending time with your daughter?

Isla was lovely from the first minute we met. It was you I didn't like."

"No! Summer, I was preparing her for disappointment. She… Her mom, Kylie, sometimes makes promises and doesn't follow through, and she doesn't always put Isla first."

Softness settled into her expression, sadness flickering in her eyes. "I see." Nibbling her bottom lip, she reached out and fidgeted with a potholder on the tabletop before her. Levi waited, suspecting she had more to say.

Seconds ticked by before she looked up, exhaled a breath, and said, "Okay. Maybe we can start over, or wait, no, I don't want to start over because there's been all this good stuff, too. And now that I know you're *definitely* not a jerk face, how about we…continue better?"

"Continue better," he repeated casually even as his mind raced through possibilities. What did "better" mean to her? He knew what *he* wanted it to mean. "I think we can do that." Because as long as it entailed spending time with her, he was game.

"I heard about your rodeo and what you're doing for your grandmother."

"Ah. Kylie?"

"No. Well, she alluded to it, but Theo got the details at this restaurant in town. The Cranky… Crowd?"

Levi tipped his head back and laughed. "Crow, actually. It's the Cranky Crow, but cranky crowd works, too. Especially these days."

"I don't know what that last part means, but what you're doing for your grandmother, for your family, is incredible. And then there's the rescuing of the animals."

"Isla," he stated because there was no doubt where she'd heard that part.

"Yes, I got the backstory on several of your adoptees. They are all precious, every single one of them. I especially adore the goats, and Bosco is extra special. I almost cried when she told me his story."

Levi smiled. "It just occurred to me that you met my ex-wife and spent the day with my daughter. Now I'm wondering what you *don't* know about me."

"Plenty! I have so many questions *burning* to be asked."

"Burning? Really? No way am I interesting enough to warrant curiosity of that…temperature."

Her smile was a mile wide, and, if he wasn't mistaken, there was an air of flirtyness about her. "Oh, I disagree, Fair Catch Levi Blackwell, barnstorming bulldogger, canniest header in the West, and all-around roping magician with the fastest hooey in the circuit."

Warmth seeped up his neck. Fair catch was a reference to his ability as the header on a roping team to consistently land his rope over a steer's horns, head or neck—a requirement for the event. Isla was accurate in that he'd never been comfortable talking about his achievements. "Don't believe everything you read online."

"Some of that came from Isla," she clarified but didn't deny she'd been googling him. "I think your record speaks for itself. You were predicted to be a triple crown winner the year you retired. One thing I could *not* find online was information about the accident where you were injured. Was it bull riding? I read that's the most dangerous event."

"Then what makes you think there was an accident?" he asked, genuinely curious. Levi had never publicly given a reason for his retirement, other than calling it personal.

"Oh." She frowned, thinking. "I guess I assumed. But didn't I read the word accident somewhere? And also, because sometimes you move and I feel like you might be in pain. I fell off a horse about six months ago, not Sacha. I was trying to help a friend work through her horse's fear of water obstacles. I won't bore you with the details because I'm sure you can envision exactly what happened when that horse put the skids on." She lifted her hands and pointed at one with the other. "That's me." Then she swapped positions. "That's the ground." She propelled the "me" hand up into an arching motion and then lowered it back down to splat against "the ground."

"It wasn't the worst fall of my life, by any means, but I messed up my back."

Levi nodded, imagining, thinking how what she did was every bit as dangerous as rodeo. He wasn't sure if it was that shared element of danger, her seeming interest in him, their horse connection or, more likely, just her. Whatever the cause, he felt compelled to keep talking.

"I've never been a bull rider. Saddle bronc was my only roughstock event with the occasional bareback ride at a smaller competition if I thought it'd give me the points I needed for all-around."

"That makes sense," she said. "I learned how the events are divided into two categories, timed and roughstock?"

"Yep. Timed events were my thing. Roping, specifically. Tie-down, team, calf, steer, anything involving a horse and a rope."

"I have tons of rodeo questions for you. Learning some of this stuff made me realize how I need to study for the rodeo, too, learn the vocabulary and stuff."

"I'd be happy to help."

"Great! We'll talk about that later. So, if there wasn't an accident, why did you quit then? Is that too personal? You don't have to tell me."

"No, no, there *was* an accident. Just not a rodeo one. I, uh…" Pausing, he searched for words and then, "I guess you could say I was bucked off my ATV."

"What?" she said, her eyes going wide. "How?"

"Coyotes were hanging around harassing the sheep. One night, they got a hold of one. I ran out and jumped on the four-wheeler and took off after them, going way too fast—especially in the dark—hit a rock, did my own version of what you demonstrated but without the water and…messed up *my* back." He winked at her. "You were spot-on."

She winced. "How bad?"

"Not as bad as you're probably thinking," he said. "Nothing requiring surgery, lots of rest and physical therapy. Sciatic nerve still gets grumpy—that's probably what you're seeing. Broke some ribs, tore a tendon in my left shoulder, but those are pretty well healed. Doctors say I'll make a full recovery. I'm nearly there, I think."

"How was your little lamb? Poor thing. Did it survive?"

If Levi hadn't already been crushing pretty hard, her concern for his flock would have sealed it. "Yes, my lamb recovered just fine. The very next week, my vet called to tell me about these two llamas she'd taken in who needed a home. That's how I got Dulce and Annabelle. Haven't had a coyote problem since."

"Why is that?"

"Llamas are like guard dogs for the sheep and the goats—all livestock. They're naturally aggressive toward canines of all types. They also bond with other livestock and then protect the herd. Donkeys do a similar thing for the cattle and horses. They don't bond the same, but, in general, they also don't like dogs so they're good for protection, too."

"That's fascinating."

"I think so."

She held up one hand. "I'm going to need to know more about that. But, back to the accident for a sec…"

He read the question in her eyes and answered, "Technically, I could compete again, but I don't want to."

"Because of Isla?"

"Mainly, yes. Traveling all the time was difficult enough, but after Kylie and I divorced, things got nearly impossible. Kylie refused to deviate from the parenting agreement, so if my designated time didn't fall on my days off, I didn't see my daughter. My sisters, Corliss and Adele, and my gran were great about bringing Isla to the closer competitions, but it was hard. And I didn't want my time with my daughter to be spent with her watching me ride. I wanted to be riding with her, teaching her all the stuff I know."

"I understand. I think that's admirable."

"Bottom line, I love horses. I got lucky when Isla inherited that gene, and I don't want to waste it. I can't imagine a life where I couldn't ride anymore. With any luck, I'll mark the last day of my life with some time in the saddle."

"Me, too." She smiled wistfully.

"And just because the accident that took me out of the game didn't happen at a rodeo doesn't mean it wouldn't have happened eventually. Over the years, I had plenty of bad falls, broken bones and more close calls than I care to discuss. They all take their toll, and

I didn't want to end up so busted up that I could no longer do all the things I want to do, whether that's riding, fishing, hiking, working in my garden, teaching Isla to ski, or how to hit a baseball or whatever she wants to try."

"I think that's amazing. But what will you do now? I know you're organizing the rodeo for your grandmother, but what comes next?"

"That's a good question. I was hoping to buy the rodeo property and turn it into an event venue for other stuff."

"Like?"

"Let's see, well… Everything from monster truck shows and tractor pulls to horse shows and dog agility competitions. I have plans for a mountain-biking course. Concerts, flea markets, Christmas bazaars—you name it."

"Show jumping?" she suggested eagerly. "Eventing? Is there enough acreage for an *eventing* course? English riding is growing by leaps and bounds. Pardon the pun. Levi, this is a truly fantastic idea!"

"Thank you. Possibly is the answer to all of those questions, and I have some questions about what you do."

"Ask away, but later. Because what do you mean, you *were hoping* to buy the property?"

Levi explained about that, too.

By the time he'd finished, outrage was stamped across her face. Head shaking, she asked, "I'd like to have a conversation with this Curtis guy about the meaning of integrity and honor."

"I appreciate that sentiment," Levi said and chuckled. "I can't wait for you to meet my grandma—she's going to love you. I had a similar inclination, but I've calmed down some, and now I'm glad I didn't press the issue. There's a part of me that can't blame him. Fifty thousand dollars is a lot of money for most people.

"The real problem is Xavier Howard and this scheme to build a new town. People are getting blinded by all the dollar signs. But you can't *buy* a way of life, and that's what we're going to be losing if he's successful. They need to wake up and see how special this place truly is."

"Well, I can't wait to see it. Theo said it's charming."

That's when something occurred to him. "Why didn't you leave?"

"What?"

"Earlier, you said you were only going to stay one night, and then you planned on leaving. What made you decide to stay?"

"Oh." Her cheeks flooded with color. "Um,

well, I guess since we're being honest, I may as well confess…"

Please say it was because of me. Say you feel this attraction, too, so I know I'm not alone here.

"It was your house."

"You…" He blinked. "My…house?"

"Yes. So, I may as well confess to you that I have this thing for barn homes. I have fantasies about barn homes. At home, I have a drawer full of photos and notes and barn home plans. And once I realized you lived in one, I wanted to stay. I wanted, *I want*, to see your house."

Levi stared. How could this be possible? Was she being honest? He was struck with the urge to look around and see if Wyatt and Nash were pranking him.

"I'm sorry. I hope that doesn't make you think I'm a terrible person."

"Why would it?"

"I just admitted that the only reason I stuck around was to get inside your house," she joked.

Levi laughed. "Summer, that answer was even better than what I was hoping you'd say. You have no idea how happy that makes me. I'm…" He needed to shut up. He didn't know her well enough yet to act on these feelings, did he?

"Well, I hope you don't think I'm being too forward when I say that *now* I'd stay for more than your cool house."

"Oh, yeah?" Levi tried to breathe, but suddenly his chest felt hot and tight. It was her tone and the way she was smiling at him. Was she flirting? Please, let her be flirting.

"Now I'd stay…" Slowly, her gaze traveled over his face before dipping to settle on his mouth. "For the cowboy who lives there."

Well. What did he do with that? Flirting question answered. And it sort of answered that "better" question, too, didn't it? He knew what he wanted to do, but it probably wasn't what he should do, was it? What was she thinking? What did she want? He didn't want to make a mistake here, which explained why he was, apparently, frozen to his seat.

But Summer wasn't frozen. No, she was not, and in the space of approximately two seconds, she answered every single one of his questions when she leaned in and kissed him.

SUMMER DIDN'T THINK she could have *not* kissed Levi at that moment. Every cell in her body had told her to do it, and none of them were currently expressing any regrets.

His lips were every bit as soft as she expected, and his enthusiastic response was even better. What she hadn't expected was how she'd feel inside, like a finger snap of fate had transported her where she belonged. Summer hadn't felt like she truly belonged anywhere but on the back of a horse for way too long. Maybe ever. Now, here she was, in the middle of "Tiny-dot," Wyoming with a man—a cowboy—who she barely knew. And yet she knew enough, didn't she? And all of it combined to make her want to know him better.

If Levi had been surprised by her advance, he'd gotten over it quick. One hand slipped around the back of her neck, and the other cradled her cheek. And the way he scooched toward her on the bench seat boosted her confidence, his leg pressing against hers like he couldn't get close enough.

The sound of a vehicle outside brought them both to their senses. They parted, but barely.

"That's probably Theo," she whispered, angling back another few inches so she could look into Levi's eyes.

"Summer," he whispered, reclaiming enough distance so that their noses were almost touching. Curving one hand around his chiseled jaw, she brushed a thumb across his cheekbone. A soft growly sound emanated from the back of his throat and sent her pulse racing all over again. And she knew that, like her, he wasn't ready for this to end. "You even taste like summer," he said before brushing his lips against hers for another soft kiss. "That was kind of corny, huh?"

She grinned. "Not at all, as long as it's your favorite season."

With a soft smile, he whispered against her lips, "It is now."

"Good." Reaching out, she brushed her fingers through his hair. "Sorry, I messed this up."

He leaned back, his gaze bouncing around absently as if he couldn't quite believe where he was or what had just happened. Summer couldn't blame him; she was reeling, too—and doubting. What was she doing?

Getting involved with him was probably a bad idea. Her life was a complete mess, and from what she'd already learned, his plate was overflowing, too. She should apologize for being impulsive, assure him it wouldn't happen again, make it clear that it *wouldn't* and—

Outside, a vehicle door closed.

"Do you want to have dinner with us tomorrow?"

"Yes," she said without even hesitating because having dinner with Levi and Isla wouldn't change a thing about her messy life, would it? And being here in Eagle Springs, in Levi's warm and cozy sphere, it was a life that felt a million miles away. "I would love that."

CHAPTER ELEVEN

"WELL, LOOK AT YOU," Theo said after Summer casually mentioned they'd been invited to dine with the Blackwells that evening. Levi had, of course, extended the offer to Theo, but he'd already made plans with Lilah. "Congratulations. You gained access in record time. How did you manage to win him over?"

"Thank you, but it wasn't exactly a hardship. You're going to be very pleased with what I'm about to say."

"Do tell."

"You were right. I misjudged him. Levi is nothing like I thought. The opposite, in fact."

"Ha," Theo chirped. "That does give me an inordinate amount of satisfaction. Hmm," he said, brushing a melodramatic thumb back and forth across his chin. "What exactly is the opposite of a jerk face?"

"A kind, generous, thoughtful, compassionate human being," Summer blurted, only to realize how smitten she sounded when she saw the look on Theo's face. Pivoting casually, she faced the kitchen cupboards and busied herself by putting away the groceries he'd purchased.

"Summer?" One word. That's all, just her name. But the inquiring lilt coupled with the hawklike intensity of his gaze had her trapped.

"Hmm?" she answered distractedly, pawing through the bags, stalling, hoping he'd let this go. "How was...? Where *did* you end up going anyway? Cody? And were you able to find any parmesan cheese?"

"Yes, Cody. And I already put the cheese away. Something going on with you and Blackwell that I should know about?"

"Like what?" Unable to face him, she turned away and stashed a can of who-knew-what in the fridge and another in the cupboard above the sink.

Theo strolled over, casually removed the container from the fridge and held it up for her inspection. "I didn't realize we were storing deodorant in the fridge now."

"Oops," she said and smiled meekly. "I, um, thought it was sour cream."

Smirking, he rolled his eyes. "No, you didn't. You are a nervous wreck, but not in your usual scary way. You've got like a wound-up colt kind of vibe. You want to tell me what's going on?"

She sighed, knowing any further attempt at subterfuge was pointless. No way could she keep this from him anyway; she couldn't keep anything from him. Besides, she needed advice. "Fine. I kissed him."

In all the years she'd known Theo, she'd never seen him speechless. Then again, she'd never seen him shocked either. She assumed that's what it was by the glaring nonverbal cues he was radiating now: body still, mouth half-open, eyes on the verge of popping out of his skull.

"You—you—you..." he finally stuttered. Another first, she noted, Theo was the smoothest talker she knew. And not in the schmoozy manner Braden often employed, but a genuinely good orator. It was part of what made him such an excellent coach. "You *kissed* Levi Blackwell—our host and your... boss?"

"Yes." She hadn't thought about that last part. Summer brought one hand up to rest on her flaming hot cheek. "I know. I don't know what I was thinking."

"Well, you managed to surprise me, so you get points for that. What did he do?"

"What do you mean?"

"When you kissed him, what did he do?"

"Theo!" She scoffed. "What do you think?"

A relieved breath spilled from his lips. "Okay, good. That suggests he wanted you to."

"What? Of course he did." Then he sputtered out a laugh and seemed way more like his usual self.

"You are incorrigible."

"Thank you." He grinned. "What's your plan here?"

"I didn't plan it! I have no plan. You know me—I've never done anything like this before. I've only had three boyfriends in my life, and my high school boyfriend really shouldn't count. Braden is the only one who was even remotely serious."

"Good!"

"How is this good?"

"Summer, for once in your life, you have a chance to do what you want. You're here on vacation in this beautiful place—relaxed and happy. No expectations from your dad. Ingrid isn't pressuring you. Braden isn't gaslighting you. You're not fretting about anything. Except for this cute boy you met and like and kissed, and isn't it nice to stress out about something fun for a change?"

"Yes," she answered simply because when he put it that way, it was. "Fun stress. Everything you said is all true and wonderful. And I know this might sound weird, but being here, it feels right somehow. I'm not sure what's happening, though, and I'm all... discombobulated."

"That's the beauty of a relationship with an expiration date—you don't need to figure it out. If you want to have some fun with Levi, then go for it."

"You think?"

"I know! We've talked about how you need to get out more and enjoy life. Your life. The one *you* want."

That was the ultimate question, though, wasn't it? What did she want? And why did even thinking about the future leave her paralyzed with fear?

"Stop thinking," he said, reading her thoughts and calming her down. "I think if you stop trying so hard to find the answer to that question, then the answer will come to you."

"But I'm only going to be here for a few weeks."

"Precisely." He shrugged and then reiterated, "Expiration date. Lilah knows how long I'm going to be here, and we're going to make the best of it. Levi knows how long you're going to be here. No one is suggesting you have to marry the guy. Besides, he has a daughter. I doubt he'd get involved with you if he was looking for more. Keep it light. Have fun. And stop thinking so much."

"Grab that side, and let's see how stuck this thing this," Levi instructed Adele the following morning. The night before, she'd sent a group text to him and Wyatt asking if they could give her a hand moving an antique wood cookstove. He'd swung through town and picked her up, and now they were waiting for Wyatt to help with the heavy lifting. Adele had brought moving straps, and Levi's pickup had a bed lift, so it wouldn't be difficult to load if they could get it out.

The stove had been installed in the corner of the old foreman's cabin on Hollow Pine Ranch. Many years ago, when a new cabin was built, this one had been relegated to storage. The owners, Kris and Ed Dunbar, had recently decided to downsize and had agreed to let Adele have her pick if she was "willing to dig it out." And willing she was. Like Levi, Adele was desperate to find a way to earn her share to pay back the bank loan that had been called in. She'd cleared away most of the junk and debris around the stove, but two of the heavy cast-iron legs had sunk into the ancient knotty pine planks, where they appeared to be wedged in pretty tight.

"I want to see if I need to get my tools and cut around this floor. Ready?" Levi asked, "On three."

"I don't know, Levi," Adele said. "Should we wait for Wyatt? I don't want you to hurt your back."

"My back is fine," he assured her, adjusting his leather gloves. Then he bent at the knees, gripped his edge and counted down. It moved, the floor cracking and splintering as they shifted the heavy bulk onto more solid ground.

Adele said, "Okay, that should do it. Let's wait for Wyatt to get it loaded."

"You have a buyer for this already? It'll be a beauty once it's cleaned up."

"I do, and I know. Major score. It's astonishing what these out-of-towners will pay for some of this stuff. Last week, I sold that old pair of snowshoes I showed you for a grand."

Out-of-towners were often wealthy new residents who'd moved here from the larger cities in search of a "simpler" life. Ironic, Levi thought, because they were known to look down on and complicate life for the people already here. Case in point, Xavier Howard.

Levi opened the stove door and flicked his cell phone light on to inspect the interior.

"Looks like the firebox might need some repair."

"I told them and emailed photos. They don't care, and they aren't planning to use it anyway. It's for decoration."

"So, they're purchasing a perfectly good stove just to take up space?" he joked.

Adele chuckled. "It's called rustic decor, Levi."

"Whatever you say, Adele. I'm happy you're making money off of other folks' impracticality. Which reminds me, did you hear about the granary?"

"Jacob Kelter's place? What about it?"

Levi told her what Molly had heard, how he'd accepted an offer from Howard.

Adele was wide-eyed and nearly as pale as Gran by the time he'd finished. "Poor Gran. How did she take it? She and Jacob have been friends forever, or at least, they were."

"*Were* being the key word, and that's exactly how she took the news—like a betrayal. But the reason I'm telling you this is so you can call Jacob and see if you can get in there before the sale goes through. Those buildings are full of cool old stuff like this. If Howard gets his way, and I'm not saying he will, the place will be flooded and everything with it.

I highly doubt he's going to care about salvaging antiques."

Features set with a thoughtful scrunch, Adele nodded slowly. "You don't think Gran would see that as a betrayal on my part? If I were to call Jacob?"

"I don't think so. Something good may as well come from it, right?" Shrugging one shoulder and dipping his head to that side, he said, "But, you know, we also don't need to make a point of mentioning it." He added a conspiratorial wink.

Adele grinned. As children, teens especially, they'd always adhered to the motto that it was better to beg for forgiveness than ask permission. Well, mostly he had, while Adele had his back. His sweet sister hadn't exactly been a firebrand. In his opinion, she'd always been a little too good, putting everyone else's happiness above her own. She wasn't one to ask for help, either, which was why when she asked Levi for a favor, he bent over backward to grant her request.

"I'll do it," she said firmly. "Today, before someone else beats me to it. Thank you for thinking of me."

"Always. We're in this together. We're going to get this loan paid off and then…" Hesitating, he thoughtfully stared up at the ceiling for a few seconds before meeting her gaze again and shaking his head. "I have no idea what we're going to do. If I can't make this rodeo deal happen, maybe we could join forces and start selling manure? That's the only commodity my little farm produces. That, and pumpkins, which seeing as how I use composted manure in my garden, that might be a selling point."

That made her laugh, and he was gratified to see it. His sister looked tired, and he knew the pressure was getting to her, too. In addition to this side hustle of buying and selling antiques, she was in the process of resurrecting the local livestock auction. Levi knew all too well the challenges of reviving a business in this community.

"Speaking of paying off loans, how are things going with your guests? You're still alive, so I'm assuming they're not serial killers, after all," she joked. "Or wait, you didn't kick her out, did you? Do I need to brush off my juggling pins?"

"Better than expected," Levi answered from where he was now crouched behind the stove. "Summer is much...nicer than I thought."

"Yeah?"

"Yeah, she um, she spent most of the day yesterday babysitting Isla."

"Levi! You asked a stranger to babysit your daughter? Did you not hear a word I said to you?"

"I didn't!" he countered and then laughed. "I didn't ask her. It was yet another bad episode of the Kylie and Brett show."

He filled her in on the incident, including his short-lived angst, and how Summer had saved the day. He then relayed the details of Summer and Isla's pumpkin harvest and subsequent baking marathon and how much fun Isla had.

He finished with, "So, she's not exactly a stranger now. Isla adores her. And Summer doesn't only ride horses, she loves other animals, too. She has the cutest rescue dog. Tiny thing, some sort of terrier, and get this—she has a thing for barn homes. She's dying to see my place, and I can't wait to show her."

"Hmm," Adele said when he'd finished. Only then did he realize the extent of his gushing ramble. Adele's knowing look made him aware and itchy. Removing one glove, he scratched his neck. She was still staring, so he pretended to study his watch. "Where in the world is Wyatt? He's turned into a fluff brain lately, have you noticed that?" He pulled his phone from his back pocket. "I'm going to text him."

"Yes, it's called *newlywed-itis*, and I think it's sweet. But, Levi?"

"Hmm?"

"Sounds like *you* have a thing for Summer Davies."

His fingers froze on the phone. What should he do? Denial? It was too late, he realized, to keep this from his perceptive sister, who knew him better than anyone. And besides, not answering was all the answer she needed.

"I see," she confirmed, her face a mask of concern. "Levi, I know I was joking around about her being a stranger, and you know I said that serial killer stuff just to make a point. But what do you know about her?"

Enough, he wanted to say. But that wasn't true, was it? Definitely not enough, considering how *serious* his thoughts had already turned. He'd lain awake way too long the night before thinking about that kiss. Not only the kiss itself, which was distracting, but what it might mean. What had it meant to her? The truth was, he wanted it to mean something. He'd never fallen so hard, so fast. Thinking back, he'd never fallen at all—not like this. What if Summer wasn't on the same page?

"Don't get me wrong—it's neat that you

have some cool things in common, but what about her background and her character? It's just that after Kylie…" Halting the thought, she changed gears and said, "I hope you're taking your time and getting to know her. And not rushing into anything."

"I'm not," he assured her confidently. Just because his feelings for Summer were so big that they were currently taking up all the extra space inside him didn't mean he had to share them with her—or with anyone. Certainly not until he knew how Summer felt.

"Good," she added reassuringly. "For Isla's sake especially. She's been through a lot, and you and Kylie are still…"

"Still what?" he said and immediately regretted the edge to his tone.

Adele opened her mouth to finish the thought, closed it and then sealed it with a frown. After a few long seconds of careful consideration, she finally plunged ahead, "You and Kylie are not exactly on the best of terms. I feel like things are still so, um, acrimonious between you two."

"That's because they are! Kylie is self-centered and impossible to deal with, and Brett is an overbearing egomaniac. But Isla is fine," he stated confidently. "She's great and an awesome kid." All of that was true, so why was he suddenly struck with this unsettling twinge of doubt?

"I know," Adele responded in a soothing tone. Too soothing—it scraped at the doubt. "My niece's greatness is not in question here. Isla is amazing. You are an excellent father, and I trust your judgment. It's just that, sometimes I think, and please, don't get upset, but…"

"But what?" he urged, suddenly aware of how uncomfortably close the conversation was to the one he'd had with Gran, the topic of Kylie feeling like too much of a coincidence. What was he missing?

"Hey!" Wyatt's voice called out, the thud of his boots reverberating on the porch. The door flung open. "Sorry, I'm late!" Their brother bounded inside. "We went on a breakfast picnic this morning. There's this spot on the old Blaylock place where there's a meander in the Blue Mist Run, like a horseshoe bend?" Arms up, fingers touching, he formed a sort of half circle. "Amazing! I didn't even know it was there. The morning light was phenomenal for photographs, and we, uh…" Shrugging sheepishly, he looked every bit like a man besotted. "We lost track of time."

"Good morning, Harper," Levi intoned dryly. "Have you seen our brother, Wyatt?

He was supposed to be meeting us here this morning."

Adele busted out laughing, dispelling any lingering tension between them.

"Funny," Wyatt returned, but he couldn't keep from chuckling. "Okay, I may have deserved that. But Harper is so…" He paused, combing his mind for a word, finally settled on a dreamy grin. He moved on. "She keeps showing me these places around here that I didn't even know existed. I don't think life with her will ever get boring, you know what I mean?"

"I'm sure it won't, Romeo," Adele teased, handing him some moving straps.

Wyatt put them on and said to Levi, "Before I forget, can I borrow your rototiller? The ranch's went belly-up, and we can't afford to replace it right now."

"Sure. What's up? Do you need a hand?"

"Nope. Mason is going to help. He wants to put in an asparagus patch, and who am I to dissuade our resident chef?" Mason was their nephew, sister Corliss's thirteen-year-old son, who did most of the cooking on the ranch. "He's already done all the research."

"That's cool. I wouldn't mind some fresh asparagus myself. I'll have to pick his brain

on that. Let me know if you need any fertil-
izer."

"Yeah, we'll make you a good deal," Adele
quipped.

Levi laughed.

"You can tell me what that means later,"
Wyatt said. "Because before I forget, Corliss
wanted me to remind you, Levi, about lunch
next weekend, and she made a point of saying that you are free to invite your guests."

"I CAN'T BELIEVE you live in this *dump*," Summer said, standing in the middle of Levi's
living room and shaking her head in disgust. "This polished barn-plank flooring is
so ugly." Crossing the floor into the kitchen,
she stopped.

Her gaze slowly traveled up over the hick-
ory cabinets to the exposed beams of the ceiling and back down to the granite countertops.
Her movements were almost reverent as she
placed an open palm on the thick wooden
butcher block that served as the room's is-
land, a gem of an antique, which Adele had
scored at an old homestead near Ralston and
then generously gifted to him. A round metal
rack was suspended on chains from the ceiling above, where his cookware hung in an
attractive circular display.

Pulling her hands to her hips, she swiveled toward the oversize apron sink and, with a nudge of her chin, stated, "This thing is too much. You could wash a VW Bug in here, so tacky." Custom made by a friend, the hammered metal face was like a work of art featuring an intricate design of horseshoes and vines entwined around the letter *B*. Stepping close, she trailed her fingertips across the surface.

"What type of metal is this, copper? Yuk."

"I'm sorry you feel this way," Levi responded, trying not to laugh. She'd been insulting his house from the first moment she stepped inside. Well, almost the first moment. Initially, she didn't say anything at all. Speechless and wide-eyed, she'd frowned the way she had during the barn tour downstairs. That was all the enthusiasm he needed. But then the insults started, and it was the cutest bit he'd ever seen.

"I know it's probably difficult to hear, but I'm only being honest."

"I appreciate that," he returned deadpan. "Honesty is a virtue, my gran always says."

She finally cracked. "Levi!" she exclaimed, blue-gray eyes sparkling as they met his. "I'm so sorry. I swear, I *want* to act like a normal person right now, but I'm overwhelmed. So, it's either this or I'm going to go fetch my suitcase and camp in your stupid pantry with those shelves that go all the way to the ceiling—what a ridiculous use of space that is. See? I can't seem to stop."

Levi's mouth curled at the corners. "You're doing fine."

"No, I'm not. I'm embarrassing myself. This place is perfect. Honestly, I'm in love with every square inch, and I have a million questions."

He hadn't seen her since yesterday's kiss, and when she'd first arrived this evening, he hadn't known what to say either or how to act. It didn't seem possible for her to be even more beautiful than his memory, but she was. And he liked how she managed to look both casual and classy in a pale pink long-sleeved knit shirt tucked into snug jeans. On her feet were a pair of ballet-type slippers, which she'd insisted on removing when she came through the door. He kept stealing glances at her stockinged feet padding around his house, which felt both familiar and pleasingly intimate.

With her dark brown hair loose around her shoulders, the light reflected the tones of red, and the contrast to her creamy-pale skin and very dark gray eyes captivated him. The same dusting of freckles lay scattered across her nose, and he was glad she hadn't covered them with makeup. The gloss on her lips, however, was just plain distracting, like a beacon reminding him of their previous encounter.

By silent mutual consent, they'd kept things at the friend level in front of Isla. After showing Summer her bedroom, Isla had opted out of the remaining tour and taken a detour downstairs to the barn. The lasagna was baking in the oven, and the tossed salad waited in the fridge. The only remaining dinner prep would be throwing the garlic bread under the broiler.

With the tour complete and the two of them alone, an electric sort of awareness hummed between them, along with a tentative awkwardness.

As Adele's warning about rushing into things played in his mind, Levi wasn't sure how to proceed. Did he come right out and ask her about the kiss? What was she looking for in a relationship? Could he sound any more needy and desperate?

Or should he take Adele's advice more literally, suggest the kiss was a mistake and propose they get to know each other better before they did it again? He hated that idea. How would you ever know when you hit that "better" mark? Plus, they were under a time crunch; Summer would only be here for a few weeks.

Maybe he should opt for honesty and tell her that he'd never felt like this before and couldn't stop thinking about her. Of all the scenarios, this one was the most true and the riskiest. What if he scared her away?

The bottom line, he realized, was that it didn't matter. He'd take whatever he could get. In the meantime, he would heed Adele's advice a bit more fluidly and try to get to know her better. Organically, yet quickly. Yes, he could do that.

"I am happy to answer all of your questions," he said, moving closer, hovering at the edge of her space. "I have a few for you, too."

"Okay," she said, mirroring his action, moving into his space, and spurring his pulse to a gallop. Inches separated them now, and with every breath, he inhaled her lavender scent, mixed with honey and a touch of leather.

Her glossy lips curved into a half smile, and this time he couldn't look away. He leaned in… And a voice that sounded annoyingly like Adele's silently chided, "Wait, you're supposed to be getting to know her."

Right. "So," he said, or tried to, because the

word was more like a rasp. Inching his body away, he cleared his throat. "Did you grow up in Louisville? Do you have any brothers and sisters? Have you ever been married? This is probably way different than where you grew up, huh?"

"Yes," she answered with a soft smile and hazy eyes. "No, no, and yes, much different and way, way…"

At some point, her gaze dipped to his mouth and stayed there, and those inches he'd worked so hard to put between them disappeared, although he couldn't be sure if that was her doing or his. He swallowed nervously because *what* was he supposed to be doing?

"*Way* better," she finished the thought. "But before we get any further into our mutual interrogation, can I press Pause so I can kiss you again? You know, before Isla gets back."

CHAPTER TWELVE

KEEP IT LIGHT. Have fun. Stop thinking.

Theo's advice had been playing in Summer's mind like a mantra, a goal, an end game. A calm, peaceful state of enjoyment she desperately wanted to achieve. Not that she didn't want to talk to Levi, but discussing her childhood and her family wasn't light or fun, and it was impossible not to think about the future when talking about her past. And her present was complicated enough.

How to explain that no, she'd never been married, but she'd *almost* been engaged to get married? And even now, was sort of fake-engaged. Did it matter? It seemed ridiculous now that she'd even considered spending her life with Braden.

Plus, and she was aware that she might not be thinking this one through, she didn't want to explain *everything*. Not now, and not…yet. They were still getting to know each other, and this felt so perfect and uncomplicated, yet full of promise.

Asking Levi if she could kiss him had not been part of the plan, per se, but had become something of an obsession ever since she'd walked through his door. She blamed phero- mones, and standing as close as they were, with every breath a Levi-scented delight, pushed her over the edge. At least, thanks to Theo, this time she'd asked.

Watching him, waiting for his answer, she feared the suspense might kill her. But not as much as she feared he'd say no. In her chest, her heart felt alive, like a bird beating against the bars of its cage. Nonverbal cues felt prom- ising; he hadn't moved away. His expression was stoic, yet she could see the rapid rise and fall of his chest. When his gaze found hers, his eyes flickered with something that looked like heat, but she hoped wasn't indecision. Did he feel pressured? She didn't want that. She wanted light and…

"Absolutely, yes," he finally whispered, and he sounded sure, too, which gave her the con- fidence she needed to close the distance.

He met her halfway. "Summer." Her name was a soft brush against her lips as his mouth found hers. One arm slipped around her waist while the other came up with a light grip on the back of her neck. Not like she was fragile, but like he wanted to hold her just so. Steady fingers slid beneath her hair, warm against her skin, and Summer melted into him.

She tried to stay in the moment, a complex undertaking with knees like butter because this time, it was… Even better than their first kiss, and she wouldn't have believed that was possible. Maybe she should warn him every time because there was something to be said about being prepared. He was focused, enthusiastic, and so, so good at it.

Beeep!

Startled, Summer jumped in his arms. "Yeesh! What the…?"

Levi held on, chuckling, and buried his face in her hair. "Lasagna is done."

"Okay, good," she quipped. "Nothing is on fire then. Should I…?"

Levi readjusted, pulling her firmly into his embrace for a hug. Summer closed her eyes, held on tight and let herself feel…everything. His hand drew a soothing circle on her back. Listening to him breathe, feeling his gentle strength, the warmth of his touch, it was almost too much. Tears prickled behind her eyes, and she quickly blinked them away. Crying most definitely did not equal light in this equation.

A tapping sound emanated from below, footsteps.

"Isla?"

"Yes." He dipped his head and kissed her neck. Keeping his face buried there, he let out a soft growl of frustration. "How am I going to keep my hands off you? Summer, I think we need to talk. I'm…"

"I know," she said, and then finding his hand and gripping it tightly, she repeated it, "Levi, I *know*."

It was the hug that did it. The kiss was incredible, yes, but in his arms, she felt this exciting sort of contentment. Could contentment be exciting? She didn't know, but what she did know was that here, being with him, checked off two out of the three Theo boxes. The fun and the no thinking about her future. The light, not so much. Because how could she keep things light when she felt this way? Like a wild horse escaped from its tether, her feelings were out there running free, and there was nothing she could do to herd them into order now.

There was, however, one person who mattered more than either of them. Stepping back, she kept a firm hold on his hand. "But for now, we will keep our distance." Squeezing his fingers before letting go, she said, "We'll do it for your daughter."

WE'LL DO IT for your daughter.

That was the moment Levi knew he was in love with Summer. A revelation that only solidified as the days went on because those words weren't just lip service on her part. That night was only the beginning. Over the next few days, she stepped into their life like a puzzle piece he didn't even realize was missing, and her insistence on putting Isla first wrapped so tightly around his heart he could barely think straight.

The next day, she picked up Isla from school, and after helping her with homework, they went for a ride. She explained to Levi that it was vital for her and Isla to develop their own friendship. Levi couldn't help but wonder if that suggested she might be thinking of a future that extended beyond the rodeo. Regardless, he appreciated the free afternoon to work uninterrupted and was surprised by how much he was able to accomplish. When he got home from work, dinner was in the oven.

Over a delicious meal of chicken pot pie and green beans, he listened to his daughter gush with excitement about their day, detailing their adventures and explaining how Nugget rode along in the saddle with Summer.

"It's a modified front pack," Summer explained. "Theo made it."

At one point, Isla and Summer spent a good long while giggling hard about something to do with a bird and a spider. Levi couldn't make out most of the story, but he didn't care. Sitting at his table in the home he loved, watching the two of them together, sent his imagination on a fantasy ride of family dinners stretching years into the future and where the empty chairs were gradually filled, one by one. She'd be such an incredible stepmom, and mom, and he wondered if she wanted kids of her own.

He told them about his chaotic day, making a point of keeping things positive. By the time they'd finished the meal, he found himself looking forward to later after Isla went to bed when he could take Summer in his arms and thank her properly.

Instead, Summer surprised him by saying good-night after dinner.

"You sure you don't want to stay?" he asked when he walked her to the door. *Please, stay,* he found himself wanting to say.

"Don't get me wrong, I'd like to, but you guys need your family time." She stated this firmly. "If you and I are going to spend time together, it's important that Isla doesn't feel displaced. And she and I need to build a relationship outside of you, too, before she knows we're…romantically involved. I don't want her to think you're the only reason I'm here."

Levi allowed himself to be encouraged by that, too.

At least, initially.

SUMMER HAD NO IDEA who the woman watching was or how long she'd been there. Leaning forward in the saddle, she patted Sacha's neck and surreptitiously tried to steal a glance. Thin with a high, bouncy blond ponytail, she executed a graceful grapevine step along the fence line, her phone held aloft, filming, Summer guessed. Reporter was her first thought, but one she quickly discarded because there were no trespassing signs posted all around the property's perimeter.

"Hey!" the woman called, all smiles as she lifted a hand to wave. "You must be Summer."

After halting Sacha, Summer dismounted and led him toward the arena's edge. "That's me."

"I hope I'm not interrupting."

"Not at all. We're finished for now."

"Great! I'm Harper Hayes Blackwell. Wow." She paused, tilting her head, a wistful expression on her face. "I wonder if introducing my married self is ever going to get old?"

Up close, Summer was struck by Harper's beauty. She'd been blessed with radiant, glowing skin, the kind that tanned in the sun rather than singed to red and caused freckle eruptions like Summer's. Sparkling blue eyes lit with what looked like a combination of joy and curiosity, and her friendly smile was contagious.

"Nice to meet you, Harper. Wyatt's wife, right?"

"Yep, and I am super excited to meet you, Summer, and just stoked that you're here in Eagle Springs. We have *so* much to talk about."

Did they? Butterflies awakened in her stomach. Had Levi been talking about her? What had he said? She'd really like to know because she wasn't even sure what they were doing. They'd agreed to keep things on the downlow because of Isla, but the last few days had been hard because they hadn't been able to spend any time alone.

Harper was not forthcoming with Levi details. Instead, she shifted her focus to Sacha and said, "Your horse is stunningly beautiful."

"Thank you," Summer said, tuning back in to the moment, because regardless, Levi raved about his new sister-in-law, and it was sweet how she'd stopped by to make Summer feel welcome. She flattened a palm on Sacha's forelock and introduced him. "This is Sacha."

"Sacha," Harper repeated thoughtfully. "Rhymes with matcha, like the tea?" At Summer's nod, she began tapping on her phone. "Is that S-A-C-H-A?"

Was she taking notes? "Um, yeah."

"And your last name is Davies?" She spelled that out, too, her fingers hovering above the screen. Definitely taking notes. How very, um, detail-oriented. Okay, and maybe slightly odd, but Summer was determined not to make snap judgments anymore. Maybe Harper was one of those people terrible with names, or perhaps she had issues with her short-term memory.

"Don't horses typically have long flashy names like... Oh, I don't know—Reach for The Sky or Trouble N Paradise?"

"They often do, Thoroughbreds especially. But other breeds, too, if they're registered. Naming a foal is fun but can also get a little complicated."

"How so?"

"Uh, for example, with Sacha's breed, there

are rules that require you to use the first letter of the dam's name for the foal."

"That's the mom, right, the dam?"

"Yes. So, Sacha's dam was Shallyn Queen, and Sacha's full name is Such a Masterpiece. But horses typically get what's called a barn name, too, which is often a shortened version of their longer flashier name."

"I get it. *Such a* became Sacha."

"Yep."

"Very cool," she said, typing again. "Girlfriend, you and your handsome horse here are about to light up my world. You are going to get so tired of me following you around."

Um, what? Not that Summer didn't appreciate her enthusiasm, but this was officially turning strange.

"Why would—"

"This is going to make my job *so* much easier. Now I have something besides a bunch of unpainted buildings and a partially renovated arena to post online. Levi hardly ever lets me include him in my shots. Which, I get. He's so busy. And a little shy, which is endearing. But, between you and me, we're getting down to the wire here, and he needs to resell some of those tickets that were refunded when Trace Baylor canceled."

Um, what? "What job?"

"Uh-oh." Harper tipped her chin down and looked up at Summer through dark lashes. "Levi didn't tell you, did he?"

"Tell me what?"

"I'm helping him promote the rodeo. Did he tell you I was stopping by, at least?"

"Oh! No and no. But the note-taking and the following threat is all making so much more sense now," Summer joked. "What a relief."

Harper scrunched her face thoughtfully, undoubtedly replaying the conversation in her head. Then she grinned. Their eyes collided, and together, they burst out laughing.

"I am so sorry," Harper said after a moment, both of them still brimming with laughter. Raising one hand, she wiped at her eyes. "Just to clarify, I am not a super stalker. I'm a social media specialist, and I volunteered to help Levi promote the rodeo. With your permission, I'd love to take photos of you and your horse and post them online. The rodeo has accounts on Instagram, Twitter, Facebook and TikTok. I'd like for you to be the face of my little campaign. Or faces, I guess it would be, with you and Sacha."

This, Summer had not anticipated, nor did she want to participate. This type of pressure was what she'd been attempting to evade. But how to decline? Theo had sent Levi her official bio and photo for promotional purposes. No other publicity requests had been made, either verbally or in the simple two-page agreement she'd signed, which had been part of the appeal. Since she wasn't competing, and rodeo wasn't an equestrian event where she would ever compete, Summer hadn't even run the job through her agent.

"What's the matter?" Harper asked, reading her silence for the indecision that it was.

"Harper, thank you so much for the offer. You seem great, and I can already see why Levi adores you, but I'm going to have to decline."

She frowned. "Are you serious?"

"Yes."

"Can I ask why?"

Typically, Summer would leave it at that, a simple no, but this was Levi's sister-in-law, the first family member she'd met outside of Isla, and she wanted Harper to like her. "I'm not…good at publicity, especially the kind you're talking about. You know what—that's an understatement. The truth is I'm terrible at it."

"I don't…? What do you mean you're terrible at it? Aren't you a professional athlete who relies on sponsors?"

"Yes, but…" How to explain? "I have to be very choosy about my sponsorships."

"I get that," Harper agreed with a nod. "So do I. You have a brand. But I promise I know what I'm doing."

"I appreciate that, but that's not it." Summer sighed and gave it to her straight. "First of all, I'm incredibly unphotogenic."

"What? No!" Harper shook her head. "That is simply not possible. Look at you! You are gorgeous! I'll be honest, when I saw you, I was so excited because I knew you'd be perfect for this."

"That's incredibly kind," Summer said. But that wasn't the problem. How to explain? Nibbling on her bottom lip, she thought for a few seconds. A picture spoke a thousand words, right? "Have you googled me, by any chance?"

"Not yet. Levi only told me you were here yesterday when I stopped by his office to discuss the campaign."

"Why don't you go ahead and do that right now?" Summer dipped her chin toward Harper's phone. "Go ahead. I'll wait."

"Okay." Harper fired up her phone. "What social media do you use?"

"None. But you'll find me."

Harper's fingers flew over the screen, typing, tapping, swiping at lightning speed before slowing to execute a series of methodical swipes. Occasionally, she'd raise a confused glance to Summer as if puzzling out a difficult equation.

"Who?" she whispered at one point. "What…?"

Summer understood and watched as Harper's sunny disposition slowly faded to cloudy disbelief. Frowning, she studied the screen for a long moment before finally looking up at Summer and clearing her throat. "How is this possible? Most of these photos don't even look like you."

"I know. You're the expert. You tell me."

"This one…?" With a funny little huff, she held out her phone so that Summer could see the image of herself at the Spencer Event Challenge. A photographer had snapped the photo while she and a group of fellow riders congregated near the course to watch their competition navigate a particularly challenging series of obstacles. Unaware of the camera, she stood next to Josiah Maxim, listening to his commentary and disagreeing with his assessment.

"What are you doing with your face? It's all twisty with disgust like the guy next to you smells like bad cheese."

Summer laughed. "I know. And for the record, Josiah smells very nice. One of his sponsors is Corbin Cologne."

"Seriously, if I made this a meme, it would go viral like this fast," Harper added a finger snap before swiping again.

Summer shrugged her agreement before commenting, "It's better than the one where I look like I've had dental work and am still coming off the anesthetic."

"Oh my gosh, that's this one!" Harper cried, tapping again and then flashing that very image. They laughed some more.

Summer could add honesty to Harper's list of virtues. Now she not only liked the woman, she wanted to be her friend.

"Well," Harper declared as if she was the final word on this subject. "This just won't do."

"I know. Trust me—it does not do."

It was a problem, one of many, if she was being honest. Braden was by far the less skilled rider, yet sponsors were constantly seeking him out. Charisma, Ingrid called it, and Summer couldn't deny that he created a buzz everywhere he went. It didn't hurt that the man was incapable of taking a bad photo. She was under no illusions about how they'd landed the "wedding package." Braden kept telling her not to worry, that he'd guide her through it. Truthfully, the only part of her job as a professional equestrian that came naturally to Summer was the riding.

"What I mean is, it is a problem for me. In my business, it prevents me from getting certain sponsorships."

Harper tapped a thoughtful finger to her lips and focused briefly on her phone again. "You look beautiful when you ride."

"Sacha makes me look good."

Harper smiled indulgently. "That's not it. You look relaxed. And your official bio photo is nice…"

"It was staged."

"Hmm, nothing wrong with that in the publicity business," Harper stated with a wide-eyed snicker of surprise. She made the photo bigger then studied the image.

"No, I mean *staged* staged. My friend Theo was behind the photographer the whole time, making me laugh. The photo is supposed to have a professional look, so my agent told me not to smile. So, yeah, that's me wanting to laugh but trying not to smile. That's literally how complicated it is for me to take a good photo."

The women shared another outbreak of laughter, and then Harper turned serious and stated, "I'm only laughing because this is not a real problem. You know this can be fixed, right?"

"What? *Nooo...*" Summer waved a hand in protest. "You can't make someone more photogenic."

"You wanna bet? Besides, even the biggest social media stars admit to taking hundreds of shots for every single one that they post."

Summer believed the statement, but she couldn't imagine taking that many photos of anything.

Harper said, "My brand has more of a natural vibe, so I'm nowhere near that fastidious, but creating an engaging photo is not as easy as it looks. But it's also not that difficult to make someone look good, especially if they already look good to start with if that makes sense?"

"It doesn't. Nothing about being a social media sensation looks easy to me," Summer replied.

"Listen, I have an idea. Why don't you let me hang around a bit, like the super stalker that you already thought I was," she joked. "I'll give you some tips about how to relax and be your natural best. I'll take photos of you and Sacha, then crop, edit and filter, and you can see what you think. I won't post anything without your approval. It'll be fun. I promise."

Summer's inclination was to stand firm, so much so that she rolled her lips to keep from declaring a loud "No, thank you." But Harper's earlier revelation tugged at her about Levi needing to resell those refunded rodeo tickets. There was so much riding on the rodeo's success. If she could help in this small way, she needed to.

"You know what? Sure. If you want to try, then I'll do it for Levi."

Harper's eyebrows jumped skyward before her face settled into a knowing grin. "For Levi?"

Oops. Shoot. She hadn't intended to say that last part. "Um, I meant… I mean, I'll do it for Denny and for the, um, you know…for the rodeo."

But Harper was also sharp as a tack, and her grin was as bright as the sun in the Wyoming sky when she turned it on Summer. "Sure, yes, of course," she agreed with overly dramatic solemnity. "Let's do this…" Pausing, she threw in a wink and added, "Hashtag—fortherodeo."

CHAPTER THIRTEEN

LEVI COULDN'T CONCENTRATE. He tapped his pencil on the top of his desk three times and stared at the endless to-do list in his notebook. Three taps, three days. That's how long it had been since he'd touched Summer in any manner other than one would when say, passing the potato salad at the dinner table as he'd done last night. Delicious potato salad, sure, but a poor substitute for a lingering hug or the taste of her lips.

Similar scenarios had played out for a few evenings before those. He came home to dinner being prepared or already in the oven. Together, he, Summer and Isla would set the table, fix their plates, then talk, laugh and enjoy the meal. Fun. Then they'd clean up. He'd begun to dread doing the dishes because immediately afterward, Summer would say good-night.

Isla had spent way more time with Summer in the last several days than he had, which on the one hand, was great. It was. Summer

and Isla were coming to know each other and
getting on famously. But on the other, Levi
was feeling silly and frustrated and selfish
because he hadn't realized that *their* spending time together precluded *his* time. Getting
creative wasn't helping either.

Each morning, out of desperation, he'd ven-
tured down to the barn a little earlier than
the day before, hoping to catch a few minutes alone with her. But she and Sacha were
already long gone, practicing in the arena.
From his roping days, he knew better than
to interrupt.

The truth was, he wanted some Summer
time, and he was growing more restless by the
hour. Prickly, even. Maybe she regretted their
kiss. Maybe she'd changed her mind about
their romantic involvement. But wouldn't she
let him know? He sighed, disgusted with himself. This was what he'd come to? Lovestruck,
grumpy and jealous of his own daughter?

"Hey, boss?" Molly called from the doorway.
Levi looked up. "Hey, Molly, what's up?"
"We have a problem."
Great. Just what he needed, another prob-
lem. Would this day never end?

KENTUCKY WAS BEAUTIFUL, no doubt about it.
Particularly, Summer believed, the Bluegrass

region in the north where she'd lived for most of her life and which had earned the state its nickname. Hallmarked by rolling green-mantled hills and fertile pastureland, the countryside was dotted here and there with patches of leafy hardwood forests. Much of it bordered old estates and elegantly appointed horse farms where sprawling white-planked fences provided a striking backdrop for long-legged Thoroughbreds grazing on lush blue-green grass. All in all, the land felt cultivated and tended. Tidy.

Wyoming, on the other hand, felt less culti-vated, wilder and unkempt, but in a good way. Even the air smelled different, earthy, she'd called it, and Theo had suggested it was the hint of sulfur from nearby geologic forma-tions. Whatever the cause, for the first time in so long, Summer felt like she could breathe.

Something about the sky here, too, contrib-uted to the sensation. And it wasn't just the vibrant shade of blue, although that was awe-inspiring in itself. It was the sheer breadth of the horizon, the way it enveloped from above and then stretched all the way to the ground, that made the country feel so vast.

Walking the length of Levi's graveled drive toward Isla's bus stop allowed Summer plenty of time to ponder all of this. Upon arrival at the small, neatly constructed hut, a miniature likeness of their home, she spun a circle, marveling at how the line of sky was broken only by the foothills. Aside from Levi's ranch animals and the attractive, unobtrusive buildings that complemented the landscape, there was no sign of anyone else. It was like being immersed in a giant fishbowl of nature. Of course, the fact that she'd walked all this way and now sat on a bench awaiting the arrival of Isla's bus, and in that time not a single car had gone by, certainly contributed to the sensation.

A few quiet moments passed where the only sounds were the chattering of birds and the feather-soft ruffle of the breeze in her hair. The deep rumble of an engine sounded in the distance. Summer stood as the school bus chugged her direction, a giant yellow loaf of bread on wheels. Brakes creaking, it coasted to a halt, followed by the unmistakable creak of the mechanical door opening. A moment later, Isla appeared around the side of the vehicle with a bright teal backpack slung over her slim shoulders.

Anticipating Isla's sunny smile and easy laughter, Summer stepped forward to greet her and then stopped in her tracks. The look of absolute misery on the child's face was painful.

"Isla, honey, what's the matter?"

She immediately burst into tears. The bus pulled away.

Heart in her throat, Summer hurried closer, took Isla's hand and led her back to the bench, where she resumed her seat and patted the spot beside her.

Sniffling, Isla sat and, with the back of one hand, swiped at her tear-streaked cheeks.

"Isla, what happened?"

"Starla Vandenburg. She's so…mean."

"Starla is a girl from school?"

Nodding, she squirmed on the bench, clearly trying to get it together. "I'm sorry, Summer. I didn't mean to cry, but then when I saw you, I lost it."

Summer draped an arm over her shoulders and gave her a squeeze. "It's okay. You can cry. Crying is allowed between us." She gave her a moment and then asked, "Do you want to tell me about this Starla?"

Isla drew a shaky breath. "Starla is this pretty girl in my riding club. She's a year ahead of Nell and me in school. Her parents are super rich, and she has this beautiful expensive horse called Charlemagne. He was trained by Hansen Remis, and all Starla does is sit there while Charlemagne does everything perfect."

Summer knew the type, but an expensive, well-trained horse would only get a mediocre rider so far. But when you were young and not as advanced, it was the ultimate advantage.

"She has all the best saddles and nice boots and cool stuff. And lucky for her, I don't care. Except then she makes Nell and me feel like our stuff is *gross*. Like, 'Oh, Isla, is that the *same* saddle you had last year?' She's horrible but acts like an angel in front of grownups—you know what I mean?"

Summer did know. In her world, Starla was called Nikki Tillman. "I have a visual. Go on."

"At lunch, I was telling Nell about how you and Theo were teaching Cricket and me jumping technique and how I want to learn to be a show jumper. Nell does, too. Starla overheard us, and she…" Her chin started to quiver, and she took a moment to stare down at her sneakers.

Summer looked down, too, and for some reason, seeing the strip of sock showing at Isla's ankles, covered as they were with tiny horses, pierced her heart—where this child had become firmly lodged in a very short time. She was bright, sweet, funny, yet focused and determined, and full of dreams—horse dreams, mainly. Similar to the ones Summer had at her age.

And now, this Starla had somehow hurt her and made her question those dreams and shaken her confidence. Summer wanted vengeance. Okay, probably vengeance was a bit of a strong reaction where grade school kids were concerned, but also a testament to her feelings. Regardless, she vowed to fix this if she could.

"What did she do, Isla? You can tell me. I promise you can trust me."

Isla bobbed her head confidently like she believed this to be true. "Starla marched up to us, and she said that Cricket isn't a good enough horse. And I'm not a good enough rider. The name Blackwell doesn't mean anything in this town anymore. Dad is a poor, washed-up rodeo has-been, so I will never be able to take lessons or have a good enough horse to be a show jumper."

Summer felt her blood begin to boil.

Isla twisted to look at Summer, her expression pleading. "Please don't tell my dad. It will upset him. Or my mom. Mom is friends with Starla's mom, and Dad doesn't like her, and they'll fight about it. They fight about everything. Don't tell them, okay?"

"I won't," she said. Isla's additional concern about her parents struck every chord within her until her entire body seemed to hum with sympathy. Summer reached deep inside, searching her own experiences for the comfort she wished someone had given to her. Reaching out, she then gathered up Isla's little hands and sandwiched them between her own. "Isla, honey, will you look at me?"

She did, and the stricken look on her face nearly brought Summer to tears. But it also fueled the determination now racing through her.

"Here's the deal. Are you ready?"

That earned her a brave nod.

"In your life, no matter what you choose to do, there will always be mean people, ignorant people, jealous people—people like Starla, who tell you why you can't. But you have to promise me that you won't believe them. No one else gets to tell you what you can and can't do. Only you. You are the only one who gets to decide that."

Her brow knitted with uncertainty, but she nodded like she wanted to believe.

"And the one thing you can do right now is not let Starla get to you. She's trying to steal your joy. Don't let her. In her heart, she's not happy, so she doesn't want you to be happy either. Does that make sense?"

Isla nodded again, looking more confident.

Summer went on, "You know what else? Starla doesn't know what she's talking about, and I'm going to prove it to you."

"DAD! HI!" ISLA CALLED OUT, bounding into his office just as he wished he could call it a day. Molly's news that the painting contractor was officially AWOL with their down payment had hijacked the rest of his afternoon. He and Molly had made call after call trying to find someone to paint the restrooms before rodeo day.

"Surprise!" She threw her arms around his neck. "We're here to take you to dinner."

The sight of his daughter's smiling face went far in lifting his spirits, and Summer strolling inside behind her boosted them even more.

"Best surprise ever," he said. "What did I do to deserve this?"

Isla giggled. "It was Summer's idea. Molly and I are going to go out and check on everything first. I haven't been here in like three days." She bounded out again.

"I hope this is okay?" Summer said with a tentative smile.

"Why wouldn't it be?"

"I don't know. All the way here, I had this weird feeling like maybe I should have asked you first."

"You think you should ask someone before you surprise them?" he teased.

"Definitely not. Surprises are the best." Edging closer, she glanced toward the door. Lowering her voice, she said, "Especially not if it makes you smile like that."

"I'm happy to see you," he confessed, dropping the volume to match hers. "That's why I'm smiling like this."

Levi felt his pulse kick up as she skirted the desk and came to stand next to him. He leaned back in his chair to get a better look. When his gaze met hers, he found that smolder he'd been longing for these last long days. Funny how fast it eased his earlier exasperation and boosted his confidence.

"You look very, *very* nice," he said. She'd paired a blue sweater with snug jeans tucked into soft leather riding boots, clean ones that she probably never rode in. Her hair was down around her shoulders, a silky smooth mass that his fingers itched to touch. He wound his hands around the empty coffee mug on the desktop before him to keep from reaching for her. "I can't decide if I like you better fancy like this or all messy in barn clothes."

"You're saying you *like* my riding clothes," she said, making the statement sound like a cross between a challenge and a revelation.

"Summer, you are the most beautiful woman I've ever personally known, in any clothes. But honestly, if I *had* to choose, I'd go with barn every time."

Her eyes flashed with what looked like heat, and then she swallowed nervously. "Levi, I—" She was promptly interrupted by the sound of the outer door opening, followed by booted footsteps on the wooden floor. A hoot from Molly preceded a round of boisterous giggling.

Inhaling deeply, he squeezed his eyes shut for a few seconds asking for patience. He opened one eye and met Summer's apologetic grimace. Well, at least, she *seemed* to be missing him, too.

"Ready?" Isla called, coming through the door. "I'm so hungry. Can I order a milkshake?"

"Sure." Levi stood to retrieve his jacket hanging on a peg by the door. "I'm feeling like a milkshake, too. Salted caramel."

Isla began listing flavors, describing their virtues, trying to land on one. Back at his desk, Levi's phone alerted him to a text.

"Molly," Summer asked, "would you like to join us for dinner at the Cranky Crow? Theo biked into town earlier and is going to meet us there, too."

Levi caught the look of absolute delight on Molly's face, which caused him to fall even harder for Summer.

"You know what," Molly said, "I think I would. Thank you."

"Yay!" Isla cried. "It'll be like a party." She skipped out of the room, with Molly close behind.

"Don't forget your phone," Summer reminded him from where she waited behind his desk.

Feeling cross at yet another interruption, he almost slipped it into his pocket without reading the message. With his most recent phone debacle fresh in his mind, he relented.

And was so, *so* glad that he did.

Summer: Dear Levi, I can't take much more of this! Seeing you and not...touching you. I. Want. To. Hug. You. Seriously, I need to feel your arms around me. And talk. I want to talk! I totally understand if you don't think this is appropriate, but do you want to meet me in the barn tonight after Isla goes to sleep?

Levi blinked and reread the message. When he looked up, he found Summer eyeing him nervously. Was this woman for real? Somehow, he managed to keep his features perfectly composed as he refocused on the screen and typed a simple two-word answer.

The Cranky Crow was everything Summer imagined it would be and more. So much more. The restaurant's decor seemed to embody every stereotype that might come to mind when one thought of The Old West, yet there were plenty of unique touches, too. She chuckled at the wanted posters featuring current employees. "This place is so much fun."

"Why, thank you, young lady," a voice said from behind her. "It's always a treat when someone educated compliments my effort."

Summer turned to find it came from a striking-looking woman. Tall and thin, she had long, pretty silver-gray hair plaited into a thick braid that hung over one shoulder. In yet another embodiment of the establishment's heavy Western flavor, she was dressed in a plaid button-down with a nice sharp collar. The shirttails were smartly tucked into a pair of blue jeans, tethered with a thick leather belt and fastened with a shiny silver buckle.

"You're Summer Davies," she stated, deliberately eyeing Summer up and down. "The show jumper. You're prettier than your picture."

"Yes, I am." Summer extended a hand and then emitted a chuckle. "I mean, yes, to the first part. And thank you to the second. You must be Harriet, the owner of this charming and fabulous establishment about which I've heard all good things. It's a pleasure to meet you."

Harriet's face erupted with a delighted smile. They chatted and discussed horses.

"Hey, there's Theo!" Isla said. "Can I go sit with him?"

Summer turned to locate Theo but not before catching the look passing between Harriet and Molly. Even though no words were spoken, Summer sensed that important information was being exchanged. Oh boy, she thought and *knew* instinctively that these two women were integral to the core of this town—and quite likely doubled as its eyes and ears. A fact that felt both comforting and unsettling at the same time.

From a large booth in the far corner, Theo waved.

They said their goodbyes to Harriet and then joined him in the dining area.

They were still studying their menus when a familiar voice said, "Hey there!"

"Aunt Harper, hi!" Isla cried. "Have you been to the rodeo today? Wait until you see the arena. It's all painted, and the floor is done. I was thinking you could take some pictures of Summer and Sacha in there while the sand is all smooth? It might be kind of neat with the empty grandstands in the background. You could make them kind of blurry—you know how you do that thing with the filter?"

"Um, excuse me?" A handsome cowboy who could only be Wyatt broke in with a teasing tone. "Harper is your aunt for what— like twenty minutes? And she gets all the greetings and excitement, and I've been your uncle for ten years, and I get…" He shrugged. "Nothing?"

Isla giggled. "Hi, Uncle Wyatt. I have some cool ideas for the Halloween maze, too."

"That's a little better. Hello, Isla. But if you give me the ideas for the maze, then you won't be spooked when you go through it on Halloween."

Levi interrupted the party planning to introduce Summer and Theo, which moved seamlessly to small talk.

But not for long because Harper was on a

mission. Her attention zoomed in on Levi. "The arena is done?"

"Yes, it is. Finally."

"Unlike the restrooms," Molly said.

"What happened with the restrooms?" Summer asked. "Did the paint guy not show up again?"

"Yeah, and he's not showing up, ever. He bailed. Took the money and ran."

"But Isla is right," Levi broke in. "The arena looks nice."

Harper seemed pleased. "This is excellent news, and your daughter is brilliant. Are photos in the snazzy, untouched arena a possibility?" Her focus shifted from Levi to Summer. "If so, is there any way you could transport Sacha to the rodeo grounds for a photo shoot?"

"Fine by me," Levi said.

Summer shrugged. "Sure, yes, absolutely."

Theo agreed, "That would be good. Summer and I were just discussing this morning how we need to get in there and take some measurements and have a look at where they'll be performing. Even better if we could get it set up for some practice."

Levi asked Wyatt and Harper, "Do you guys want to join us for dinner?"

"Oh, we've finished," Harper said. "I want

to get back to the Flying Spur before Denny goes to bed."

Wyatt's expression was a snapshot of sweet tenderness as he looked at his wife. "Harper's been playing cribbage with Gran in the evenings."

"That's sweet, Harper," Levi said. "Thank you."

Harper smiled. "Just trying to take her mind off of everything, you know? It's fun. Denny is so great, and I love her feisty opinions."

"Feisty," Levi repeated. "Mmm-hmm. In the same way that an angry mountain lion is rambunctious." They all laughed.

Wyatt took Harper's hand, and Harper said, "Summer, there are a few other details about the promo project that I need to discuss with you. I have so many ideas. I'll text about all of this and see if we can meet up soon."

CHAPTER FOURTEEN

"IT'S BEEN A long time since I sat on a hay bale and kissed a girl," Levi informed Summer later that evening. They were sitting outside Luna's stall where earlier he'd stacked some bales.

Summer's pulse took off all over again, thinking about Levi's earlier response to her invitation:

It's appropriate.

How could two such simple and innocuous words leave her heart racing with anticipation? She'd taken a screenshot. Then time had seemed to stretch on and on until they'd finished dinner, arrived back home, taken care of animals and then Levi had finally texted to let her know Isla was asleep.

"Yeah?" She gave his shoulder a playful nudge with her own. "How long?"

"Oh, hmm, let me think, it would have been

in my teens, so maybe Annie or Becca? No, wait, it could have been—"

"You know what?" she interrupted light-heartedly, patting his knee. "Never mind. I don't need to know."

He chuckled and then said, "Trust me when I tell you, I never enjoyed it this much. Obviously, or I would remember." He leaned in and gave her another quick kiss, which quickly turned... Not-so-quick.

When they parted, he immediately spotted her uneasiness. "Hey?" The pad of his thumb felt rough, but his touch was gentle as he smoothed the furrow between her brows. "What's this? What's the matter?"

"Nothing, really. Except..." Tipping her head, nibbling her bottom lip, she pondered the topic for a few seconds, not sure if she wanted to venture into this territory quite yet.

"But what?" he urged. "You can ask me anything."

"Didn't you live here with your wife?"

"Oh." He scoffed. "Yes, briefly. No special memories of Kylie and me here, though. We divorced soon after we moved in, and we were already fighting. She did not like it, especially *this* part." One arm came up and made a sweeping motion.

"What do you mean?"

By the time he'd finished explaining, sympathy had tied a knot in her chest. He'd relayed the details matter-of-factly, but she knew the experience had hurt.

"Zoo?" she repeated lightly. "How is that an insult, though? What kid doesn't dream of living in a zoo?"

She liked the sound of his deep rumbling laugh. "Good point, but she was convincing and adamant that no reasonable person would ever want to live like this. It made me protective of my lifestyle choice here and my privacy."

"Oh. Levi, that's…" *Messed up*, she wanted to say but refrained. She was going to end up in the middle of something if she wasn't careful. Not that she minded going to bat for Isla, which she was planning to do in a different way. But was it her place to lecture him about his relationship with his ex?

Instead, she said, "I'm so sorry. She's wrong—you know that, don't you?"

"I do know that. Your reaction went quite a ways in cementing that—thank you very much. I don't know why I let her get to me. She pushes my buttons."

It was like he was inviting her to comment. Spending time with Isla, hearing her anguish over her mom and dad's "fighting all the time," was rapidly making it more and more difficult not to voice her opinion on this topic. In the stall behind them, Luna made a sound like a cross between a snort and a snuffle before resuming her soft rhythmic snore.

They chuckled together, and Summer took the opportunity to herd the subject in a different direction. "Sacha does that, too, and I think it's the cutest thing. I always imagine he's dreaming. I love the sounds that horses make."

"Me, too. When I was a kid, I'd sneak out at night and hang out in the barn, listening. Sometimes I'd fall asleep in the hayloft."

"I did that, too! Okay, it's possible I still do that. When I can't sleep, I go to the stables, which explains why I was so excited about the bed in your tack room. You could relax in there and let the barn sounds lull you to sleep. You know how they sell those recordings of whale songs? I think they should do one called horse nickers."

"Horse nickers," he repeated. "That is brilliant. I was thinking I would sell manure if this rodeo gig doesn't work out, but now I might go in a different direction. I have the raw material, your idea—we could go into business together." With an exaggerated finger tap to his chin, he gazed up at the ceiling briefly before focusing on her again. "Expounding on this concept... What do you think of goat bleats?"

"Delightful," she returned deadpan. "People could play it super loud at bad parties when they wanted to annoy their neighbors."

"Boom. Now we have our marketing campaign, too."

She laughed and then broached the idea she'd been pondering, "So, Isla was telling me that she has a riding club meeting this weekend. Do you take her to those?"

"Yes, I do. Unless it's here. A few of us who have riding facilities rotate hosting the meetings depending on what's on the agenda. Sometimes, they'll do a trail ride after, and my place is popular for that."

Even better. "Do you know the leader, this Melody Howe?"

"Sure."

"What is she like?"

"Melody is terrific. Fun, outgoing, horse lover—excellent barrel racer. You'd like her."

"Mmm-hmm, so Isla tells me they practice exclusively Western riding."

"That's true. That's what Melody knows. That's what I know, and all her rodeo friends know... Where are you going with this?"

"Isla and I were talking, and she mentioned how sometimes riders will come to their meetings and demonstrate or help with certain skills. I heard this rodeo champ even shows up occasionally and teaches the kids about roping."

"I've heard that, too. I've also heard that he's very good-looking and funny, and all the women love him."

"Yeah? Hmm. I didn't hear that part. However, I did hear that he thinks very highly of himself and smells like horse because he basically lives in a barn."

Levi choked on a laugh. "I can't believe you…"

"Too soon to joke?"

"No, it was funny. You are so… I can't believe how cute you are."

"I'll take unbelievably cute." She gave him a little grin. "Anyway, I was hoping maybe Sacha and I could do a jumping demonstration for her club. Theo could talk about technique and different methods for teaching jumping.

"If I called Melody and she agreed to have the meeting here, we could have a really cool course all set up. I'm willing to transport Sacha wherever, too, but this way would be best. What do you think?"

"I think that's a very generous offer, and you have my blessing."

"Yes!"

"And aren't you going to make Isla the most popular kid in her club?"

That's the plan, Summer thought.

"So, YOU HAD a lot of horses growing up at the Flying Spur?" Summer asked. Levi noted, not for the first time, how skilled she was at steering the conversation away from herself. But tonight, he was determined to stay the course Adele had recommended.

"We did. The barn was generally full. Gran bred horses and trained them, and taught us kids. We had tons of cattle back then, so we used the horses a lot, too. Ranching and horses and rodeo all go hand in hand so that all makes sense. But what about you? Tell me about this show jumping and eventing stuff. You must have had horses as a kid, but how did you get started? Do your parents ride? Or maybe you, I don't know, come from a long line of fox hunters?"

That earned him a chuckle. "My parents do not ride, nor do they fox hunt. As far as how I got started, it's going to sound rather fantastical, but if you knew my mom, you wouldn't be surprised. When I was about eight years old, she had a whim, which was a regular occurrence, and decided she wanted to be a horse person. Never had horses in her entire life, didn't even know how to ride. So, we moved to a new house with a barn and stables where she bought herself some horses and hired a stable master and a trainer."

"Just like that, huh? Wow. That's cool."

"No, it wasn't. Like most of her interests that don't involve martinis and sunbathing, it didn't last. While I, on the other hand, fell in love with riding. My poor dad."

"Why is that?"

"He did all the work. Then, about a year later, my parents got divorced. I stayed with my dad, but my mom was, *is*, the one with the money. My horse, Daisy, was already my life, and Dad couldn't bear to take that away from me. As you know, horses are expensive, and I'd already been taking riding lessons. At nine years old, I was obsessed—I wanted to be a professional show jumper. Meanwhile, my mom decided she wanted to be a sailor, bought a boat, hired a captain and hit the high seas. She took her money with her, and because she's a trust fund baby, she could."

"I don't think I've ever met a real-life trust fund baby."

"It's not as cool as it sounds. In my experience, there's a reason why they're called trust fund *babies* instead of trust fund grown-ups, trust fund citizens, or even trust fund people. Bethany, that's my mom, basically sits around in the sun all day with other trust fund babies sipping martinis and buying more stuff they may or may not be truly interested in to appear more and more wealthy."

"Wow, that's…"

"Exhausting," she glibly interrupted. "Yeah, I know. That's why they have to spend *all day* doing it. It's an unsolvable dilemma."

Levi laughed, even as he knew the humor had to be covering a painful wound. "How did he manage?"

"Not well, it turns out. Child support eventually covered some of it. The court ordered my mom to pay a pretty good amount, and it would have been plenty if Dad had scaled back his spending, sold the horses, or at least most of them, and moved us to a smaller place. But we were already living this life, and he couldn't bear to take it from me, or from himself, since I'm being honest. I could go on, but that's the gist of it. I didn't learn all of this until way later, and by that point, it was too late."

"Too late?"

"This part is embarrassing, but I only recently discovered how much debt my dad was in, much of it due to me and my riding."

"Why would you know? Parents don't usually discuss their finances with their children. At least, not the ones I know."

"I've, um, I've been under a lot of pressure because of it, trying to find a way to keep riding and support myself."

"Seems like you're doing pretty well if your RV is any indication."

"Oh no, it's not. It belongs to one of my sponsors, Matilda Motorcoach. They specialize in luxury equine transport."

"Wow."

"Yep, so as you can see, I couldn't survive in my sport without sponsors."

POETRY. THAT WAS the word that came to Levi's mind as he watched Summer and Sacha navigate a series of complicated jumps in his arena, which was kind of embarrassing and such a strange thing for him to think. He didn't even like poetry. But he certainly enjoyed watching Summer.

If the expressions on the eager faces assembled around the opposite side of the fence were any indication, he wasn't the only one. Melody had not only been amenable to Summer's offer, but she'd also expanded on it, inviting clubs from all over the area.

Summer and Isla had been riding every day for nearly two weeks. Summer had loaned her an English saddle, and with Summer and Theo both teaching her, his daughter was on cloud nine. Already he could see an incredible amount of progress. Summer was a patient and gifted teacher, and Theo knew horses. They were an impressive combination.

Now Levi felt himself holding a breath as Summer guided Sacha over an impossibly tall fence, rounded the end of the arena and cleared two smaller obstacles before slowing him to a trot. He'd spent his life in the saddle and competed in rodeo and livestock competitions for nearly two decades. Roping, cutting, barrel racing—he'd watched and competed against some of the best riders in the world. Even then, some of the hard-core cowboys he'd met on ranches scattered around Wyoming, Montana and Idaho would put *those* guys to shame.

This was similar but also different. The symmetry between Summer and Sacha was unlike anything he'd ever witnessed. For sheer skill, Nash on a cutting horse was the best comparison Levi could make. Yet she rode with Wyatt's panache, and there was a dash of his bold confidence thrown in there, too. Truthfully, she had it all. And her horse was perfection; Sacha trusted her completely. Levi'd spent a fair amount of time watching them jump now, and he was pretty sure Sacha would follow Summer wherever she asked him to go.

"Hey!" a voice rang loudly in his left ear while an elbow simultaneously jarred his ribs from the right.

"Ouch!" He looked over to discover the flying elbow had come from Wyatt. "Might want to think about laying off the protein powder, Wyatt."

"Whatever, wimp," Wyatt said, sputtering with laughter.

Nash, the shouter, stood on Levi's other side, chuckling and shaking his head.

"Hey," Levi said to him while pointing a finger at Wyatt, "I know this was his idea, but you're no better. My eardrum is ringing like a cowbell on a green-broke. Why are you guys sneaking up on me?"

"Sneaking up on you?" Nash repeated and then barked out a laugh. "You were so far into that daydream, brother, you were essentially comatose."

"I wonder why?" Wyatt remarked sarcastically, head tipped toward the arena. "Couldn't be the scenery, could it?"

"You're hilarious," Levi said flatly. Had he been that transparent? Yes, and the fact that he'd allowed his brothers to ruffle his feathers was a dead giveaway. Best to let it lie now before they figured out how far gone he truly was. "What are you both doing here anyway?"

"I'm borrowing your rototiller, remember? Nash wanted to come along and catch Summer's performance, and Harper is taking photos for this rodeo business."

"Right," Levi said. "I can't believe how successful Harper's been at selling rodeo tickets." With the rodeo only a week away, she wasn't letting any grass grow under her feet. Last weekend, Summer and Theo had loaded Sacha into his horse trailer and taken him to the rodeo grounds, where Harper had spent hours photographing them there.

"Hey," Wyatt said. "If my wife can convince *thousands* of people to buy a pair of glasses by simply wearing them in a selfie, she can sell your rodeo tickets."

Every bit of Nash's attention was focused on the arena where Summer had moved on to a series of complex dressage moves, something most Western riders didn't do—at least not the ones he knew. However, Isla had informed him that Western dressage was indeed a thing. Summer had explained how dressage could be more difficult than jumping because it took an incredible amount of focus and technical precision. He could see how that was true.

They all watched in silence for a moment as she did it again. Then Nash commented, "Man-oh-man, they are even better in person. I'm going to give you a pass for the, uh, laser focus you displayed earlier. I can't take my eyes off of them either, and I'm *not* infatuated with the rider."

"Just the horse?" Wyatt quipped.

"He is…incredible, but Summer's technique and soft hands are a perfect complement. *They* are incredible. Last year, at the Marin-Mac Invitational, they won the *eventing* portion and—"

"Wait, Nash, you know Summer?" Levi interrupted.

"Sure," he confirmed. "Well, I know of her."

"How would you…?"

"I like to watch equestrian competitions online."

Levi rolled his eyes. "Of course you do."

Nash shrugged a shoulder. "A horse is a

horse. Sort of like a classical musician taking in a rock concert or a hip-hop dancer going to the ballet. Doesn't matter what the performance is so much as how it's performed. I appreciate dedication and training, and skill when I see it. And heart, which is what gives the truly great ones like these two an edge. You'd be surprised what you can learn by studying a discipline that isn't your specialty."

Levi hoped rodeo goers would appreciate that, too.

"That is impressive," Wyatt agreed, his attention now on the duo, too. "But the important question is, can she rope?"

Levi chuckled, but he feared rodeo goers would also wonder that. He could only hope they'd lean more toward Nash's way of thinking than Wyatt's.

CHAPTER FIFTEEN

MELODY WAS EVERY BIT as great as Levi claimed. Enthusiastic and keen to expose her little band of riders to something new, she'd accepted Summer's offer and then run with it. The turnout exceeded both their expectations. Somewhere around fifty people, including parents and other curious family members, were on hand to view the demonstration.

Theo jokingly called it her rodeo dress rehearsal, which Summer could only hope came off as well. On top of their game, she and Sacha executed every jump with textbook technique. It had been way too long since she'd performed for the sheer joy of the sport. And Sacha, taking a cue from her enthusiasm, rounded out the course with a rambunctious high-stepping trot he was prone to when feeling particularly proud of himself.

Summer laughed. The crowd went wild, erupting with applause and cheers.

Theo stepped forward with the microphone Melody had provided for him and began his talk about how to get started in jumping. Summer led Sacha out of the arena and turned him into the small corral. Then she headed to the barn where Isla was waiting with Cricket.

"You ready?" she asked.

"Yep."

Isla was adapting well to the borrowed English saddle, but still, Summer checked the position and girth. You could never be too careful. "Perfect," she declared. "Nervous?"

"Not really," Isla confessed and then shook her head as if she couldn't quite believe it. "I'm more excited than nervous. I know we can do this."

"Yes, you can."

Summer loved how Isla always talked about herself and Cricket as "we." She already understood the concept of horse and rider being a team, working together, trusting each other. It was a huge responsibility to handle such a powerful animal, at the same time that it took courage to put your trust in it. This mutual confidence was the key to effective riding, especially at the competitive level.

They went outside, where Isla mounted and got settled in the saddle. Summer checked her stirrups and went over a quick checklist. As planned, by the time they made it back to the arena, Levi and Theo had set up a series of training exercises. Poles were laid out on the ground in various configurations. The goal was for the horse and rider to navigate over the obstacles with smooth and even pacing. Gradually the poles would be elevated, and the horse and rider would transition to jumping.

Summer scanned the crowd, noting where Starla stood with her mother, Felicia, and a couple of girls from their club. Summer had spotted the Vandenburgs from the moment they'd arrived. Even if Isla hadn't described Starla, she'd have picked her out of the crowd. Decked out in all her finery, she'd be difficult to miss—her boots alone cost more than a good saddle. And it wasn't difficult to see where the attitude came from—her mom wore matching boots with a complementary handbag slung over her shoulder.

"Now," Theo announced to the crowd, "I've asked Isla and Cricket to demonstrate these ground exercises so you can see how a new horse and rider team might fare."

Isla took the cue, urging Cricket toward the spot Theo indicated. Summer felt a lightning bolt of adrenaline hit her bloodstream. Her pulse began pounding hard, sounding like a drumbeat inside her head. She never got this nervous for herself, not where riding was concerned, but she was suddenly a wreck with Isla in the saddle.

Cricket snuffled with a spirited head bob, letting Isla know he was ready to roll. Isla leaned forward and patted her neck, talking softly, calmly holding her at bay. The horse's ears pricked with attention. Watching Cricket respond, Summer felt a sense of calm come over her, too. Confidence replaced her jitters; Isla knew precisely what to do, and she knew how to convey that to Cricket.

"First, Isla will walk Cricket through these poles, letting him get a feel for the spacing…"

Isla urged Cricket forward, and the horse easily adjusted his pacing to navigate the poles.

"Excellent," Theo said. "Now a trot…"

From the corner of her eye, she watched Starla's haughty expression morph through a series of emotions that Summer would describe as surprise, wonder and then envy. Felicia leaned over and whispered in her ear. That was all the attention Summer could spare, turning her focus to Isla and Cricket again.

"Way to go, Isla!" Theo cried and then addressed the crowd, "Let's do it again. Remember, gang, these two haven't been practicing this for long, but I can tell you from the short time I've worked with Isla, she is a strong rider with the natural talent, instincts, dedication and work ethic required to make a superior show jumper. Cricket is a graceful, athletic horse with flawless conformation. He's got energy, power and courage, and most importantly, these two are in synch. A true horse and rider team."

Bless you, Theo, Summer thought and felt her heart smile. That wasn't part of the script, and she knew he would never have said it if he didn't believe it to be true.

Theo paused, letting the crowd absorb his words, and for a moment, the only sound was the rhythmic pounding of Cricket's hooves. Theo went on, "Isla and Cricket are advancing very quickly. So, please, whatever you do, don't compare yourself. Everyone proceeds at their own pace. And that pace, as Summer can attest, is like a ride through the Rocky Mountains, full of hills and valleys. Some days, you're on top of the world, and others, you're slogging through a muddy bog..."

Theo kept talking, teaching, encouraging Isla through each challenge. By the time they'd finished, Summer felt like she was on top of the world. At some point, Levi had joined her by the fence.

"Thank you," Levi said softly.

Reaching over, Summer took hold of his elbow and clutched it hard. "Did you see her, Levi? That's your daughter."

"But she's your student," he countered. "You and Theo. And, Summer, I know you arranged all of this for Isla's sake."

Summer exhaled a breath as Isla and Cricket finished the demonstration. The audience broke out with a final round of enthusiastic applause. Nell jumped up and down, and Summer felt like joining in. She'd never been so proud of another human in her life.

SUMMER HAD JUST FINISHED signing the last autograph when Harper came to stand beside her. "Summer, hey, can I talk to you for a minute?"

"Hi, Harper. Of course. Autographs, how cute is that?"

"Super cute," she agreed. "I got a couple of great shots of you with these kids." But Summer could see her usual verve was waning.

"What's up? Is something wrong?"

"No, maybe? I hope not." Shifting from one foot to the other, she glanced over her shoulder to where Levi was huddled with his brothers.

"What is it?" Summer urged.

"So, your posts are incredibly popular. People are loving the photos and videos of you and Sacha. Engagement is off the charts, and we're seeing an impressive uptick in ticket sales, and people are visiting the rodeo's website." All facts for which Summer credited Harper. She'd delivered on every promise of making Summer look way better in photos than she ever had or dreamed she could. And she had to admit that while she wasn't about to start "Instagramming" or whatever it was Harper did, she made the experience fun. "All good news."

"Definitely," she agreed.

"I asked Levi if I could beef up your bio and add some photos to the site. I wanted personal tidbits to share about you, fun stuff that might not be included in a traditional bio, so I googled you again."

"Okay."

Harper inhaled a deep breath and then announced, "I found this."

Summer took the phone and felt her stomach plummet. The photo quality wasn't great, and thankfully the light was dim, but she knew instantly where it had been taken.

At Chauncey's on the night of the ring toss, Braden on one knee, looking handsome and sincere. And for once, Summer looked… good. Although, she knew the truth, that the smile was far from a happy one. Apparently, a mix of disbelief and disdain was the emotion she should strive for in her photo shoots.

"That's not what it looks like."

"The caption says this is you being proposed to by a man called Braden Keene."

"That part is true."

"Summer, are you engaged to this guy?"

"No."

"Maybe you should tell him that." Harper retrieved her phone and began tapping the screen. "Because it's all over social media that you two are secretly engaged. Well, not *all over*—not yet. But people have mentioned it in the comments on a few of my posts, and someone posted this photo."

"No, Harper, no, it's not true."

"Great," she said, exhaling with relief. "So, can I end this rumor by putting up a post of my own saying you're single but allude that you're being wooed by a mystery cowboy? Who is Levi, obviously. Fans love that kind of thing. And take it from me, people love cowboys."

Summer hesitated a beat. "Not yet. Because while Braden and I are not engaged, we are…connected."

Harper's gaze narrowed before traveling over her face, no doubt attempting to puzzle out the meaning. "Connected?" she finally repeated.

"Yes. It's a long and messy story, but it's part of the reason I'm here. We are linked professionally with some mutual endorsements. It's very complicated. Can you please not say anything to Wyatt until I've had a chance to explain to Levi?"

"Fine. I will do this for you because I already consider you a friend. Levi is over the moon about you, and I can see the feeling is mutual. Luckily for you, none of the Blackwells are very into social media. But I'm warning you, Summer, plenty of people in this town are. Tons of them follow me. If I saw this, others will, too. Possibly even Wyatt, and if he asks me, I'm sending him straight to you. I won't tell him, but I won't lie to him, either."

"I understand."

"My advice to you is that you *disconnect* from this Braden guy sooner rather than later."

"I will," she said. And she would, too, she

vowed even as the thought churned her stomach. *As soon as I find the right time.*

"Mom!" Isla cried while an unpleasantly surprised Levi felt annoyance bubble inside of him as they watched Kylie stride toward them. Levi swallowed a sigh. She hadn't even called to say she was coming. Typical of her habitual inconsideration.

"What are you doing here?" Isla asked, clearly surprised by her presence as well.

Kylie hurried forward and wrapped Isla in a hug. "Surprise! Isla, sweetie, I am so proud of you! You looked like a rock star out there."

"Thanks. Summer and Theo have been giving us lessons. It's so fun!"

"Awesome! I knew Summer would help you out. I could tell right away she was good people."

Levi rolled his eyes.

Kylie shot him a glare and said, "What is your problem, Levi?"

"Don't start, Kylie. You're lucky I haven't asked you to leave. This is still my time, remember?"

Isla shuffled her booted feet and glanced over to where Nell was waiting. She tugged on Kylie's sleeve. "Why didn't you tell us you were back, Mom?"

"I wanted to surprise you. I missed you. I can't wait to hear about your riding lessons and tell you all about my trip."

Levi sighed. "Kylie, this really isn't a good time. She has plans. A trail ride with her friends."

"Really, Levi?" Kylie snapped. "Let me talk to our daughter for five seconds. Like she can't go trail riding every day."

"No, she can't because half of the time, she's stuck in town." With a babysitter, a thought he didn't vocalize and then patted himself on the back for his restraint. At least she'd had the good sense not to bring Brett along. "You can tell her all about it tomorrow."

"I haven't seen her for two weeks!"

"Whose fault is that?" he muttered. "Do you remember what happened when I showed up at your mom and dad's house on Easter—after your mom invited me—when it wasn't *my time*?"

"That was two years ago, Levi. You need to get over it."

"Get over you calling the cops on me? How about when Brett threatened me? That was two *weeks* ago. Should I get over that, too?"

"Hey, Kylie!" A smiling Summer joined them. "Nice to see you again. How was your trip? Judging from your beautiful tan, it was amazing."

Kylie chatted easily with Summer about her skin, the sun, snorkeling and all-you-can-eat buffets. And just like that, Levi felt his anger subside. What was it about his guest that calmed him so? Whatever it was, it seemed to work on Kylie, too.

"So, listen," Summer said when Kylie finally came up for air. "We're taking Isla and Nell and two other kids from her club on a ride later. But first, we're having a quick bite to eat. It's not much—sandwiches, fruit and chips. Sorry, no guacamole!" she cried, and they laughed together. Levi had missed this reference, and he wasn't sure what to think about his current love interest making jokes with his ex-wife. "But there's plenty. Would you like to join us?"

Or about her inviting his ex to lunch.

THAT EVENING, LONG AFTER the trail ride and a quick dinner of leftovers, Levi shooed an exhausted Isla down the hall to shower and get ready for bed. Theo was relaxing in the RV, and Summer and Levi headed down into the barn to get the animals settled for the night.

The goats were uncharacteristically quiet, bedding down in their stall, where they climbed on their sleeping platforms to nestle in their piles of straw.

Levi said, "These guys are exhausted, too, after being showered with so much attention today. Bosco can't keep his eyes open."

"Well, it's tiring being the cutest goat in three counties."

"True." Levi joined her in front of Cricket's stall, where Summer had just finished with the curry comb. She came out and shut the door, a contented Cricket sighing softly behind her.

He leaned a shoulder against one of the barn's thick timbers and crossed his arms over his chest. "Sorry about Kylie showing up today."

"No problem." Ugh, she didn't want to discuss this. "It worked out fine, I think."

"I don't know. I…" He looked frustrated and maybe a bit nervous as he shook his head. "Listen, Summer, I don't know where things are headed with us, and I don't know what kind of future we can have if you're in Kentucky and I'm here. But I don't want this to end with the rodeo."

She brightened because this was a better topic and one she did want to discuss. "Me either, and I'm hoping we can figure something out." After Harper's reveal, she'd made a plan. She would tell Levi about Braden, get through the rodeo and head back to Louisville to straighten out her messed-up life. Then, when she was free to focus on their relationship, she would tell him she loved him and talk to him about Isla and Kylie. And figure out what their future held.

Relief settled over his features, his mouth curving with a satisfied smile. "Good. I don't want things to be awkward because of my ex."

And back to this again. She'd hoped that diffusing the situation would be the end of it, for now. But with Levi laying these cards on the table, she realized she had no choice. She'd have to lie and say things weren't awkward when they were, and she couldn't have a relationship with him if he and Kylie were going to continue to drag Isla along on their path of destruction.

"Mmm-hmm," she said, trying to decide where to begin. This wasn't going to be an easy conversation.

"If we're going to keep seeing each other, and I want that more than anything, then you should know that our relationship is pretty messed up."

"Yeah, I caught on to that from my first meeting with Kylie."

Levi's cheeks filled with air, which he exhaled with a quick breath. "I can only imagine what she said about me."

When Summer didn't answer immediately, he said, "I'm sorry if I'm making you uncomfortable. This is too much information, isn't it? It feels like I'm assuming that things with us will continue. And I know you have to go back home after the rodeo, and we haven't even talked about our future."

"It's not that. It's not too much information. I want things to continue. I want a future. Levi, I…" Looking over his shoulder, she inhaled and drew strength from the familiar, comforting scents of hay and horse. She wanted to tell him she loved him but not like this, and it would feel forced, like she was saying it to mitigate the hurt she was about to cause.

"As I mentioned the other day, I'm a child of divorce myself. What I didn't say was that it was a bad one. Really bad. Like epically terrible. So, I sympathize with Isla."

LEVI FELT RELIEF course through him. This was great. Not great, but it meant she got it. Summer understood. Why was he surprised? Everything about her was pretty much perfect. Plenty of sympathy and comfort coming his way, too.

Capturing his gaze, she said, "That's why I'm going to tell you something. I wouldn't— I wasn't going to, but if you mean what you said about us, then I have to. Because I feel the same way. I care about you, Levi, and I'm not ready for this to end with the rodeo.

"But I care about Isla, too. This connection that I have with her, it's… Well, she's stolen my heart. I'd like to come back after the Meadows Cup when I've taken care of some things in my life. There are things, complicated things, that you don't know about, and after those things are resolved, then I'm… free."

Was it possible that he'd found a woman who loved his daughter as much as he did? Levi had to bite his cheek to keep from blurting out his love for her. Instead, he went with, "I'd like that, too. Let me know how I can help."

"Okay, good. Here's how you can help. You and Kylie need to stop the sniping, arguing and name-calling."

"What? But she just showed up and—"

"No," Summer interrupted gently. "End of story, Levi. I don't care that Kylie showed up early or that she went on vacation without telling you or whatever. No buts, no excuses, no holding on to past hurts and slights. It has to stop. Isla doesn't need to hear anything from either of you about the other, except how you both love her and want what's best for her."

"Summer, you don't understand. You don't know everything that's happened. You don't know what she's done to me and—"

"That's exactly what I'm talking about, and I'm sorry if she hurt you. Wyatt told me she cheated on you, and that's the worst. That stinks, and I know because I've been cheated on, too.

"But Isla is *all that matters* going forward. You are her father, the most important man in her life. She worships you. She also adores her mother. Whether you believe Kylie deserves that adoration or not, she has it. All kids have it. And no, I don't know Kylie well, but I can see that she loves her daughter. Is she a little lost right now? Yes. Will she come around? I think so. Regardless, I see a good heart in there. And how bad can she be if you loved her once?"

Levi stood stock-still, anger and frustration urging him to flee even as the shock had him immobile.

Summer squeezed her eyes shut as if the

words were causing her pain. Opening them, she said, "Isla is such a smart kid. She's basically you in a smaller female form, which no doubt has much to do with why I like her so much—and probably isn't as much fun for Kylie. My point is, and please trust me here because this is where my own personal experience comes into play, she can pick up on even the slightest hint of your unhappiness, especially where her mother is concerned. And vice versa. So, imagine what this blatant hostility is doing to her. Soon, she's going to start thinking things are her fault."

"That's ridiculous!" Levi countered. "She knows none of this is her fault, and she understands why her mother and I do not get along."

"No, she doesn't. My parents did this, too. All. The. Time. They couldn't see it from a kid's perspective—I liked them both, so why couldn't they like each other? It got to a breaking point whenever I knew they were going to be near each other.

"Did you see Isla today while you two were arguing?" She held up pinching fingers. "She was this close to tears. My parents told me terrible things about each other—Bethany was much worse than Dad. She was overt, whereas Dad was more subtle. But still, I couldn't handle it. I started having panic attacks. My horses were my saving grace. But eventually, I had to choose. I had to go to court and choose because they couldn't get along."

"Summer, I get that you think you're trying to help. But this situation is complicated. You're not a parent. You could never understand."

"That's true, Levi. I'm not a parent. But I was a child. I'm *still* my parents' child. And their hatred for each other—" She stopped herself. "No, it's not even that. It's their behavior. That they refuse to at least be civil to each other while they're around me tells me that I don't matter to them. How they act still affects me to this day. Ironically, it took being here and getting away from them for me to see that clearly. I don't want that for Isla. I can promise you that if you don't find a way to make things work with Kylie, Isla will pay the price. She's already suffering."

"Suffering? You don't know what you're talking about," he said, hearing the stubborn tilt to his tone. How had this all gone so wrong? How could she be so misguided? "I'm sorry about your situation, but my relationship with my daughter is different. I love

Isla, and every single day I want what's best for her. And she knows that."

"Yes, she does. Anyone can see that you love her. And one day, hopefully, when you meet my dad, Roland Davies, you'll find a kindred soul. A man who would do *anything* for his daughter. Which is a wonderful quality, don't get me wrong. But, in my experience, you have to know when *not* to do things for her or in front of her, too."

CHAPTER SIXTEEN

LEVI PARKED HIS PICKUP next to Corliss's and checked the time. After dropping Isla off with Kylie at the designated time, he'd driven straight out to the Flying Spur, which put him here early. A luxury that his busy life hadn't been able to afford him often enough lately. Leaning forward, he rested his forehead on the steering wheel and took a moment to ponder what lay ahead.

Hurt and fear churned inside him, along with lingering bits of anger. He and Summer hadn't spoken since the incident in the barn the night before. He was pretty sure she wouldn't show up for lunch with his family, and could he blame her? Before their... discussion, they'd agreed to meet here at the ranch to save time because she and Theo had plans to check out a horse for sale in Carson, which was the opposite direction.

As the morning ticked by, Levi had reached for his phone roughly a thousand times. But what could he say? He didn't know, and he had no idea how to make this better. The problem was he couldn't see the situation clearly. That's when he spotted his big sister sitting all alone on the front porch. Straight talk was her specialty.

Before he could lose his nerve, he got out of his pickup and headed directly there.

"Hey, you," Corliss called out as he approached. "You are early, and that is awesome. It'll give us a chance to catch up. I feel like I haven't seen you in ages. Come and sit with me."

Feet heavy, he climbed the stairs. "Corliss, can I talk to you for a minute? I, uh, I need your help."

"That depends. Are there goats involved? Because the last time you asked me for help, we went on a two-day goat hunt. And, honestly, Levi, I have zero spare time for goat catching these days."

That almost made him smile. "No goats."

"Llamas? Sheep?"

"No animal rescuing is involved. Um, Corliss, this is serious. I need *advice*."

"Oh." Surprise sparked her expression before it settled into concern. "Then yes, absolutely. Can't guarantee it, but you know I'm always good for it." He forced a smile, and she said, "Levi, out with it. You are never this serious."

With a ragged sigh, he scraped a calloused hand across his jaw. "It's about me and Kylie and how our…divorce might be affecting Isla."

"Oh, thank goodness. This is about the fighting, right? And how tense it is making Isla?" She sounded relieved and then asked, "Did Gran talk to you? Or was it Adele? We were going to do rock, paper, scissors, but then we decided…" Catching the scowl on Levi's face, she grimaced and said, "Uh-oh. Whoever it was, I'm guessing it didn't go well."

"It wasn't either of them, although now I can see how they both tried. And obviously, all three of you thought it, but none of you said anything. What's that about, Corliss? Since when did you start pulling punches with me? Of anyone in this family, I can always count on you—and not only for honesty, but for laying it all on the line. And if any subject deserves both, it's my daughter."

"True," she answered carefully. "Which is why we decided we needed to mention it. But, Levi, it's tricky. Sticking your nose into someone else's parenting business is tough, and it is not to be taken lightly and only attempted when you really, *really* love someone. Like your family does. Plus, you're so… bristly where Kylie is concerned that the timing needed to be right."

"I'm not—" Except, he was, wasn't he? He'd proven that when Summer raised the topic, too.

"I'm sorry—we should have mentioned it sooner. We love you, so we meant to, we planned to. But you've been under a lot of stress. We all have, and we've all had a lot going on, and I think, at least in my case, I thought-slash-hoped it would get better. You know, as time went on. But, and please remember how much you value my honesty when I say this, it seems worse lately."

Levi placed a hand on his chest where his heart was currently imploding. He'd never felt like a bigger failure. The one job in life you most wanted to get right, and he'd blown it. How could he not have seen this? Isla, his child, was the most important person in his world and the one he absolutely did not want to let down.

The worst part was he *had* seen it. He recalled the day Summer had babysat when he'd told Isla how he wasn't happy with her mother; she'd looked dejected. He'd done that, not Kylie, and that's what he hadn't been able to see. No, he couldn't control Kylie's actions, but he could control his.

Sure, his choice of words might not be as brazen as Kylie's. He didn't call her names, but he made his opinions clear. The sarcasm, the snark, and yes, the arguing, he was guilty of them all. This truth was hard to hear, but Summer was right. Gran, Adele and Corliss—they were all right.

That's when Corliss's earlier words about doling out parenting advice plowed into him like a bull at a stampede. *"And only attempted when you really, really love someone."* Summer loved him. Corliss was right; it was the only thing that would have prompted her to tackle this topic. And now, he'd probably blown it with her, too. How could he fix this? Both of these things?

"I can see in your eyes that you're beating yourself up. Stop it. Just don't. You are an amazing father, and that's the most important thing. You and Isla are so similar, completely simpatico, and that is such a beautiful gift. And I have news for you—no parent is perfect. In fact, I think it's impossible to parent exceptionally well in every area of life all the time. It's a give and take, isn't it? We do well in some areas, but that makes us lack in others. Then we fix *that*, only to slip in some other way. But what is possible is to recognize the areas where we lack and then do better. Recognizing our shortcomings is half the battle."

Levi nodded.

"Was it your show jumper?"

He needed to call or text her, but what could he say? How did you simultaneously apologize to someone and tell them you loved them?

"What?" he asked, aware that Corliss had asked a question.

"Summer, your show jumper? Is she the one who mentioned this?"

"Yeah."

Corliss grinned. "In that case, I have one more piece of advice. If she was brave enough to breach this topic with you, Levi, you'd be wise to do whatever you have to, to keep her."

THE FLYING SPUR was exactly how Summer imagined a ranch in Wyoming would look—if all the animals went on vacation. There were acres and acres of neatly fenced fields but no livestock in sight. It was almost spooky, and a glaring reminder of the hardship the Blackwells had endured. Not to mention the pressure Levi was under to ensure "Denny's Rodeo" was a success.

As she neared the house, the barn came into view, and she spotted a few horses grazing in a pasture beyond. That was a relief. She wondered if they were the ones Nash was training for cutting. Levi had invited her to come out and meet them, and she'd been looking forward to the visit. But that was before their... She wasn't even sure what to call it—an argument? A disagreement? It was awful; she knew that much. Butterflies churned in her stomach. What if Levi didn't appreciate her showing up?

She'd debated skipping the outing, but he hadn't officially uninvited her, and she knew his family was expecting her. It would be rude not to show, and what possible excuse would she give? *Sorry, Grandma Denny, but I had a falling out with your grandson about his parenting style and didn't think he'd want me here. No, I'm not a parent myself, just the product of dysfunctional parenting, and for some reason, I thought that gave me the right to lecture him.* Yeah, no.

Lying was unacceptable, and she refused to begin a relationship with Levi's family that way. Besides, if she and Levi were going to make a go of things, she certainly couldn't bail every time they disagreed.

None of this self assurance helped to quell

her nerves as she gathered the bundle she'd brought and climbed out of the pickup. At least the house looked welcoming. Blue with white trim and fringed with the kind of wide front porch that felt like a cozy extension of the home, a place to gather and talk shop, or in this case, horses. A topic about which she felt confident that she could converse.

An attractive log fence marked boundaries and enclosed a garden that appeared to rival Levi's in scope and variety. An image of a little Levi in dirty jeans and scuffed boots sprang to mind, roping fence posts, roping Wyatt and catching frogs with Wyatt and Adele. What a great place to grow up and to raise a family. She wondered if Levi wanted more kids. Instinctively, she knew the answer was yes. What surprised her was how desperately she wanted to be their mom.

A cacophony of barking startled her from her daydreams.

"Howdy," a deep voice called, "you must be Summer."

Turning around, she discovered a man walking her way. Tall, with the lean muscles and broad shoulders brought about by long hours doing hard work, he was accompanied by an adorable and enthusiastic canine duo. Friendly and super sweet, the dark Lab and diminutive terrier seemed a surprising combination for a ranch. She couldn't help but wonder if Levi's penchant for animal rescue had played a part in the choice.

"Yes, hi." She'd already met Wyatt and Nash, so she deduced he must be Corliss's husband. "I'm guessing you're Ryder?"

"That I am. Ryder Talbot. Pretty sure you're Summer. Nice to meet you." Nudging his chin toward the house, he asked, "Stalling?"

"Absolutely," she confessed.

A short, sharp laugh drew her attention to his handsome features. The twinkle in his warm brown eyes paired with his welcoming smile was comforting. "Honesty," he stated. "I like that. You have nothing to fear." Tipping his head to one side, he turned serious and added, "Okay, in keeping with the general spirit of truth that you introduced, let me amend that—you have very little to fear."

"Am I…?" Was he the sentry designated to inform her that Levi uninvited her?

His deep chuckle sidelined the question she'd been about to ask, and she found herself smiling. She liked this guy already.

"Come on. We'll go inside together."

They continued toward the house. Before they could get there, the door opened. Summer looked up and into a keen, assessing gaze that reminded her so much of Isla, she felt her heart skip a beat. This striking woman had to be Denny Blackwell.

"Ms. Blackwell? Hello, I'm Summer Davies."

"Denny, please."

"I'm honored to meet you, Denny. I've heard so many intriguing things about you. Thank you for having me. I hope we have a chance to chat. I have so many questions for you."

"Intriguing things, huh?" Denny repeated flatly, but her mouth hinted at a smile. "Not wonderful things or nice or good things?"

"Oh. Yeah, sure, there was plenty of that kind of stuff, too," Summer answered. "I could list the usual adjectives. But, to me, the interesting stuff, the stuff I'd like to hear about, is how you single-handedly built this ranch with nothing but two pair."

"Two pair?"

"A pair of wild mustangs and a pair of wild boys."

Denny chuckled. "Two pair, I like that."

"From what I've heard, this town wouldn't even be here if it wasn't for you."

Her expression softened slightly into something that might be approval. But it was impossible to tell. Like Levi, she was difficult to read, and from what he'd told Summer, she wasn't easy to impress. He'd warned her that she wasn't susceptible to the usual compliments and accolades. With good reason, Summer believed. There wasn't anything "usual" about the woman, and she figured honesty would get her further than flattery.

Denny said, "I have to say when Levi told me he'd hired a show jumper to replace Trace Baylor, I had my doubts."

"You're not the only one," Summer answered. "I'm *still* having them. Who am I showing up in my riding *breeches* and blazer to show a bunch of ranchers how to leap over obstacles that no self-respecting cowboy would jump in the first place? But here I am. And I promise, I'm going to do my best to show you all how to do it. You know, in case someone suddenly throws up a bunch of fences and hedges and giant mud puddles all over the state of Wyoming."

Denny laughed, and it sounded pure and genuine, and Summer felt as if she'd struck gold.

"Gran, are you monopolizing our guest?" A pretty, dark-haired woman joined them on the porch, flanked by a young girl.

Levi's sister Corliss introduced herself and her stepdaughter Olivia.

"Actually," Ryder quipped, "Summer is charming the boots off your gran."

"Impressive," Corliss said dryly. "And not an easy feat."

"Feat, feet," Olivia repeated and then giggled at her pun. "That's a good one, Corliss."

A teenage boy stepped out behind her and groaned. "Oh, Mom, we've talked more than once about you being *punny*." But he was smiling as he introduced himself as Mason. The chef, Summer silently acknowledged. She was enjoying putting faces to the names she'd already cataloged in her conversations with Levi, Isla, Harper, Wyatt and Nash.

"Yeah, I've been practicing just to embarrass my son," Corliss joked. "How am I doing?"

"Summer." Levi's voice cut through the din of the crowd like a knife. He stood at the bottom of the porch steps.

"Hey," she said, doing her best to keep the nervous tremor from her tone. "There you are."

"You made it," he said in that smooth tone that revealed nothing. Was he upset? She analyzed his stony expression and thought she saw a flash of relief in his eyes.

She couldn't tell that either because now he was looking at his nephew. "Mason, how long until lunch?"

"Half hour," Mason answered confidently.

"Okay, great. Summer, can I talk to you for a minute?"

"Um." Summer felt her stomach twist with apprehension as she glanced at the curious faces of his family. She didn't want to say no, but she didn't want to be rude.

"Please," he said. "It's important, and it won't take long, I promise."

"Okay, sure." Knees weak, she descended the stairs and then walked beside him toward the barn. She imagined multiple pairs of laser-like eyes burning into her back.

The second they stepped inside the barn, Summer faced him and said, "Levi, I'm sorry. Are you upset that I showed up after our disagreement? I should have waited to see if you still wanted me to, but I told your family I'd be here, and it would be rude to cancel."

Bobbing his head, he repeated the word, "Upset? You think I'm upset after I criticized you when you were telling me something I desperately needed to hear? And then I disappeared up the stairs, leaving things unresolved? You think I'm upset that, astonishingly, you still decided to drive all the way out here and meet my family? And with the thoughtfulness to bring my grandmother a gift?"

"Um, no?"

"Summer, I can't do this…" Raking a frustrated hand through his already mussed hair, he assured her, "I am going to apologize for *all* of that and tell you that you were right. We'll talk about it, and about how I'm going to do better with Kylie.

"But first, and I know this is probably too soon, and maybe I'm going to ruin everything. But it has to be said." Palms up, he shrugged his shoulders before letting his arms fall helplessly. "I love you. I am in love with you. I know that's a lot, and I'm terrified of scaring you away. But it's true, and I can't help it, and I'm having thoughts of forever."

Summer went hand to heart in an unsuccessful attempt to stop its flight. "Levi," she whispered. "I love you, too."

Tipping his head back, he took a few seconds to gaze at the rafters above and mutter something under his breath. She thought maybe she heard "grateful" and "lucky" and "deserve," but then he was moving, and so was she, and it was… He was.

One delightful hug and long kiss later, they parted, and he said, "I was afraid you wouldn't show up, and I would have understood."

"Well, cowboy," she said with her best, but still very bad, combo John Wayne–Old West style impression, "That's not the way we're going to run this outfit. Here at the Summer and Levi operation, we stay. We show up. We keep our word. We…"

"We're honest," he supplied, turning serious again. "Summer, I know it wasn't easy for you to say what you did about Kylie and me. To give me that honesty."

"Levi, I only said what I did because—"

"I know," he interrupted with a confident smirk. "Because you love me."

"Yes. And I love Isla, too. She's…" She brought her hand up again to where her heart was nestling comfortably back inside her chest, her love for Levi and Isla tethering it and binding it tight. "Right here. You are both right here."

CHAPTER SEVENTEEN

SUMMER ROSE ONTO her tiptoes, stretching the paint roller as high up on the wall as she could reach. Yesterday at lunch when Levi revealed how he'd been unsuccessful at finding anyone to finish painting the rodeo's restrooms before the event, she'd volunteered. She'd never painted a thing in her entire life, but when Theo heard what she'd signed on for, he'd jumped in to help.

They'd had fun, and it felt good to do this for Levi, to ease this small burden, one of many. Painting, she'd discovered over the last couple of days, was not only satisfying, it was cathartic. She'd spent much of the time daydreaming, pondering and planning. And now that Theo had gone to fetch them some lunch, her mind wandered once again to yesterday's life-altering turn of events.

Meeting Levi's family on Sunday, touring the Flying Spur, dining with them all in the house Levi had grown up in made the relationship between her and Levi feel official.

Real. The exchanging of "I love yous" hadn't hurt either.

In fact, she decided as she stepped back to analyze her efforts, she couldn't imagine how the day could have gone any better. Denny had been her biggest concern. The woman was formidable for sure but in the end it was Adele who'd given her the most pause. Summer felt a reluctance on the part of Levi's sister and sensed she'd have to win her over, earn her trust.

So busy was she pondering whether to invite Adele out for coffee or possibly a horseback ride that she didn't even hear footsteps approaching.

"Summer, what in the world are you doing?" The familiar, deeply unpleasant voice jolted through her, causing her to splash paint everywhere.

"Braden!" she shrieked.

"Oh, good grief," he said. "Now you look…" He shook his head and sighed dramatically. "It's going to take even longer to get you cleaned up. You've even got paint in your hair."

"I look fine," she countered calmly even as shock and consternation twisted into a tornado inside her. Because Braden! Here. Where Levi… Levi! *Panic… No! Breathe.*

Thank goodness Levi was currently not on the premises, although she had no idea when he'd be back.

And where was Theo? He'd gone to get them lunch and hadn't yet returned. She pulled out her phone and texted a quick SOS.

"What are you doing here? How did you find me?" She should have known Braden would come looking for her when she didn't respond to his messages, but now she needed to get him out of here before Levi returned or someone else saw him.

"Rescuing you from a prison sentence of hard labor?" he joked. "And I found you because news of this little rodeo gig you've signed on for is currently sweeping our social circles. A rodeo? Seriously, Summer. What were you thinking? Would you put that paint thingy down? What if someone sees you? There are cameras everywhere."

"It's called a roller," she said, his comment making her aware that she'd been brandishing it like some sort of shield to hold him at bay. "And, yes, apparently, secret cameras are even in restaurants where people are supposedly proposing privately."

He smirked. "Nicole sent you the video." He stated it proudly as if she hadn't infused the statement with a heavy dose of sarcasm.

"There's a video, too?" That's all she needed.

"Of course, I had Cort film it. That's why they were there. You look stunning in it, by the way. I told you you'd thank me for those shoes. At least, he got a good angle of your legs before you so callously tossed them into the lake.

"We can't use the video, given how it *ends*." He added a meaningful, chastising look. "But we don't have time to stage anything else now. It was Cort's idea to make some stills from the footage, which turned out fabulous. The bad lighting doesn't even bother me. It makes the whole thing look more authentic."

"Braden, what are you even talking about? Nothing about that fiasco of a proposal was authentic."

"No one needs to know that." He waved her off. "Ingrid is here, too, and we need to have a confab about when to leak the photos. Also, you need to call your father. Are you aware that he thought you were in Nebraska this whole time?"

"I don't want to talk about my dad. Why is Ingrid here? Why are you here? And we are not *leaking* anything. Braden, this is not happening. Me and you, it's a no-go. We are done."

"Summer, honey—"

"Don't call me that," she snapped.

"Fine, but I think you'll be changing your tune once you hear my news."

"I'm listening," she said because she wanted to get this over with once and for all.

"Remember how I promised I would make this up to you?"

"Braden! We covered this ground before I ever left Louisville. It is not possible to make this up to me. Infidelity is a hard line for me."

"Summer, we aren't married, and I would never cheat on my *wife*. Like I told you, I wouldn't have been with anyone else if I had any inkling you were going to get serious about me. We hadn't been dating that long, and I didn't even think you liked me that much."

"There's no excuse for cheating, Braden! That's the last time I'm going to say it."

"I'm sorry I hurt you," he said.

Summer felt herself thaw ever so slightly. Not about what he'd done but about her reaction. Because while his betrayal had hurt, she could see now that it hadn't been as painful for her as it should have been. He'd bruised her heart, but he hadn't broken it.

Her new feelings for Levi made that so

clear. And she could also see how Braden hadn't been the priority he should have been. If she was being honest, he was somewhere around fourth or fifth, after Sacha, Dad and Theo. Even Nugget, for that matter, often came before him as she would regularly decline going out because her dog had been alone too long. But that was on Braden, too, because he didn't like staying in. Bottom line, they were mismatched from the start.

She sighed. "Braden, I am sorry, too. I wasn't a very good girlfriend." Completely different than her relationship with Levi, where she looked forward to every second and spending time together felt effortless. She wanted to do things for him. Seeing him smile, making him laugh, was now something she looked forward to. The point being that Levi's happiness felt linked to her own.

This realization prompted her to look at Braden and add, "To you. I often didn't put our relationship first."

He waved her off. "I forgive you, and I'm willing to put all of that behind us."

"I forgive you, too," she said gently. "But not enough to forget or to take you back. Now, I need you to go so I can—"

"Summer, Summer, Summer, I'm not going

anywhere because this is the part where I tell you why we *have* to get married."

"Hey, boss," Molly said, shooting to her feet as Levi walked through the door.

"Please, do not tell me there's another problem, Molly. I am in too good of a place today." With Summer and Theo nearly finished painting the restrooms, the latest "problem" had been tackled.

"Hoping not to," Molly said with a wide-eyed anxious cat expression. Levi took note. Stopping before her, he listened as she went on in an exaggeratedly professional tone— one an actual employee might use, "There is a woman in your office."

"Who?"

"Her name is Ingrid Finch. She says the matter is urgent, and she is…" Molly paused to capture his gaze, lifted her brow into a deliberate look and mouthed the word, *Scare-ee.* "Anxious to speak with you," she then finished primly.

Levi shrugged a shoulder, conveying that he had no idea who she was, and no, he hadn't left Molly out of the loop. Continuing into his office, he found the woman in question standing in front of the largest window, looking out at the arena.

"Hello," he said. "I'm Levi Blackwell. Can I help you?"

"Ingrid Finch," she replied and stepped forward to shake his hand. Distinctive looking with angular features, she had hair the color of an overripe wheat field that she wore sheared off in a straight line just below her pointed chin. In her green pantsuit, she reminded Levi of a praying mantis, long legs and narrow, bony shoulders outlined beneath her snug jacket. As her gaze swept over Levi, one word came to mind: shrewd.

"So, you're the rodeo organizer?"

"Yes, ma'am."

"Ingrid, please. I'm Summer Davies's agent, which you would know if you had booked her through the proper channels."

"Uh, okay. I'm unaware of any channels, much less proper ones."

"Is that supposed to be funny?" Ingrid retorted, her face pinching into an expression that was part scowl, part condescension. Molly's assessment was spot-on, and Levi resisted the urge to take a step back.

"No. It's supposed to convey that I don't know what channels you're referring to or why you're here."

"I'm referring to Summer's unauthorized hiring to perform at your event, and I'm here to let you know that she will not be performing or emceeing or whatever it is she's scheduled to do."

"As far as I know, Summer hired herself. Or maybe Theo did, although Summer signed the deal."

"Neither of whom are authorized to do so. Besides, I doubt *the deal* is even legal."

"Summer isn't *authorized* to hire herself?" Levi asked, this time allowing the doubt to creep into his tone.

"Of course not," Ingrid said. "Do you know who she is? Are you aware of the dollar value attached to her image? Her horse alone is probably worth more than this entire venture."

The sound of a ringing phone interrupted any response Levi might have given, which was good because he had none. What in the world was going on here?

Now scowling at her phone, Ingrid sighed and said, "Will you excuse me for a moment? I need to take this call. I dropped everything in Louisville to come to this place and clean up this mess."

"Sure," Levi answered as if he had a choice. Something told him it was better just to let this woman say her piece before escorting her out and locking the door behind her.

Removing his phone from his shirt pocket

to call Summer, he noticed several texts. The first one was from Wyatt:

Have you seen this? Is this Summer? What's going on?

Two images were attached. The first appeared to be a classic engagement photo: guy down on one knee, woman in a fancy dress and high heels, her hand in his.

He tapped on the next image and discovered a screenshot of another photo, same couple, slightly different pose. A closer shot, so their features were more discernible, and this one with a caption reading:

This just in! Equestrian superstar Braden Keene pops the question in the middle of romantic Chauncey's Restaurant. Sources say show jumping champ Summer Davies was ecstatic with the elegant three-carat diamond and sapphire engagement ring.

The following text was from Harper:

I know this looks bad, but please, don't jump to conclusions. Trust me, social media isn't always what it appears to be. Talk to Summer.

"WE AREN'T GETTING MARRIED, Braden. It doesn't matter what you say."

Summer's phone vibrated with a text. With her free hand, she removed it from her pocket and opened the message from Harper:

Code Red! Levi has seen the photo! As I feared, Wyatt spotted it and then did a search. It is officially big news in the equestrian world that you and Braden Keene are engaged.

Summer's irritation at Braden's and Ingrid's high-handedness was rapidly over-riding her panic over Levi finding out. No matter what had happened with Braden, she and Levi were solid. Even though she wished it wasn't going to be like this, he had to find out eventually. The only reason she hadn't told him was that he had so much to worry about already.

Stomping to a nearby bench, she tossed the phone into her bag. Then she glared at Braden and demanded, "Did you *leak* news of our non-engagement engagement already?"

"I didn't," he denied quickly. "But Ingrid may have. In an effort at damage control."

"What damage control?" That's when a glaring omission occurred to her. "Where is Ingrid?"

"She's inside waiting for the rodeo organizer dude, so she can break it to him that you have to resign from his cow-and-pony show."

Without another word, Summer took off walking. She was vaguely aware of Braden behind her, but she didn't stop until she reached Levi's office.

"Summer!" Ingrid cried. "Come in and join us. We were just talking about you. What are those splotches all over you? Please, don't tell me you've been photographed looking like that."

"Ingrid, the answer is no."

"It certainly is if the question is 'Ingrid, can I perform at a rodeo in Podunk, Wyoming?' But since you never asked me that question, I'm here to answer it now. If you want to keep riding, if you want to compete in the Meadows Cup, you cannot do this rodeo performance."

"That's ridiculous. Of course I can."

Couldn't she? Doubt crept over her as she looked at Levi. Usually, he was stony-faced and unreadable in times of stress, but now he looked shocked or possibly terrorized. Ingrid had that effect on people.

Ingrid droned on, "It is counter to your brand and violates your contract."

"But it's only a demonstration. I'm not competing."

"That does not matter. Participating in any activity that is counter to your brand is not allowed. If you had taken the time to run this little gig by me before you went AWOL, I would have explained these fine-print details to you. There's a reason why I pick and choose your events and appearances. *Rodeo* is not who you are. Your image is an integral part of your package, Summer. That much you do know. We've talked about it extensively. And your image is high-class, elite, elegant. It is not dirty boot stomping and loud, messy bull riding."

"I didn't know I had to clear *every*thing with you."

She shrugged. "Well, you do. Maybe I should have made that clearer, but I never dreamed something like this would happen. If someone had bet me you were going to run off and join the rodeo, I would have lost a lot of money."

This could not be happening. "Okay, Ingrid," Summer said. "First of all, you don't run off and *join* the rodeo. It's not a traveling circus."

"It may as well be. It might be better if it was. Because if you insist on doing this rodeo, Juniper, Bundy and Matilda, as well as about eight of your other sponsors, will all terminate their contracts with you. Several have already threatened."

After a quick glance at Summer, Levi stepped forward, reached out a hand to Braden and introduced himself. "Levi Blackwell. And you are?"

Summer could see a muscle twitching in his jaw, and she knew he already knew about Braden. Could this get any worse?

Smug and unaware, Braden flipped the switch on his smile and said, "Pleasure to meet you. I'm Braden Keene, Summer's fiancé."

"No, Levi, he's not," Summer said. "I can explain."

Ingrid and Braden both stared at her.

"Summer." Braden slowly enunciated her name. "Why do you need to explain anything about our impending nuptials to this cowboy man?"

"Indeed," Ingrid agreed and seemed to shake off the possibility that was before her. She said, "One thing I am pleased about is how you've become fluent in internet promotion while you've been away. Well done. We're going to do a livestream this weekend where you and Braden will announce your engagement on horseback. And then—"

"No!" she said firmly. "There will be no livestreaming horseback engagement, and there will be no wedding."

Ingrid pressed two fingers from each hand to her temples. Then she looked up and sighed. "Summer, I have worked my tail off these last few weeks beefing up this ad campaign. You'll be pleased to hear that I've more than tripled your potential earnings. I've secured you and Braden a spot on the series *Wedding Wows*. Your advance alone will—"

"I can't, Ingrid."

"Summer, if you don't do this, you won't have the funds to continue riding."

"I'll figure something out. I'm going to do the Meadows Cup and then...reevaluate."

Not surprisingly, Ingrid had anticipated this move. "Even if you compete at the Meadows Cup and win, word will be out that you violated your contracts. No one will want you, Summer."

Levi was watching her; she could feel it. All she wanted to do was reassure him that none of this mattered, and she would figure this out. She focused on the aspect that was probably bothering him the most. "I don't care, and I'm not marrying Braden."

For the first time, Ingrid looked shaken. She scowled at Levi before asking in a dubious tone, "You don't care? Do you have any idea how much this is going to cost you?"

"It's not about the money."

Braden asked, "What about your dad?"

"What about him, Braden? I am no longer using my dad's money to fund my riding, and you know that."

"Do you care that he's about to lose everything?"

Summer felt a sharp pain in her chest as panic tightened her lungs. "What are you talking about?"

"Roland is in some seriously dire straits, Summer. He came to my dad last week and asked for a loan—a big one."

CHAPTER EIGHTEEN

"SUMMER, IS THIS all true?" Levi asked a few minutes later after inviting Braden and Ingrid to leave his office.

"I'm not sure." She forced herself to remain calm and took a moment to think. "Probably. Ingrid wouldn't be here if it wasn't. Everything but the engagement. That is not true."

"Wyatt sent me a photo of you and…him. It sure looks like a proposal."

"Yeah, it was, but I didn't say yes. That night, right before this happened, someone sent me a video…" She went on to explain. And then, "I was sort of in shock. If you look closely at the photo, you can see that on my face. Seconds later, after he asked me, I threw the ring off the balcony and into the lake.

"I realized my mistake almost immediately. I was afraid someone had seen what I'd done. But I didn't want a public breakup, and I couldn't afford one at that point. As I'm sure you've gathered, we have sponsorships contingent on our engagement, an ad campaign centered around our wedding. The biggest problem for me was that I'd used the money from my advance to get me to the Meadows Cup. My plan, admittedly more desperate than foolproof, was to win at the cup. An eventing championship would likely earn me new sponsorships of my own. So, I wanted to wait until as close to the cup as possible before Braden and I officially split."

"Okay." He nodded, and she felt a tiny spark of hope. Maybe this wouldn't be so terrible, at least not the Levi part. He had absolutely nothing to worry about where Braden was concerned, and she could prove it by showing him the video. So focused was she on the issue of Braden that the meaning in his next question wasn't immediately evident.

"But what about the rodeo?"

"The rodeo? What about it?"

"You didn't come here to Wyoming for the rodeo, did you?"

"Oh. No. Theo heard about it from his aunt Stella, who as you know is a friend of Molly's."

"So, it was all about running away from all of this…chaos." He gestured toward the parking lot where, presumably, hopefully, Braden and Ingrid had gone and would disappear forever. "All you were doing was getting out of Louisville and away from your problems."

"Yes," she answered, feeling unsettled but not sure why. "I wanted to get out of town. I was so stressed—my riding was suffering. Sacha could feel it, too. I needed a place to go where I could think and figure out what I was going to do, where Sacha and I could practice without distractions, without anyone breathing down my neck. But that was before I met you and Isla and everything—"

Shaking his head, he interrupted. "I should have known that someone like you wouldn't deliberately sign up to perform at a small-town rodeo. And that stuff about making it a vacation with your horse… Adele knew something wasn't right, and I didn't listen."

"Someone like me?" she asked, uncertainty crawling up her spine.

He shrugged. "A rich socialite who happens to ride horses."

"Levi, I am not rich, nor am I a socialite."

"Yes, you are. You may as well be. That's the life you live. You claim you don't like it, but you haven't done anything to change it. You can't even break up with a guy when you have video proof that he cheated on you. Instead, you ran away, but what you don't understand is that you can't run from your problems. And now, you've made your problems mine."

Summer flinched, his words cutting deep and true.

"You never considered that this rodeo might be important beyond being a convenient escape for you, did you? It didn't occur to you to make sure your legal bases were covered? Now I have to cancel another headliner, refund tickets, and how do I explain that? That I hired you when you weren't technically available to hire? I don't even know what that means.

"How is this going to make me look to the town, to my family? Why would the town support me in a new business if I can't even make a tried-and-true one successful? Why would Curtis Holloway sell the property to me if I can't manage to pull off one rodeo?"

He was right. All of this was true. In her selfish quest for avoidance, she'd inadvertently jeopardized not only the rodeo but his future success.

"Levi, I can still do the rodeo. I will do it. I made a commitment, and I'm not going to break it."

"You still don't get it, do you? You *can't*, Summer. What are you going to do? Give up your career, your life, Sacha's future in the show circuit, or whatever you call it, and for what? For a single rodeo performance? And what about your dad? It sounds like this is a disaster for him, too. No, that makes no sense, and I won't let you."

"You can't stop me from—"

"I can. I couldn't live with myself if I let you do this."

She'd done this. She'd put him in this impossible position of having to choose between destroying her career, her life, or jeopardizing the rodeo, the Flying Spur and his future.

"Levi, let me talk to Ingrid. Maybe I can negotiate with some of my sponsors and—"

"No," he stated flatly. "I heard Ingrid, Summer. I know from my rodeo days the importance of sponsorships, and they're even more vital in your sport. You told me yourself that you couldn't ride without them. I get it, and I won't let you do it. You have far more to lose by doing it than I do if you don't. I can still have a rodeo. It just won't be as advertised. Twice in a row."

"You can't—"

"I can. Read your paperwork. Technically, I'm your boss, and you're fired."

"Levi…" That was as far as she got because her throat seemed to be closing in on her. Panic threatened and she forced herself to breathe.

"You told me that I needed to see myself

more clearly where Isla was concerned. That was true, and I acknowledged that, and I appreciate how you helped me get there. But this is a classic case of you needing a dose of your own medicine, as Gran would say. You need to stop avoiding your problems and start facing life."

"You don't understand."

"No, I probably don't. But I know what I see, what I've learned from you. By your own admission, you've been avoiding your father's financial issues for years. You avoid your mother altogether. Instead of ending things with Braden and handling the fallout, you ran away. You even dodged your agent, knowing there'd be consequences.

"I can see now how your interest in Isla, in me, even the rodeo, was a way of distracting yourself, stalling, so you wouldn't have to deal with any of it."

She felt those words like a blow, and he must have seen the agony on her face.

He looked miserable, too, as he said gently, "I'm not saying your affection was contrived. I believe you care about us. What I'm trying to say is that you need to take care of yourself first. You need to clean up your mess of a life and stop sweeping your problems under the rug. You need to figure out what you want before deciding whether you want us. Make some decisions, Summer. Not decisions that someone else makes for you, or that you think you should make."

Tears burned her eyes, but somehow she managed not to cry. "Levi, I've never wanted anything as much as I—"

"Please, Summer, don't say it. Don't…" Bringing his hands up, he linked fingers around the back of his neck and tipped his face toward the floor. "Right now, I just need you to go."

SUMMER FELT HOLLOW as she exited Levi's office. She was relieved to discover no one was waiting in the entry. She knew she needed to call her dad, but she wasn't ready to tackle that yet. Was that proving Levi right? Probably. But she needed a moment.

Theo was parking their rental pickup when she exited the building. He climbed out as she crossed the freshly painted pavement toward him. Nugget, who'd gone with him, trotted over to greet her.

"Summer, did I just see Braden and Ingrid pulling out of here?"

"Yes, we've been discovered, my life is now officially a disaster and… It's a long story. Where have you been?"

A frowning Theo glanced toward the road. "Now, I'm guessing where I've been is part of a larger story."

"What are you talking about?"

"You know Heidi from Matilda Motorcoach?"

"Of course." She liked Heidi. Theo had dated her a few times, but she was located in Maryland, and the distance between them kept things casual.

"I was at the Cranky Crow waiting for our burgers when she called to say they'd sent someone to confiscate the motorcoach. She was giving me a heads-up so I could get our stuff out. I tried to call you, but you didn't answer. So, I took off and packed up as much as I could. I didn't know what to do. It's all sitting in Levi's barn."

Summer closed her eyes. Her phone was in her bag, which in her haste to get to Levi, she'd left beside the women's restroom.

"And here I thought I'd already hit rock bottom. Now we need to find a place to stay." Her thoughts landed immediately on Sacha; she could only hope Levi wasn't so angry that he'd kick her horse out, too.

"Do you think we can camp out in Levi's barn?"

"No, he told me to go." The tears she'd been holding at bay filled her eyes.

"He...what?" Over her shoulder, Theo scowled at the office.

Swiping at a few errant tears, she inhaled sharply, scooped up Nugget and said, "Let's go clean up the paint mess, and I'll tell you everything."

"Wow," ADELE SAID to Levi when he'd finished venting. "I feel so bad for her."

They were waiting for their pie order at the most out-of-the-way corner table in Sweetwater Kitchen. They'd purposely avoided the Cranky Crow because he knew Harriet would take one look at him, and at he and Adele huddled together and conversing in low tones, and report back to Gran.

"You feel bad for her? Adele, this woman has ruined my rodeo and my..." Heart. *She's broken my heart*, he added silently, but he could see from the look on Adele's face that he didn't need to say it anyway.

"Oh, Levi, I feel worse for you, of course."

The server swung by with their orders, apple à la mode for Levi and lemon meringue for Adele.

"There's a *but* in there, Adele. I can hear it, so you may as well spit it out. Come on—I trust your opinion. You're the only one who saw through her right from the beginning."

"I didn't exactly see through her. It just seemed odd to me that she would choose to be here, that's all. But then I met her at lunch, and she seemed so down-to-earth and genuine and fun. I mean, she passed the Gran test, for goodness sake! And clearly, she is head over heels about you."

"I know," Levi said. "It would almost be better if she was a serial killer. It would be so much easier to get over her."

"Get over her?" Adele repeated sharply. "Are you saying that you can't forgive her for this?"

This situation was impossible. "No, I'm not saying that, but a relationship is pretty much off the table. This rodeo fiasco will always be there between us. I know she didn't outright lie to me, but not telling me any of this makes me feel like a chump. The woman practically has a fiancé, and she didn't say one word. She's got too much baggage, and I can't help her carry it. I don't need any more drama in my life."

"I get that—I do. I think you could find some local talent to replace her. I know that's not ideal, and this is a major inconvenience, and before you argue that point, let's go back to you and Summer for a sec. We are all maxed out right now, but..." Pausing, she gave him a brow-raised grin. "That's right— I have another *but*." In a deliberate display of stalling, perhaps searching for words, she scooped up a bite of pie and placed it in her mouth.

Levi waited impatiently, but when she looked up, her gaze flitted past him, and her smile soured to match the lemon of her pie.

A proverbial shadow fell over their table with the looming presence of Sheriff Grady McMillan. Brooding and intense, he reminded Levi of a superhero's alter ego. Tall, somber, with these impassive dark blue eyes, which, when prompted, narrowed into an impressively intimidating scowl.

"Sheriff, hey!" Levi greeted the big man. "How are you?"

Polite to the point of formal, he answered, "Fine, thank you, Levi."

Adele swallowed her bite. "Good evening, Sheriff."

"Evening, Adele," he muttered, and Levi couldn't help but note how long the man stared at his sister before finally shifting his gaze to her plate.

"Don't worry, Sheriff," Levi quipped. "The

pie's on me. No need to arrest my sister for dessert larceny."

A flicker of what looked like discomfort crossed his face while he shifted his weight from one foot to the other. "I wish the same could be said for the motorcycle in the back of her pickup."

The air seemed to go still as Adele carefully lowered her fork to rest, tines down, upon her plate. "Excuse me?" she said.

"You have a motorcycle in the back of your pickup?" Levi asked.

"It's an antique, a Jethro."

"Nice," Levi said. "I'd love to restore one of those. Do you have a buyer?" Not that he could afford it at the moment.

"Do you have the title?" The sheriff asked, steering them both back on point.

Adele waited a beat before saying, "I will. He's getting it from a friend and bringing it to me this weekend."

The sheriff sighed. "There is no title, Adele. It was stolen."

"Stolen?" she repeated, the color fading from her cheeks. "No, I bought it from Sam Green. You know, Councilman Green's son. Ned Green."

Uh-oh, Levi thought. Sam Green had turned into a skilled con artist and notorious delinquent whose affable charm would be no match for Adele's trusting nature.

"I believe you, but that doesn't matter. I'm going to have to take you in for possession of stolen property."

"Take her in? Come on, Grady!" Levi cried. "Are you serious? She got conned by Sam Green, and you're going to arrest her?"

With a voice tighter than haywire, he replied, "Unfortunately, I have no choice here."

Adele flattened one hand across her forehead. "Sheriff, I don't have time to be arrested tonight. I have to... So many things to do. And the twins!" She glanced down at her phone. "My babysitter is leaving in less than an hour. What am I supposed to do with my children?"

Scratching the back of his neck, he glanced to one side, out the window to where two kids on skateboards glided by. At least he had the good grace to look uncomfortable as he suggested, "Can you, uh, call someone else?"

"Who do you suggest, Grady?" Adele said, the calmness of her tone echoing with derision. Levi was so proud. "Can *you* find me a babysitter in less than an hour?"

Sheriff McMillan did a narrow-eyed half scowl, prompting Levi to jump in. "Adele, I got this," he assured her. She'd recently been arrested for violating a bunch of bizarre city ordinances: no need to make matters worse. "Let's not engage lest the sheriff here decides to charge you with something else. For all we know, eating pie after 5 p.m. is illegal in the Eagle Springs city limits. Isla is with Kylie. Don't worry—I can stay with the girls for as long as it takes to straighten this ridiculous mess out. I'll call Wyatt and have him run out to my place and take care of the animals." Then he looked up at the sheriff. "But come on, Grady. Can't you cut her a break here?"

"I wish I could, Levi."

"If you really wished you could, you would. And I don't—"

"Levi," Adele interrupted sharply. "We aren't engaging, remember? The best thing you can do for me right now is to go and be with your nieces."

"Fine," he said, focusing his glare on the lawman.

"Adele Blackwell Kane," Grady droned quietly, "you have the right to remain silent…"

She stood and held out her hands, wrists up, and the familiarity of the gesture chafed at him further. Levi silently fumed while the sheriff secured the cuffs on her wrists because his sister, the kindest, sweetest, most generous person he knew, shouldn't be an old hand at getting arrested. But then… Was it his imagination, or did Grady give her hands a reassuring squeeze before letting them go? Hmm. And then he couldn't help but wonder if the sheriff secretly agreed.

THEO SUGGESTED, "We could go to Aunt Stella's, but we need to find a place for Sacha. I don't want to leave here without him."

"Agree," Summer said, her heart squeezing with affection at his concern for Sacha, and for her. "We need a trailer. Maybe I could call Melody, Isla's riding club coach, and see if she has one we could borrow."

"That's a good thought," Theo agreed. "Okay, we're getting somewhere. We'll figure this out."

"Thank you, Theo, for being so easy on me about all of this. I'm sorry I dragged you into it."

"Summer, there was no *dragging*," he said and then nodded. "This was my idea, remember? I've wanted to come out here for ages and see Aunt Stella. I feel bad for *bringing* you here."

"Don't! It's the best thing that's ever happened to me." Saying the words aloud made her realize both how true they were and how drastically she'd messed it up. "Despite what's happened, I'd do it all over again. I would just do it differently. Properly. I would break things off with Braden, I'd clear the rodeo performance with Ingrid, I'd straighten things out with my dad and…"

There was more, and she could see how her pattern of avoidance had started years ago. But none of that mattered now, did it?

Scrolling through her phone, she found Melody's contact and tapped the screen. With a new determination stirring inside her, she looked at Theo and said, "Unfortunately, I can't go back. All I can do now is try and figure out how to solve some of the problems I've created."

CHAPTER NINETEEN

The town of Eagle Springs had exactly one judge on its payroll, the Honorable Verna Pickett, who was also the owner of the Bait & Tackle shop and herself an avid angler. Unfortunately for Adele, Judge Pickett was currently camped out near her favorite fishing hole on the Blue Mist Run, which meant his sister had to stay the night in jail. Poor Adele.

For his part, Levi didn't mind. He enjoyed babysitting, and he particularly liked it that evening because it kept his mind off Summer and all the accompanying problems she'd created. Well, not completely off, but it was a good distraction.

He knew he needed to figure out what to do about the rodeo; Adele was correct in that he could probably find someone local to replace her. But Harper had so masterfully built anticipation for Summer and Sacha's performance he didn't even know how to begin to announce her cancellation or how to deal with the consequences and complications. And so, for the evening, he focused on his adorable, hilarious and exceedingly industrious nieces.

First on the agenda was a rousing game of dog pile on Uncle Levi, followed by several rounds of piggyback rides, which seamlessly morphed into a simple, virtually rule-free contest of who can make the most noise. He attempted to wind them down with dinner, which consisted primarily of ketchup—enjoyed soup-style with a French fry serving as a spoon—apple slices and a few nibbles of a chicken strip.

Bath time came next along with the mystery of how there could be approximately six inches of water on the bathroom floor when he'd only filled the tub with four? By the end, the girls were clean, and he was drenched, forcing him to borrow a T-shirt and socks from Adele's closet. Attempting to outfit two squirming toddlers in their pajamas turned out to be a contact sport. The ordeal went smoother after the promise of a cookie and a makeshift session of hide-and-seek. Quinn found a great spot, which she opted to use every single time thereafter, much to Ivy's delight.

Finally, bedtime rolled around, and three stories later, they were down for the count. Levi collapsed on the sofa, exhausted, hopeful that sleep would quickly overtake him. Sleeping equaled not thinking.

It didn't take long to realize that his aching heart was not so easily dismissed. He couldn't stop thinking about Summer. How could something that felt so true and so promising end so miserably? How was he going to let her go? Regardless, he needed to find a way to say goodbye. He wasn't proud of how he'd invited her to leave his office, and he certainly didn't want things to end with bitterness.

And Isla! How was he going to explain to his daughter that Summer wouldn't be performing in the rodeo? All of her riding friends had bought tickets, and she was so proud. Summer had filled a need in her life that Levi hadn't even known existed. In his, too.

"THERE'S ANOTHER ALTERNATIVE." Theo's voice broke the silence as they traveled down the road, on their way back from Melody's, who'd been happy to loan them a horse trailer. Even better, she didn't ask a single question about why Summer needed it.

Where exactly they were going to take Sacha was still uncertain, as was the means of getting him back to Louisville. The thought of going home no longer made her queasy. Now it felt like something she needed to do, a to-do list, a tough one, for sure, but one she was eager to tackle. The specific items and their priority were the current topics of conversation.

"What are you talking about?" Summer said, glancing over at Theo. Nugget was nestled between them, snoring softly.

"Don't freak out when I tell you this, but I'm not going back to Louisville."

"What?" Summer said, experiencing a jab of something that felt suspiciously like jealousy, and followed quickly by despair.

"Yep. I'm moving back here to Wyoming. I like it. You know how I've been saying forever that Louisville is too crowded for me. Aunt Stella is here, and she's terrific. I'd like to spend more time with the only blood relative I have who I like. Plus, I love to ski, and I haven't been in years.

"I've made some acquaintances here in Eagle Springs who I think could help me get established, assuming the town remains. Even if it doesn't, Mountain Ridge will."

"You could get established on the moon," she said and then swallowed around the lump of emotion in her throat. "I want you to be happy, but I can't bear the thought of life without you."

"Same. You are my family, Summer."

"I don't want to be in Louisville without you."

"So, stay with me."

"I don't think Levi would want…" She couldn't say the words; Levi wouldn't want her around, a perpetual reminder of the hurt and disaster she'd caused. Her heart was already cracked wide open. For the same reason, she couldn't stay. Even if she figured out a way to mitigate the rodeo damage—and she was working on that—she wouldn't want to be here if she couldn't be with Levi.

"Stay for yourself, Summer. It's a big state with a lot of space. We could find a place closer to Jackson or anywhere that suited you. Consider your options for a minute. Don't think about Levi or your dad or anyone else. What would you do if you could have any life you want? Would you stay in Louisville?"

"No," she said quickly. The answer came easy because she'd been thinking about this nonstop since the day before. Forced as she now was to face the future, she couldn't seem to stop thinking about it. Likely because the repercussions of avoiding it for too long had proven dire.

"And I wouldn't compete anymore. I would miss the excitement, the competition, the mental toughness it gives me. But the promotion part isn't worth the stress, and I don't want to do what's necessary to get sponsors."

"Okay, now we're getting somewhere. You're considering it."

"I am. But, Theo, what would I do here? I have no college degree. No skills. Very little work experience that matters."

"That's not true. Riding is a skill. One you possess to a degree that very few people have. And you are an incredible teacher. I watched you with Isla, with those kids from her club, and you're a natural. You had the time of your life teaching her. Since we've been here, it's the happiest I've ever seen you."

"It's the happiest I've ever been."

"Here's my idea. We could open a riding school together. We're a perfect team. Me with the horses, you with the kids, or people of whatever age. Never too old to learn to ride, right?"

Yearning flamed to life inside her, surprising in its intensity. Sharing her love and knowledge of horses with eager young equestrians and people who'd always wanted to learn but didn't have the opportunity truly appealed to her. Ideas flooded her brain, and she realized she'd been having them ever since she'd started teaching Isla. A riding school? The anticipation, the very possibility, left her breathless. But...

"How? I have no money. I have nothing to contribute financially. We would need... facilities. Here in Wyoming, we'd need an indoor arena."

"I'm going to sell my house. I've been saving for something like this for a long time. I just didn't know what. And you have Sacha." A gift from her mother; Sacha was all hers.

"I can't sell him!"

Theo chuckled and held out a calming hand. "I would never suggest that. However, if you and Sacha won—"

"Ugh. I don't want to compete anymore."

"You don't want to compete, or you don't want to compete with sponsors?"

"It's one and the same for me."

"You're still not thinking outside your box, not far enough, anyway. Plenty of people compete without sponsors, and others could, too, if they wanted."

"Only rich people, Theo."

"What if I had a way around that, too?"

Summer laughed. "What are you going to do, find a way for me to make a million dollars?"

"Not a million, but maybe…enough."

SUMMER WAS GONE.

It took Levi a while to process what he was seeing. After pulling into his driveway, he sat in his pickup staring at the spot where her motorcoach had been parked. It now looked barren, forlorn. So much for figuring out a way to say goodbye. He grabbed his phone to see if he'd maybe missed a call or a text. Nothing.

How could she leave without saying goodbye? Yes, he'd been upset, but that hadn't warranted her rolling out of town without a word. Except… Now that he thought back on it, he'd told her to go, hadn't he? But he'd only wanted her to leave his office, so he didn't say something he'd regret. He'd just needed time to think.

Why hadn't he said that? Dipping his head to rest on the steering wheel, he tried to get a grip. But it hurt. Knowing she was gone was excruciating. How was he going to get over her when he couldn't even bring himself to get out of the pickup? He wished he could see her at least, hug her and tell her goodbye. There were so many things he'd like to say…

His phone chimed with a text. Fingers fumbling, he nearly dropped it in his haste to see if it was from Summer.

It was Adele:

Hey, thanks again for watching my babies. I slept easy knowing they were in good hands. Jail = sleep. Who knew? Maybe I should get arrested more often?

He tapped out a response:

The fact that you're making jokes suggests that you're getting arrested too much. You're welcome. We had a blast. You're out of ketchup.

Adele: I'll put it on my grocery list. We didn't get a chance to finish our conversation last night, and I forgot to tell you my "but" before you left this morning...

Levi: I was wondering what you were going to say before our arrest-aholic sheriff dragged you off in handcuffs. But...?

Adele: You said you didn't need any more drama in your life, BUT I don't think that's true. By its very nature, love is drama. And, Levi, we all need love.

Levi felt his eyes well with tears. She was right. He was currently embroiled in the fight of a lifetime for his family, their ranch, his town, a way of life because he loved them. And it was a fight that rivaled Hollywood on the drama scale. He loved Summer, too. So why wouldn't he fight for her?

Levi: I changed my mind. If we can't save the ranch and this town, you can be a philosopher. You're right. I love you.

Adele: Shut up. Family love doesn't count, and you know it!

Levi: It absolutely does count, Adele. AND I do love you. Thank you. I get it now.

Adele: Oh! Good. In that case, I know I'm right, AND I love you, too! Now go get her back.

He was going to try. The only problem now was how to find her?

"THANK YOU SO MUCH for your help, Wyatt," Summer told him, shutting the stall door behind her. "Please tell Corliss I'll pay by the week."

Yesterday had been a long day. She and Theo had picked up the horse trailer from Melody and then headed back to Levi's. She'd been both sad and relieved that he wasn't home. Somewhere along the journey, she'd remembered Levi mentioning that the Flying Spur bordered horses. She'd called Wyatt, who'd arranged for Sacha's arrival. They'd dropped the horse off in the evening, headed back into town and gotten rooms at the Barn Door Inn where they spent the night. She'd driven back out first thing this morning.

Wyatt and Nash were already up and completing chores when she arrived.

"Sounds good," Wyatt said. "Do you want to go over his feeding schedule and routine so I can take care of that for you?"

"I would appreciate that," Summer said. "I plan on doing it myself, but I typed it all out in case something comes up, and I can't get here. I'll text it to you."

"So…" Wyatt drawled as Nash walked inside to join them. "How, uh, how long do you think you might be utilizing our facilities?" Summer wanted to laugh because she could tell it pained him to ask. Much to his credit, it was the first question either of them had asked.

"Not sure yet," she said. "Theo and I will

be looking for a place to rent for a while, so that depends on whether we can find something suitable." Summer lifted a thumb and hitched it in the general direction of the house. "Is your grandmother home? I'd like to say hi, if possible."

The old Summer would have avoided every Blackwell in the vicinity, but the new Summer wanted to explain, *needed* these people to understand how sorry she was, and hopefully, they'd back up her plan.

"Wait, you're staying?" Nash asked in a not quite unfriendly tone, but there was an air of suspicion. "Here in Eagle Springs?"

"Yes," she said, and liked how firm she sounded, how resolute she felt. "We are. I'd love to chat with you later about our plans, and I could use your advice on a few horse-related matters."

"Uh…sure?" he answered.

Hands latched on to his hips, Wyatt inflated his cheeks with a deep breath and released it. Summer almost laughed, imagining him warring between curiosity, concern and minding his own business.

"Summer! You're still here. Good." Corliss appeared from the other end of the barn, striding purposely in their direction and, in keeping with everything Summer knew about her, did not possess her brothers' qualms. "Wyatt told us Levi said you quit the rodeo. Is that true?"

Harper had come in behind Corliss and offered a tentative, encouraging smile for Summer as she approached. There was a glint of determination in her eyes. Summer had already stated her case to Harper on the phone the previous evening, and it felt good to have at least one Blackwell in her corner, hoping, if not thinking, the best. And now, she appreciated the show of friendship.

That's when another Blackwell voice joined the mix, "I'd like to know if that's true as well."

Summer turned to face the imposing family matriarch, Denny Blackwell, the person she most definitely did not want to let down.

"Good morning, Denny. I was just asking if you were here. Any chance I could have a moment of your time?" She'd come here this morning determined to seek her out and explain and maybe, hopefully, gain her support. She hadn't intended to do so with an audience, but Summer suspected there weren't many secrets where this clan was concerned.

"Sure, you can start by answering Corliss's question."

Summer nodded, and after a fortifying breath, she charged ahead, "No, that's not true. Levi fired me from the rodeo."

Nash's brow shot up, his expression reflecting pure surprise. "Did he tell you that, Wyatt?"

"No…" Wyatt replied hesitantly, thinking. "Not exactly. He said Summer had a conflict of interest and wouldn't be performing."

"That is true. But he didn't give me a chance to decide which conflict interested me the least, or however that works. He went ahead and decided for me."

Arms crossed, Corliss questioned her, "What does that even mean? The way we heard it is that if you do the rodeo, you give up your career and a barn load of money. Are you saying you would choose the rodeo?"

"That's not entirely accurate about giving up my career. It's a long story, but yes, I would choose the rodeo."

"But—"

"No more buts," Adele said, walking up to join them. Summer hadn't heard her come in a different door behind them. "It's Summer's decision. Right, Levi?"

Levi. Heart pounding, Summer turned to face him.

"You left," he said. "You left without saying goodbye."

"You told me to leave."

"I meant for you to leave my office, not pack up your RV and take off. Where is it? Where are you staying?"

"Oh. The motorcoach was confiscated. Theo and I stayed at the Barn Door Inn last night. You weren't home, or I would have said goodbye and told you where we were headed. When I didn't hear from you, I thought it didn't matter."

Adele raised a hand. "That's my fault. I got arrested, and Levi was babysitting the girls."

"Arrested? Adele, are you—"

"I'm fine." She waved a breezy hand. "It's fine. It was a misunderstanding."

Levi's gaze bounced around at the curious faces around them. "Summer and I have a few things to discuss in private. Summer, will you come outside with me?"

"Now, hang on a minute here, kiddo," Denny said. "Summer and I were having a conversation. Is it true what she told me? Did you fire her from the rodeo?"

"Um." Scowling, Levi did that neck scratch

thing he did when he was uncomfortable. "Yes, but—"

"Numbskull," she said.

"Gee, thanks, Gran," Levi said wryly. "Love you, too."

"Quit trying to deflect. My love isn't in doubt here."

"It's your intellect that she's questioning," a grinning Wyatt supplied unhelpfully.

"Ergh." Corliss ground out a sound of frustration. "It's that temper of yours. Levi, what were you thinking? Didn't we just have a discussion about that?"

Adele crossed her arms over her chest and frowned at him. "You *told* Summer to leave? Not classy, Levi. You never mentioned that part to me."

Nash was slightly more diplomatic. "Summer is more than willing to do the rodeo, Levi, so I think you should hear her out."

"Wow," Levi said with a heavy dose of sarcasm. "As thrilled as I am to have *all of you* chiming in with your opinions, advice and…" He delivered a deliberate look to Wyatt. "Hilarious wisecracks. I think Summer and I can handle it from here. Summer?" He swept an arm toward the door, indicating she should lead the way.

"Denny?" Summer asked. "I'd like to talk more about this later if you have time."

"Come on inside and have a coffee with me when you're finished telling my grandson what you think of his foolish and impulsive behavior."

Summer's smile came straight from her heart. "I would like that." She looked around. "Thank you," she said. "All of you."

She exited the barn and then followed Levi around to the back, where he halted, faced her and said, "When I got home this morning and saw you were gone, I... I figured you were halfway to Louisville."

"I wouldn't do that, Levi. I told you how this was going to work between us—I stayed, I showed up here to talk to your family because I owe them an explanation and I'm trying to keep my word to you."

"Honesty," he countered, but his tone was gentle enough that it gave her a sliver of hope. "We decided on that, too."

"I never lied to you. It's true I didn't tell you everything, and that was wrong. But I didn't purposely keep it from you. At first, it didn't seem relevant, and then it was partly my own fears and, yes, avoidance and partly because I wanted to protect you from the fallout I knew was coming eventually. I intended to do the rodeo—help you make it a success, and then go home to Louisville and straighten it all out."

"And now?"

"Now I'm not going back."

CHAPTER TWENTY

LEVI STARED AT SUMMER, seemingly unable to process her statement. "You… What do you mean, you're not going back? How can you not go back?"

"Theo and I are staying here, whether you and I are us or not. This is what's best for me. And Theo. And Sacha. My dad, too, even if he hasn't quite landed on that yet. I'm going to keep competing, but on my terms. No more pandering to sponsors and trying to be someone I'm not. I'm going to enter the competitions I want, and Sacha and I will rack up some wins to increase his stud fee. With the funds from that and the sale of Theo's house, we plan to open a riding school. Until we have the funds, I'll give lessons, and Theo will buy and sell and train horses for English events.

"I'll have to go back to Louisville at some point and sort things with my dad. He's on the cusp of financial ruin, and I've invited him to come here and live with me once I get settled. And then—"

"Summer?"

"Hmm?"

"Stop, please. Can you stop talking for a second? I'm happy that you have all of this figured out."

"Yeah, me, too. It's been a lot of thinking and deciding. I put so many of these decisions off for far too long, but now, I can't seem to stop... Sorry, you asked me to stop talking."

Levi stared at her and wondered what he'd done to deserve this chance, this woman, who was everything—more—than he could ever have hoped for.

"Summer, I love you. I didn't even understand what love was until I met you. You are... *it* for me."

"Levi." She choked out his name, then brought one hand up to cover her mouth as if she could squelch the accompanying sob.

"There's more. I'm grateful for everything you've done for Isla. I'm grateful to even know you, but—"

She held up a hand. "Wait! You heard Adele, no more buts. Don't try and talk me out of it. My mind is made up, and I'm doing the rodeo."

"Okay," he said. "You can have your job back, and I'll be honored to have you perform at our rodeo."

Stepping close, he wrapped his arms around her. "Honored and relieved, quite frankly," he joked. "Adele is pretty good at juggling, but I'm not sure she's headliner good. I think she was secretly hoping she'd get called up."

She laughed against his shoulder.

"Summer." He hugged her tight. "You give me hope for the future. No matter what happens with the rodeo, the Flying Spur, Gran, the town, I can honestly say that my life will be better with you in it."

"Mine, too." She sniffled into his shirt. "I love you. Can Theo and I stay in your barn until we figure out where we're going to live?"

"Of course. Now, let's make this the best rodeo this town has ever seen."

AND SO THEY DID, Levi silently decreed the following Saturday evening from his spot in the booth next to Summer, overlooking all the action.

To say that the Eagle Springs Rodeo reboot went off without a hitch would be a bit of an exaggeration. The microphone kept cutting out during the steer roping, the cash registers at the food court quit working for nearly an hour and one-quarter of the toilets in the women's restrooms didn't function properly. Since there were so many, no one cared. Plus, the parking lot overflow plan didn't exactly flow smoothly. Yes, that's right, overflow! Not the worst problem to have.

A sold-out show was the icing on the cake. Seeming to draw energy from the crowd, Summer and Sacha had nailed their demonstration, a graceful, athletic exhibit of dressage and show jumping. Summer may not have come to Eagle Springs intending to stay, but she couldn't have set things up more beautifully for her future.

All of his family was in attendance. Directly across from the booth, in the lower portion of the middle section, Adele, Corliss, Ryder, Mason and Olivia were seated together. Isla was a few rows below them with Nell and some friends from her riding club. Thanks to Melody and Summer's earlier demonstration, members from other clubs across the state were also in attendance. There was even a contingency from Montana. They'd cheered wildly after Summer and Sacha's demonstration, and Isla was still beaming. Summer and Theo wouldn't have any trouble finding students.

Near the bottom of the stands, he zeroed in on Gran in the handicap-accessible area where she sat beside Angus, who was using his wheelchair. Nash was on her other side.

Nash's five-year-old son Luke sat beside him. His nephew's attention was glued on the action in the arena. Levi grinned. The kid reminded him so much of himself and Nash at that age: horse crazy and rodeo obsessed.

Wyatt appeared in the aisle, jogging up the steps, probably on his way to check on Levi. Gratitude and affection welled inside him; Wyatt and Harper had proved invaluable during this last week of preparations right up through this evening's events. A couple walking hand in hand caught his eye when Wyatt paused to talk to them.

Levi felt his stomach drop as he recognized Helen, Nash's ex-wife, their former sister-in-law, and mother of Luke. Helen was good people, but what in the world was she doing with Phil Mitchell? Conceited and smug, the guy was a decent cutting horse trainer and competitor but so swollen with pride, Levi wondered how he didn't float away. Helen was way too good for Phil. Maybe Levi was letting his own disappointment at the end of Nash and Helen's marriage color his view. They'd all been sad to see Helen go.

His attention was pulled back to Summer as she announced the name of the next competitor. He was making plans to ask her if she'd be the next addition to the Blackwell clan. She and Theo had contentedly moved into the barn and were busy making plans for their new business venture. Levi had offered his facilities for their use and felt confident Summer would soon, hopefully, if all went according to plan, be a permanent fixture there anyway. It made the most sense, economically and logistically. Maybe he'd finally have a ranch that didn't lose money.

Summer had talked to her dad multiple times now. Levi, Summer and Theo were going to travel to Louisville together next month so Levi could meet him and Summer could help him sort his finances. Summer calculated that if he sold the house, let the staff go, liquidated the expensive antique furnishings and she sold two of her horses, he'd be able to pay off a good portion of his debts. The rest would entail a dramatic lifestyle change, which, she hoped, would help convince him to relocate.

Levi and Summer would then travel back to Wyoming with her remaining two horses and belongings while Theo put his house up for sale. He would follow as soon as he could.

Ingrid had been shockingly amenable to Summer's bailing on the wedding and all its ensuing entanglements. She'd issued a tasteful press release asking for privacy and understanding for the couple during their amicable parting. She and Summer were even working on a new agent-client agreement where Summer would have a more active role in the business side of her career. Who would have guessed the woman had a soft, romantic side?

Even Braden appeared to be moving on. He was now dating a well-known British dressage champion who had ties to the royal family. He was making plans to relocate.

Meanwhile, Summer appeared to be having the time of her life.

"Congratulations to Matt Carnes out of Falcon Creek, Montana!" she declared. "That steer isn't going anywhere. There is ice in that boy's veins. Fastest time of the evening. Let's give it up for Matt."

The crowd went wild. What a night! Summer might not be a natural in front of the camera, although Harper had worked wonders in that area, but she was incredible behind the microphone. Clever, witty and spot-on after three weeks of studying rodeo vocabulary and Levi's intense coaching. Levi sat beside her, "co-hosting," but happy to have her do most of the commentating. She owned the crowd.

After the events were complete and the prizes awarded, Levi thanked the crowd for their attendance. Then he paid tribute to Angus and his achievements as the town's winningest rodeo cowboy. Levi gratefully acknowledged his grandmother and a few other long-standing Eagle Springs residents who'd been instrumental in establishing the rodeo. He and Summer signed off with heartfelt thank-yous.

Holding Levi firmly by the shoulders, Summer declared simply, "We did it." Her smile was so beautiful, so filled with satisfaction that he ached with love for her. Both of them were euphoric; they embraced with a long hug.

"Yes, we did," he answered and then kissed her. "Thank you."

Then she surprised him by flattening one hand to his chest and stating somberly, "Don't go anywhere yet. There is someone here who wants to talk to you."

She disappeared into the hall and moments later returned with a man by her side.

"Levi, congratulations!" Curtis Holloway cried. "That was a great show tonight!"

"Hello, Curtis. Thank you! I didn't know you were coming."

Curtis slid a glance at Summer. "I didn't

know either until this fine lady called and invited me."

What?

Smiling brightly, Summer gave Levi a short version of a typically complicated small-town happenstance. "I heard from Lilah, who is friends with Curtis's daughter Veronica, that her daughter Lexie is interested in English riding."

"Lexie is my granddaughter," Curtis added proudly.

"Yes, and she sure is a sweetheart. Anyway, Curtis and Monica were shopping for an Arabian for Lexie, who is interested in getting into eventing. Lilah put them in touch with me, and Theo found them Felix."

"Felix is a gorgeous horse," Levi said.

"Is he ever." Curtis nodded. "Still can't believe the bargain Theo got us. And my goodness, does my granddaughter love that horse."

"They're a good match, Curtis," Summer said. "I can already tell they're going to be one of my stars. Anyway, Curtis and I were chatting on the phone one day, and I mentioned the rodeo, and you and one thing led to another."

Curtis took it from there. "Summer invited Monica and me to attend and sent us tickets. I gotta tell you, Levi, I got tears in my eyes when I saw what you've done with this place. Almost couldn't get Monica out of the ladies' room, nice as they are. She's impressed with how it's three times as big as the men's, thinks you're a genius." He chuckled. "Place hasn't looked this good since… Well, ever."

"Thank you," Levi said. "It's been a labor of love."

"I can see that. The only way this town is going to survive is with investment in its future. That's what you've done here, Levi, and I commend you for it. I'd like to come here and visit my daughter and granddaughter and see this town thriving instead of it sitting at the bottom of some lake. I've reconsidered. If you can meet me halfway to that fifty thousand, we can make it legal."

Twenty-five thousand more than his original offer. Levi had no idea where he'd be sitting after the evening, but with the sold-out show bolstering his confidence, he felt emboldened, and hopeful. He'd find a way to make this work. He had to.

"You've got yourself a deal." Levi shook the man's hand. "Thank you, Curtis. I can't tell you how much this means to me."

"I'll tell Howard. But I feel like I need to warn you, Levi. I don't trust that man. He's a vulture, and he's got something up his sleeve.

Something bigger than…" Curtis gestured to the rodeo. "All of this. If I do this, if I sell you this place, he will not be pleased. You'll be in his sights. He's very determined in his plans for this place."

"I'm aware of that."

"I hope so, Levi. You need to be if you're going to make a go of this. I'm gonna be honest—this whole thing kind of freaks me out. Howard reminds me of a TV villain or something. Monica thinks he's obsessed."

"It's a chance I'm not only willing to take, I'm looking forward to it. We're going to find a way to beat him and save Eagle Springs, and if you sell this place to me, you'll be helping us do that."

"Proud to contribute in this small way." Curtis reached out a hand. Levi gripped his hand and knew in his soul that he may have won this battle against Howard, but Curtis was right; the war for Eagle Springs was far from over.

"COME ON, GRAN, time for the zombie hayride."

Corliss, dressed as an old-time livery driver complete with a top hat, tall boots and a jacket with a satin lapel and long tails, steered the horse-drawn wagon right up to the front porch.

"I don't do zombies," Denny called back from her chair on the porch, where she'd been doling out candy to the trick-or-treating partygoers. "Only witches," she quipped, and then cackled. Gathering her black flowing robe in one hand, she stood, and then adjusted the oversized, cone-shaped witch's hat on her head. Long, frizzled locks of gray hair tweaked out from beneath and green grease paint tinted her face. It was so fun how she'd embraced the role.

Summer was thrilled with how well everything had come together. She, Harper, Adele and Corliss were a great team. Gauzy ghosts and purple-black bats with glowing green eyes hung from the porch beams and twirled in the breeze. Orange, purple and white lights were strung here and there, lighting the path from the house to the barn, where the games and fun for their family and friends would commence after the zombie hayride. Later, they'd move to the house for a festive pumpkin-themed dinner.

The day before, Summer and Isla had loaded up Levi's pickup with pumpkins and brought them to the Flying Spur. Along with Corliss and Adele, all the kids had spent hours carving jack-o'-lanterns. They'd placed them all around the ranch, and by the time they'd arrived this evening, Nash had managed to get them all glowing with battery-powered lights.

"Great-Gran, you can sit by me," Nash's five-year-old son Luke, dressed as a fully-fledged cowboy from the Wild West, called out, patting the hay bale beside him. "Don't be scared. I'll protect you."

Summer and Harper shared a smile while Summer made a mental note to slip some extra candy and prizes in Luke's bucket.

"You got something that protects against zombies, huh?" Denny asked, carefully navigating her way down the porch steps. "Who could turn down an escort like that?"

Who indeed, Summer thought? The kid was irresistible.

"Yep," he assured her. "Uncle Wyatt said all I need to fight zombies is fire, and he gave me my own fire torch."

Denny stopped and squinted toward the wagon. "Uncle Wyatt gave you a fire torch?"

"What?" Amelia Earhart, a.k.a. Adele, had stepped up beside them, looking authentic and fabulous in vintage aviator gear she'd scored at an estate sale. She glanced at Summer and Harper and informed them in a low tone, "One time when we were kids, Wyatt made a bonfire to roast marshmallows and almost burned down the woodshed."

Harper laughed. Summer was slightly concerned until Luke shouted, "Watch this, Great-Gran!" There was a click, and then the beam of a flashlight glowed from his hand.

Adele puffed out a "Phew!"

"Of course he did!" Denny called, in keeping with the spirit of the holiday. "Your uncle Wyatt is a champion zombie fighter—only stands to reason you would be, too." She continued down the stairs. "Zombies beware."

They all laughed while Levi and Nash stepped forward to help her up into the wagon, where she claimed the seat next to Luke, while Ryder's daughter, Olivia, adjusted her cape. She'd put together the excellent superhero costume herself. Summer had no doubt the little genius would one day take the world by storm.

Isla and her best friend, Nell, were hilarious as a vintage foil-covered astronaut and her green alien friend. Isla had invited a bunch of kids from her riding club, which currently included a penguin, a cat and a pair of scarecrows. The other kids had all invited a friend or two as well, and they rounded out the rest of the passengers.

Nash and Levi hoisted Adele's toddler twins, Ivy and Quinn, up next. They were dressed as peanut butter and jelly in purple-and-tan tutus with sweatshirts corresponding to their respective condiment and matching tights. Adorable. Adele hopped up to join them.

Conspicuously absent were Corliss's teenaged son Mason and his friend Betsy, who had dressed as zombies and were waiting along the course to "scare" the riders. Corliss had lectured them firmly about not being too good at their job.

Wyatt and Harper, outfitted as a scar-faced Frankenstein and his bride, climbed in next. Nash gathered his black flowing robe and hopped up beside Corliss. With his skin powdered snow white and his dyed black hair combed flat against his skull, he made an inspiring vampire.

Levi had volunteered himself and Summer to skip the ride and get the games set up in the barn. They waved as Corliss urged the two-horse team into a walk, and the wagon rolled away.

"Good luck, Dad!" Isla called out while Nell giggled beside her.

"Good luck?" Summer repeated. "What was that about? Did she tell you I've been practicing so I could challenge you to the Halloween hoop shoot?"

"Nope. But all the practice in the world will not help you,," Levi joked, taking Summer's hand in his and heading toward the barn. "I am unbeatable. But have I told you how beautiful you look today?"

"Only seven times," Summer said. "This princess thing is really working for me, I think," she joked. Adele had found her the gorgeous medieval princess costume at a thrift shop in Cheyenne. It was emerald-green velvet with long flowing sleeves and gold-threaded accents. The woman was a marvel with a sewing machine and had altered the garment one evening while Summer played with the twins. Levi was her handsome prince.

Not that it mattered what she was wearing; he told her she was beautiful multiple times a day. She liked how he wasn't shy about telling her he loved her either.

They stepped inside the barn where the hay bales had been set off to one side. Other games were planned, too, including the hoop shoot, pin the hat on the witch's head and a fishing game that constituted a sheet decorated as the ocean where the little ones could cast their line over and "hook" a prize.

Summer looked around; her heart felt full. She was grateful to spend time with this family. It was amazing to have a purpose and finally know what she wanted out of life.

"Huh," she said, hands on hips studying the festively decorated room. Twinkle lights were sparkling, jack-o'-lanterns were all aglow, the plastic skeleton was fluorescing, and ghosts and bats floated overhead. Snacks laid out, drinks on ice, games were ready to roll. "Now that we're here, there's not that much to do, is there? Besides moving the hay bales into a circle, and I already have 'Monster Mash' queued on my phone."

"Summer?"

"Hmm?"

"I need to ask you something."

"Sure," she said and spun around to face him. Only to discover he was sitting on a hay bale.

"Can you come here?" he patted the spot beside him.

"Only if you promise to protect me from zombies. Do you have a fire torch?" She crossed to him and took a seat.

He chuckled. "No, but I have this." He held out a fist and then opened his fingers to reveal a ring in the center of his palm.

She gasped. "Levi." Her gaze snapped up

to meet his, and his gorgeous gray-green eyes were overflowing with love and joy and laughter. She'd thought her heart was full before, but now she feared it might burst.

"You're surprised," he said, and there was so much satisfaction in his tone she had to laugh.

"I'm stunned, but in the best possible way."

"Good. Marry me?"

"Happily," she answered even as her mind ignited with thoughts, the most important of which was that for the second time in her life she was shocked by a proposal, only this time everything about it felt right. Almost. "But…"

"Uh-oh. I thought we agreed on no more of those." He exhaled a playful sigh. "Let's hear it."

"Will I have to move upstairs out of the barn?"

"Yes, I'd like you to live upstairs with Isla and me."

Slowly, she let her head tip to one side as if considering the notion. "I suppose I could do that. As long as I can spend the occasional night downstairs surrounded by horse nickers."

He laughed. "I'll be more than happy to join you. What else?"

"Um…" How to gently articulate the thought that Isla should somehow be included in this?

"If you're worried about Isla, this was her idea."

"What?"

"Yep, I wanted to propose in a barn—our barn, but she thought you'd be more surprised if I did it here. And I also chose it since this is the one I grew up in, and I spent a lot of time here as a kid, dreaming about finding a girl like you someday."

Oh, wow.

"She helped me pick out the ring, too." He held it out for her, and she removed it from his palm to examine the simple platinum band engraved with an intricate swirling design. It was stunningly beautiful and wonderfully unique. "If you want something fancier with diamonds and gems, I understand, and we can do that later when our finances are more solid. But Isla was adamant that you'd want something like this, something you didn't have to take off when you were in the barn, or with the animals, a ring you could ride in. That made sense to me."

Summer gripped it tight, then brought her hand to her chest, where it seemed to connect with her heart. She squeezed her eyes shut and shook her head in wonder. "She's absolutely and completely spot-on." Then she slipped it on her finger. "Levi Blackwell, I will marry you, but don't you dare buy me any diamonds."

"Okay," he agreed with a laugh. "Summer Davies, you are the most surprising and un-expectedly wonderful woman ever. And—" he leaned in so that his lips hovered over hers "—you are the only girl I ever want to kiss on a hay bale for the rest of my life."

"Let's make sure we do that every day," she said and then kissed him.

EPILOGUE

"YOU'RE BACK," DENNY SAID, hoping she didn't sound as relieved as she felt. Relief, she assured herself, that didn't have anything to do with sisterly feelings. Her only concern was for the man's safety and his health. Elias Blackwell was no spring chicken, despite his seemingly endless abundance of energy with which to meddle in her life.

"And aren't you a sight for sore eyes," Big E said, scaling the porch steps like a man half his age. "You're looking good, Delaney."

She rolled her eyes toward the sky, where rich blue velvet streaks were tangling with rays of sunlight and slowly turning the color of ripe peaches. Another stunning Wyoming sunset was in bloom, and these days, Denny was increasingly grateful for each and every one.

"Don't start lying to me now, you big oaf. I look every bit of my age and my health, and you know it. Now take a seat."

He chuckled and did as he was told. "I

know better than to argue, so all I'm going to say is that you've always been more beautiful than you know." Before she could argue or insult him further, he said, "Fine evening for a Halloween bash."

"It's been a hoot. The girls have outdone themselves. You missed the zombie hayride. Adele found this old horse-drawn wagon at an estate sale, and she and Corliss got it all rigged up. Mason and his friend Betsy dressed up like zombies, jumped out and scared the kids, but they weren't too scary. They loved it.

"But don't worry, the haunted maze is up and running, thanks to Nash, Wyatt and Ryder. Summer and Mason have a pumpkin-themed dinner brewing in the kitchen. Soup, pasta, chicken—every single dish has got pumpkin in one form or another."

Big E guffawed. "Thanks for the heads-up. I'm not sure about all of that. Pumpkin is for pie."

"On that we agree." They enjoyed a moment listening to the kids' screams and giggles and squeals of delight drifting over from the maze on the rapidly cooling breeze.

Big E said, "Heard Levi's rodeo was a hit."

"Oh, Elias, I wish you could have been there. I have never been prouder of that boy, and he's done a lot to make me proud over the years." And she wasn't only talking about the event, which was a huge success. He'd proved himself to be the man she knew he was. "He bought the property—did he tell you?"

"He sure did. Texted me that night, said Summer invited Curtis to the rodeo."

"Clever, huh?" Denny chuckled approvingly. "Appealing to Curtis's sentimental side. Looking forward to having another great-granddaughter-in-law soon, too. Levi proposed, and I couldn't be happier about it. I like her. Levi needs a woman who understands him. On the one hand, he's tough as nails, determined, stubborn and temperamental. But on the other, he's got this soft side to him. Real soft, like a downy chick."

"Hmm," Big E pondered dryly. "Wonder where he gets that?"

"You better not be implying I have a soft side," Denny shot back. "Summer is going to keep him on his toes, too, which we'll all enjoy. The best part is how good she is to Isla. And now that Levi and Kylie are revamping the custody arrangement, Isla will get to spend more time with Summer. Don't even get me started about their mutual love for horses. Summer thinks Isla has what it takes to be a champion show jumper."

"Horses and Blackwells go hand in hoof. This is all excellent news. What else did I miss?"

"Speaking of hooves, Nash is working himself ragged training those horses, and Adele got arrested again."

"For what?"

Denny told him. Big E sighed and pondered, "I'm wondering if I need to talk to that sheriff. Starting to think that's personal, too."

"You keep your nose out of my granddaughter's business."

"She is my great-niece, too. Adele needs to learn that she's stronger than she thinks. That girl is way more like you than she realizes. Sure, she's a whole lot *nicer*, but that generosity looks awfully familiar."

"I don't have time for nice." She flapped an annoyed hand at him. "Now stop trying to goad me. Before you give me your news, I have some more for you. Adele told me tonight that we lost Hollow Pine Ranch."

Big E whistled softly through his teeth. "I thought the Dunbars were solid. They seemed as intent on not selling their property as you are."

"So did I," Denny answered. "But it's family owned. They voted, and they split three to two. I gotta tell you, Elias, I'm starting to feel like nowhere is safe. Friends are betraying friends, and family are turning on one another."

"Oh, Delaney." He heaved out a sigh, a big troubled one. "That makes it even harder to tell you what I have to. This thing is bigger than either of us could have imagined."

"Elias, you're scaring me."

"Well, that's because I'm scared, too."

Denny became even more concerned when he didn't explain but instead stared off into the distance.

Finally, he shifted, squarely meeting her gaze and said, "It's Frank."

"Frank?" she repeated, needing clarification because surely, he didn't mean Frank Wesson? Her brother-in-law, the brother she'd rejected for the one she loved.

"Yes. Frank Wesson is the brains behind Xavier Howard. Not just the brains, he's the money, too. Or, at least, the biggest share of it. Mountain Ridge is his development project."

Denny felt the blood rush from her head, only to return with the force of a thousand prickling needles beneath her skin. She struggled to find enough voice to ask, "How much money?"

"More than enough to destroy this town. He's going to buy up every inch he can get his hands on, pick the bones and then bury it all underwater. As we suspected, this is about more than a new town. He wants to destroy what you've built here, Delaney. He wants to wipe out your legacy and replace it with his own."

"But, but..." Her chest felt so tight she feared her heart would take her out before her bum kidneys could. "This is all my fault? Oh, Elias, what have I done?"

Elias's expression turned fierce. "Don't you dare think for one minute this is your fault. Frank has... Well, I don't know what Frank is thinking. But the question we need to be asking is, what are *we* going to do? We need to formulate a new strategy."

"That's the part I don't get. How is he going to convince the holdouts, like me, like Levi, Harriet, the Bannons and there are plenty more, to sell up? Some of us won't be bought, and he can't force us to sell up."

"No, he can't. And he knows that. Which means, eventually, he's going to have to seek alternative means. I got a map here..." He unrolled the paper in his hand. "That shows which properties would need to be flooded to make this reservoir." Using his index finger, he traced a line, which included the downtown area and stretched toward the mountains, encompassing the Flying Spur and several other ranches.

"After he's purchased all he can, it'll be up to the town to decide."

"You mean...?"

"If he can buy enough properties and convince the town council that the benefits of relocating the town up here..." he tapped the area proposed for the new town of Mountain Ridge "...are greater than remaining down here, it will go to a vote. And he might try to buy votes just as he's buying land."

Denny knew very well he didn't mean that literally.

Big E confirmed it. "He's got plans for a new school, a community center with a pool, a park. He's got buildings designed, construction lined up and tax incentives for the businesses that choose to relocate. The list goes on. He's going to make promises that are too tempting to pass up. The thing is, there are no guarantees behind these promises. But he's very convincing. And he's had success with other similar developments on a smaller scale."

Denny felt a wave of frustration and despair so powerful she gripped the arms of her chair. "How are we going to compete with that? What are we going to do?" she asked, fully aware that she'd said "we."

"For now, we're going to keep this information between us. I don't want the grandkids to know, or Molly or Harriet. There's no need to upset folks more than they already are. Yet. First, we need to decide who we can trust. See if we can figure out what Frank's next move is. Then, we need to find a way to convince the town council not to put the relocation of the town on the ballot. At least, not until we're sure how they'll vote."

Struck with a feeling of vertigo, Denny squeezed her eyes shut. Instead of getting better, this situation was spiraling out of control. After all these years, Frank was out for revenge? It didn't seem possible. If he'd been harboring ill feelings for this long, he'd been planning it for a while, too. Suddenly, she feared she no longer had the energy for a fight this big. But she couldn't quit, not when her family, friends, the town she'd helped create were at stake. How was she going to do this?

Intuiting her thoughts, Big E said, "You're not alone here, Delaney. I'll be with you every step of the way."

Denny felt the sting of tears prickling her eyes, but she wouldn't let them fall. It was a skill she'd become very adept at over the years. For her entire adult life, she'd prided herself on not needing anyone, solving her own problems—and those of others, too. She'd been a leader, a pioneer, even a daredevil at times. Sure, she'd made mistakes, too, but only had herself to blame. The point was that she'd done it all on her own.

But the truth now was, she didn't want to fight this fight without her brother. Irritating as he was, he'd finagled his way back into her life, and she no longer had the desire to keep him out. She needed his help, but that didn't mean she had to say so, right?

Nodding, she reached over and placed her hand on top of his, drawing comfort from the warmth of his skin, a stark contrast from the deep cold radiating from her very core. "Thank you, Elias."

"Anything for you, sis."

She sniffed. "In that case, go fix us a couple plates and I'll meet you inside."

"Sure thing." He shoved to his feet. "I don't know about you, but I've suddenly got a hankering for some pumpkin soup and pumpkin salad and maybe pumpkin chicken. I'll be sure to heap up your plate."

"Don't you dare," she warned him. "All I need is pie."

"Don't worry, Delaney. You can count on me." Chuckling, he strode toward the door.

"I hope so," she whispered into the breeze. "For all our sakes."

* * * * *

Don't miss the next installment of
The Blackwells of Eagle Springs, coming
next month, from acclaimed author
Cari Lynn Webb
and Harlequin Heartwarming!

Visit www.Harlequin.com
to preorder the story —Adele and Grady's
charming romance
Her Favorite Wyoming Sheriff.

COUNTRY LEGACY COLLECTION

19 FREE BOOKS IN ALL!

Cowboys, adventure and romance await you in this new collection! Enjoy superb reading all year long with books by bestselling authors like Diana Palmer, Sasha Summers and Marie Ferrarella!

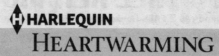
#443 HER FAVORITE WYOMING SHERIFF
The Blackwells of Eagle Springs
by Cari Lynn Webb
Widower and single mom Adele Blackwell Kane must reopen the once-renowned Blackwell Auction Barn—if she can get Sheriff Grady McMillan to stop arresting her on town ordinances long enough to save her ranch. Can love prevail in county jail?

#444 THE SERGEANT'S CHRISTMAS GIFT
by Shelley Shepard Gray
While manning the NORAD Santa hotline, Sergeant Graham Hopkins gets a call from a boy who steals his heart. When he meets the boy's mother, Vivian Parnell, will he make room in his heart for both of them?

#445 THE SEAL'S CHRISTMAS DILEMMA
Big Sky Navy Heroes • by Julianna Morris
Navy SEAL Dakota Maxwell is skipping Christmas—and not just because his career-ending injuries have left him bitter. But Dr. Noelle Bannerman lives to heal. And she'll do that with physical therapy...and a dose of holiday magic.

#446 AN ALASKAN FAMILY THANKSGIVING
A Northern Lights Novel • by Beth Carpenter
Single mom Sunny Galloway loves her job as activities director of a seniors' home—then Adam Lloyd shows up, tasked with resolving financial woes. They have until Thanksgiving to save the home. Can working together mean saving each other, too?

HWCNM0922

HARLEQUIN
PLUS

Announcing a **BRAND-NEW** multimedia subscription service for romance fans like you!

Read, Watch and Play.

Experience the easiest way to get the romance content you crave.

Start your **FREE 7 DAY TRIAL** at
www.harlequinplus.com/freetrial.